# A MODEST PROPOSAL

When Jessica informed the earl that she had been dismissed by the Barries without references, he looked at her thoughtfully and asked, "What are your plans?"

"I shall seek other employment," she replied.

"As what?" he asked. "You cannot be a governess. Or a lady's companion. Or a librarian. Or even a lady's maid. Probably not even a scullery maid. Nor do you have a family to return to. Your options are alarmingly few."

"I am not worried," she said, lifting her chin. "Something will turn up."

"Probably," he agreed. "In fact, Miss Moore, I am in a position to offer you employment that is well paid and would place you in a position for some security and comfort."

Jessica's eyes widened as she waited.

"I do not believe you would regret the decision to become my mistress," the Earl of Rutherford said.

MARY BALOGH, who won the *Romantic Times* Award for Best New Regency Writer in 1985, has since become one of the genre's most popular and bestselling authors. She also won the Waldenbooks Award for Bestselling Short Historical in 1986.

# The Ungrateful Governess

## Mary Balogh

A SIGNET BOOK

SIGNET
Published by the Penguin Group
Penguin Books USA Inc., 375 Hudson Street,
New York, New York 10014, U.S.A.
Penguin Books Ltd, 27 Wrights Lane,
London W8 5TZ, England
Penguin Books Australia Ltd, Ringwood,
Victoria, Australia
Penguin Books Canada Ltd, 10 Alcorn Avenue,
Toronto, Ontario, Canada M4V 3B2
Penguin Books (N.Z.) Ltd, 182–190 Wairau Road,
Auckland 10, New Zealand

Penguin Books Ltd, Registered Offices:
Harmondsworth, Middlesex, England

Published by Signet, an imprint of Dutton Signet,
a division of Penguin Books USA Inc.

First Printing, October, 1988
9  8  7  6  5  4  3

 REGISTERED TRADEMARK—MARCA REGISTRADA

Printed in the United States of America

# 1

THE EARL OF RUTHERFORD was aware as soon as he opened the library door that someone was there before him. He could see the faint glow of a single candle set somewhere behind the door. He frowned and was glad that he had approached the room and turned the handle with some stealth. He had not wanted to wake any of the sleepers of the house. It was past midnight. He held his own candle at arm's length away from the door opening so that it would not be seen from inside the room unless the occupant were looking exactly in his direction, and began to close the door as quietly as he could. He certainly did not relish the thought of another dull encounter with his host.

Before the door was quite shut, however, there was the thud of a falling book from inside the room and the sound of a mild exclamation. In a distinctly female voice. Rutherford could not resist the temptation to ease the door open again and peer cautiously around it. A moment later he had stepped quietly into the room and was closing the door slowly behind him.

What good luck! The little gray governess.

But she was looking neither very gray nor very uninteresting at the moment. Quite the contrary, in fact. She was wearing only a white nightgown. The blue shawl she must have worn downstairs had been flung onto a table beside her. She was stretching up to replace a book on a high shelf and revealing to his delight two small bare

feet and one very trim ankle. Her hair—that light brown
mass that was usually scraped back from her face and
confined ruthlessly into a large bun at the back of her
head—was hanging loose. It reached to her waist and
even lower, tilted back as her head was. It was shiny,
thick, and wavy.

He had suspected for the past week that she was not
the gray creature that one tended to take her for at a
superficial glance. The rather loose, shapeless dresses
she wore, unadorned gray and covering every inch of
her except her hands and head, did a good job of
conveying an impression of sexlessness. Indeed, they
helped her almost disappear into the background
entirely. And her hairstyle, demurely lowered eyelashes,
and unsmiling face suggested no femininity whatsoever.
But he had suspected.

The Earl of Rutherford considered himself something
of an expert on female servants. The obviously pretty,
brash ones, the ones who spilled out of their dresses,
eyed one boldly, and made their availability patently
obvious, were almost always a disappointment. They
were as unsubtle in bed as they were out of it. The best
one could hope for was a few minutes of energetic
animal pleasure. Frequently one had to endure vulgar
flattery and shrill giggles while one was taking one's
pleasure. It was the other kind of servant that generally
interested him far more. Miss Moore's kind.

They tended to glide around unobtrusively so that a
man of less discernment and experience than himself
might not even notice that they were there. And those
men thereby would quite unwittingly deny themselves
great pleasure. Such creatures, Rutherford had discovered from his not inconsiderable experience, almost
invariably were intensely passionate. It was as if they
repressed all their sexuality in the normal course of their
lives and released it unstintingly for the satisfaction of
the man who had seen it hidden there.

Governesses frequently made delightful bedfellows.
They generally considered themselves a cut above the

ordinary servant and usually were. They would not open their treasures readily to anyone else of the servant class. And yet they could not mix freely with the gentry. They were usually very ripe indeed for a bedding when a gentlemen came along who saw beyond the gray disguise. They almost always wore gray, and it was almost always meant to conceal. Any governess who did not boast personal attractions would probably not be uniformed in gray. Why conceal one's governess if there was no danger of her attracting the roving eye of one's husband or one's sons?

Miss Moore was kept in a particularly heavy disguise: the loose dresses, the severe hairstyle. She must be an unusually attractive girl. So he had concluded when he had first cast assessing eyes on her the week before. And it seemed his host did not avail himself of her personal services. At least, Rutherford had been able to intercept none of those knowing glances that usually told him if a man's wife was being cheated in her very own house. The chances were that Miss Moore had passion just waiting to explode at the first invitation.

It was true that he had been unable to come any closer to her than half a room away during the past week. True too that he hardly knew the sound of her voice. And he did not know the color of her eyes. But then it was very understandable that Lady Barrie would not allow him any chance encounter with her daughter's governess when the daughter looked as she did. Who could blame a mother?

The door was finally shut behind him, and the book was finally on its shelf.

"Do you suffer from insomnia too, Miss Moore?" the Earl of Rutherford asked conversationally, moving a few steps into the room.

The governess whirled around, her eyes wide and startled. She grabbed for her shawl and fumbled with its folds before throwing it, bunched untidily, around her shoulders.

Dark eyes, Rutherford thought, though he was not

close enough to know their color. He observed the blush
that flooded into her face. And he noted with some
interest that her breasts, unconfined beneath the linen
of the nightgown, were firm and high. What on earth
did she do with them beneath the gray dresses? Bind
them?

He felt a distinct stirring of desire.

"Oh," she said. "My lord. I did not realize that
anyone else was still awake."

Low and soft, he thought. A seductive voice.
Naturally so, he suspected. She did not seem intent on
seducing at the moment. She was clearly agitated. She
was still wrestling with her shawl.

He walked closer to her. "It is twisted at the back,"
he said. "I fear you are fighting a losing battle. Allow
me."

And he took the shawl from her suddenly nerveless
fingers and straightened out its folds. He stood directly
in front of her, his arms reaching over her shoulders,
and finally set the shawl down on them. He had not
touched her at all. He looked down into her eyes as he
held the ends of the shawl for her to take from his
hands. Blue. Her eyes were blue, a darker shade than his
own.

She seemed to realize suddenly that he intended her to
take the shawl from him. She grasped it clumsily,
brushing her hands against his own as she did so. She
took a step back so that she almost touched the book-
shelves.

"I came to choose a book," she said. "I did not have
a chance earlier today. I have been busy. If you will
excuse me, my lord, I will not disturb you any longer."

"But you still do not have a book," he said. She was
no longer looking at him. Her eyes were resting on the
top button of his shirt—at least, the top button that was
done up. The top two were open.

"I shall choose one tomorrow," she said. "It is too
late to read tonight anyway."

"I could not agree with you more," he said. "Unfortunately, when one is unable to sleep, reading seems the best way to induce slumber. If one is alone, that is. Of course, if one has company of suitable gender, there is another, more pleasant way of doing it.''

She looked up at him a full second before comprehension brought the color flooding back into her cheeks. He reached out and took a lock of her hair between his thumb and forefinger. She bit her lip.

"It seems we have a choice, Miss Moore," he said. "And I can tell without even having a closer look that Barrie has no book of any interest on his shelves."

She stared mutely back at him. Her hands fidgeted with the fringe on her shawl.

"Shall we put each other to sleep, Miss Moore?" he asked softly. His eyes were on her lips, which were parted with what he thought was probably unconscious provocation. "After suitably pleasurable exercise, of course."

He sensed a change in her suddenly, though she did not move and her hands continued busy.

"I think you are under a misapprehension, my lord," she said, her voice low and steady. "I am not available for dalliance."

He smiled and raised his eyes to hers again. She was looking full at him, her gaze startlingly direct. "Why do you hide your beauty?" he asked, though he knew the answer full well. "Why the daytime disguise?"

"I am a governess," she said. "I dress in a manner suited to my calling."

"With some encouragement from your employer, I would guess," he said.

She did not reply.

"It must be a very dull life," he said.

"Life is what one makes it, my lord," she said. "I do not complain. I do not seek the kind of diversion that you suggest."

"You wish to be persuaded," he said. "I believe I have some skill, Miss Moore. And I am not the sort of man who considers only his own gratification. I believe that a woman is as entitled as a man to be thoroughly pleasured in a bed where she has chosen to give herself. Come, let me give you a foretaste of what you may expect."

His hand moved around and twined itself into the thick silkiness of her hair. He had to make a concerted effort to give her time to respond. He wanted to drag her against him without more ado. He suspected that those firm breasts were not the only delight hidden from view beneath the loose nightgown.

She raised her chin an inch. "I will not be ravished, my lord," she said. "If you do not release me immediately and let me pass, I shall scream very loudly. I shall of course be dismissed from my employment without a character for having had the audacity to have tempted the Earl of Rutherford to seduce me. But I shall do it nonetheless."

He took a rueful half-step backward. There were, of course, always those few gray creatures who were so from choice, whose virtue was unassailable. A great shame in Miss Moore's case as she was a rare beauty even clad in the unbecoming and virginal nightgown. She would have been far more satisfying in his bed than any of the books ranged behind her. And a far more effective sleeping potion. He moved his hand forward until it held only the one lock of hair again.

"You need put neither your lungs nor your employment in jeopardy," he said. "I have never been driven to rape any female, Miss Moore. I see no reason to begin on you. I foresaw an hour's mutual pleasure, that is all. You are quite free to step around me and leave, your virtue intact. My apologies if I have wounded your dignity."

He grinned down at her and let his hand rest on her shoulder for a moment. He was about to step back and sweep her a mocking bow. He anticipated the only pleasure that was to be granted him that night, it seemed: that of watching her cross the room with her indignation and her bare feet, knowing herself watched.

The next person to enter the room was clearly less intent than he had been on not disturbing the house. And the sight of two candles within did not set the new arrival to withdrawing quietly as he had begun to do earlier. When the door opened, it did so quite abruptly and noisily, and its sound was succeeded by the immediate entry of Lord Barrie, a whole branch of candles in his hand.

Lord Rutherford turned toward him, one eyebrow raised. "Three of us suffering from insomnia, Barrie?" he said. "I only hope that you have enough good books to satisfy us all. What would you recommend?"

And he was not even to be granted the pleasure of watching the governess withdraw, he thought with an inward sigh, as she muttered something indistinct and disappeared from the room while he surveyed the shelves languidly and hoped that his host was not about to be his usual garrulous self. Not at an hour well past midnight. And not at a moment when he was still smarting from a strong dose of sexual frustration.

Jessica Moore took one last look around the room that had been hers for the past two years. She knew there was nothing left inside drawers or wardrobes; she had just double-checked those. There was nothing lying on surfaces either. She had everything, then, stuffed inside one small trunk and a valise. One did not accumulate much as a governess. She had arrived two years before with scarcely less than she had now.

There was not much in the room to make her wish to linger. It was a small box of a room on the floor above the family bedchambers, next to the schoolroom. It was too cold in winter, too hot in summer. Facing north as it did, it was never brightened by the direct rays of the sun. Its curtains and bed hangings were an uninteresting shade of pale brown. There was almost no hint left of the floral design that had brightened them in the long ago days when they had hung in a more important bedchamber.

The only thing that made her at all reluctant to leave was the fact that this room had been her only refuge for a long time. The only place where she could go to avoid Sybil's petulant moods, to escape Lady Barrie's waspish temper, to recover from the frequent insults that as a servant she must endure meekly.

Was she sorry to be leaving? She thought not. She had never been happy in this house. Not nearly so. She had no friends, except perhaps the vicar's wife, who was more than twenty years her senior. The servants were awkward with her; the family despised her. And she had outgrown any usefulness she might once have had when Sybil had won a shrill argument with Lord and Lady Barrie a few months before and been officially released from the schoolroom. Jessica had expected to be given notice. Instead, her role had been converted to that of "companion." That is, she was expected to trail around after Sybil, a silent and virtually invisible shadow.

She wished now that she had resigned of her own free will. At least then she would probably have been given a letter of recommendation, even though she would have expected no warm praises from Lady Barrie. But she had procrastinated. Unhappy as she was, at least she was familiar with her situation. The thought of having to start all over again in a new household had filled her with dread.

Well, Jessica thought, dragging the trunk across the floor to the door of her room, she did not have to worry about any such thing now. Dismissed without any period of notice whatsoever and without any recommendation. There was no earthly chance of finding herself another situation. And what was she to do? A wave of panic grabbed at her stomach as she tied the ribbons of her gray bonnet beneath her chin and drew on her gray cloak.

What *was* she going to do?

She was to leave on the stagecoach to London in one hour's time. But why she had chosen London she did not really know. What was there there for her? But what was there anywhere for her? The stagecoach went to London. That was why she was going there probably. Two days she would have on it. Two days in which to decide what she was to do with the rest of her life. And she could not hope for employment as a governess or companion. Even as a lower servant she would doubtless need a character from someone. And who was there who would be willing to speak for her?

Really, Jessica thought, the panic threatening to overwhelm her for the moment, there seemed to be only one avenue open to her. And she would not take that. Could not. Her pride was far too great. What was she to do?

She picked up her valise with a resolution she was far from feeling and left the room without a backward glance. She would ask Terrence to bring down her trunk. He was the only footman—the only servant, for that matter—who had ever shown her any warmth of feeling. He would carry it for her. She could not expect any sort of farewell from anyone, of course. She was leaving in disgrace. She had not even been granted a maid to help her with her packing. Besides, it was too early for the famiy to be up yet. Lady Barrie had probably returned to her bed after summoning her very early that morning in order to dismiss her.

And probably *he* was not up yet either, for he had had a late night.

A little more than an hour later Jessica was seated in the stagecoach between two large persons, one male and one female, both of whom were displaying their disappointment at her late arrival to take the empty middle seat by ignoring the fact that she was there at all. Not that she wished for their conversation. But it would have been far more comfortable if they had at least acknowledged her need for room on the seat. She resigned herself to two days of discomfort. Indeed, she must enjoy these two days. At least while the journey lasted she belonged somewhere. Her meager resources would not keep her for very long in London. She had had to pay for her own ticket on the stagecoach.

Had he asked that she be dismissed? Jessica wondered. Did he even know that she had been? She had expected it, had lain awake all night wondering what her punishment would be and fully expecting that it would be dismissal. After all, this was not like the time when Lady Barrie's brother had kissed her beneath the mistletoe while his wife and all the rest of the family had looked on, laughing merrily. Her punishment that time had been merely nine days confined to her room and the schoolroom abovestairs until the visitor she had enticed with her wicked ways had finally taken himself and his wife home.

This was different. This time she had practiced her wiles on the intended husband of Sybil. There could be no forgiveness for such a heinous crime, even after a suitably harsh punishment. A suitor had arrived from London, and the suitor was to be converted into a betrothed and a husband with all due speed so that Sybil could have the great distinction of being a countess at the age of seventeen. Despite the extreme plainness of her face and figure and despite her petulant and bad-tempered nature. No governess was to be allowed to distract the attention of the suitor.

And so she had been verbally abused early that morning by Lady Barrie, called whore among other insults, and told that she might take herself away from the house within three hours. She was not invited to speak a word and indeed did not attempt to do so. She had stood quietly before her employer, looking her calmly in the eye, a daring action that had only stirred the other into further wrath. Servants were expected to direct their eyes at the floor when Lady Barrie condescended to speak to them, like Moses, afraid that the light from the Godhead's countenance would blind them if they looked into it.

Jessica was too accustomed to her former employer to feel any great anger or bitterness at her treatment. It was to be expected. But what about *him*, the Earl of Rutherford? Was she angry with him? Did she now hate him? She tested the idea in her mind and came to the conclusion that no, she did not really blame him for the course events had taken. Not unless he had asked for her dismissal, that was. But she did not believe he had. What would be his motive? She had refused to go to bed with him. That would not be of sufficient importance to provoke the Earl of Rutherford into vicious revenge. She could say with some certainty that at least three of the chambermaids would have been only too willing to warm his bed at any moment of the night or day.

"Some persons thinks they can turn up at the last moment and take the whole seat that decent folks has paid good money for," the large female at her left remarked loudly to the large male on her right. She was attempting to locate something in the covered basket she held on her knees.

"Some persons do like to put on airs," the male agreed with a wheeze. "Prob'ly used to traveling around in their private coaches where they can spread out all along one seat and stretch their feet on the opposite one."

"Nobody better not try to put their feet on this seat," a passenger of superior wit across from them said. "Not unless they wants ter walk on stumps that begins above the ankles for the rest of their born days, that is."

Jessica was further squeezed by the hearty laughter of her neighbors. She wisely chose to ignore all remarks and won a sniff and a charge of being "uppity" from the female beside her for her pains.

She had found him powerfully attractive from the day of his arrival. As who would not? she asked herself. The Earl of Rutherford was a good-looking man by any standard: tall, athletically built, his aristocratic features, very dark hair, and blue eys designed by heaven to make any normal female heart skip a beat. To a lonely, love-starved young lady he appeared quite irresistible.

She had rarely been in the same room with him, had never been closer to him than the width of a room, had spoken not a word to him. He had not even noticed she existed, she had believed. But she had looked when no one was observing her, and what she saw had filled her with longing, the longing for pretty, flattering gowns, for wearing her hair about her face, for the freedom to smile and lift her eyes to the world. She had longed for one of his looks, one indication that he knew she existed, one sign that he knew she was a woman.

She had been kept severely in the background. Even her usual task of chaperoning Sybil during visits and walks was usurped by the girl's middle-aged abigail. She had been sent back to her room one morning when it was judged that her hair was not tightly enough pulled back and some wave remained.

She had not expected him to notice her. Indeed, she had not thought he would stay long. He had come there by some chance as a prospective suitor for Sybil. It seemed unlikely to Jessica that he was as firm in his intentions as Lord and Lady Barrie seemed to believe. Such a man would have no trouble at all finding a wife. Even if his pockets were to let, he could surely find a more amiable wife among the ranks of the wealthy than Sybil. Jessica did not believe that in two years she had made any impression on the girl's character whatsoever. She was as bad-tempered, as selfish and uncontrolled now as she must have been from childhood. And she had no beauty with which to blind a suitor to the defects of her character until after a marriage had taken place.

But he had been there a whole week, and he had noticed her. He had even known her name last night. Of course, he had noticed her in one way only. She was a governess. A servant. And apparently presentable enough in her nightgown and with her hair down to be deemed worthy of a night in his bed. There was nothing remotely flattering about such notice.

But oh, she had been tempted!

He had looked quite suffocatingly masculine, dressed as he was only in his breeches and a silk shirt open at the throat. His hair had been tousled, as if he had just risen from his bed. And those blue eyes, seen at close quarters, had been disturbingly direct.

She had felt almost instant desire. She had wanted to be held against that tall, strong body. She had wanted his hands and his mouth on her. And truth to tell, she had felt her knees weaken at the thought of going to his bedchamber with him and allowing him any intimacy that he chose to take. Virtue, chastity, virginity had seemed dreary taskmasters for a few mad moments. She had had but to say the word. She could have experienced delights to dream of for a lifetime. He had assured her that he was skilled, that he liked to give as well as receive pleasure. And she had not doubted him for a moment.

Why had she held back, then? Why had she denied her own desire, her own deepest need? Perhaps it was just the knowledge that what for her would have been the experience of a lifetime would have been merely the delight of a moment for him, something he would have forgotten after a few days and the next woman. She had found when it came to the point that she could not degrade herself to that extent. She could not allow herself to become what all men seemed to expect female servants to be: ready bedfellows. Not persons at all. Merely the human instruments through which they could satisfy their sexual appetites. She could not do it and live with herself the next day.

But she was not at all sure, Jessica thought, sighing inwardly as the large female changed position and jostled her further with hip and elbow, she was not sure at all that she would be strong enough to make the same decision if it were hers to make all over again at this very moment. It would be something indeed, something worth having, to be granted just a few minutes out of a life of neglect and insult in which to be the full focus of a gentleman's attentions. To know that for those minutes he would be intent only on her, on both pleasuring and being pleasured. To be seen fully just once, wanted fully.

But wanted for what? For Jessica Moore? Or for the woman's body in which Jessica Moore just happened to be housed?

She shifted sideways so that some of the pressure was taken off her left arm at least. She wondered how far they had traveled and how much farther they would travel that day.

# 2

THE EARL OF RUTHERFORD cursed aloud as he turned his curricle into the cobbled yard of the Blue Peacock. It looked to be a large enough inn, but he had never heard of it before and had no way of knowing if it was worth his patronage. Besides, he had a feeling that the stage-coach he had passed an hour before must use this particular inn as a stopping place. There seemed to be nowhere else of any size to rival it. And darkness would be upon the coach by the time it got this far. He did not relish the thought of spending a night amid the noise and vulgarity of stage passengers.

He had hoped to travel much farther himself that night, but the rain that had begun half-heartedly a while earlier was now setting in for the night and was becoming something of a downpour. And the coolness of the November day had turned to an uncomfortable chill. It would be madness to continue on the road in an open curricle. Apart from the personal discomfort of raindrops dripping from the brim of his hat and somehow finding their way down his neck, the vehicle was not solid enough to cope with muddy roads. At least a heavier carriage could be relied upon to stick fast and safe. A curricle would slither and slide until it overturned into a hedgerow.

Even the Blue Peacock offered a less unpleasant prospect than that. Rutherford vaulted from the high seat of his vehicle, handed the ribbons to a lackey, and

strode into the dark but blessedly dry taproom of the
inn.

He was feeling somewhat reassured ten minutes later,
having found that the inn was as yet empty of guests
with the result that he had been allotted the best room in
the house and, he suspected, the only good one, a
bedchamber complete with private parlor. His rooms
were clean, he had discovered, the mattress dry and
reasonably free from lumps, the sheets clean, and the
maid, whom he had passed on the stairs, a potentially
satisfying armful.

He did not have a great deal of baggage and was quite
unsure if his valet would catch up to him with the
carriage that night. But no matter. All he really needed
was a change of shirt for the morrow and his shaving
gear, both of which he had in his leather bag. He never
encumbered himself with a nightshirt on his travels for
the simple reason that he did not wear one. He had
never found that his companions of the night objected
to the lack.

Lord Rutherford toyed with the idea of ordering his
dinner to be brought to his parlor immediately, but he
decided that it was too early. He had eaten luncheon
only a few hours before. But what was he to do with
himself? He did not have so much as a book in his bag.
He could not take a walk as the rain was now streaking
down outside. He would go down to the taproom, he
decided, and look over any new arrivals. And the innkeeper had seemed like a garrulous fellow, who might
have some interesting stories. Innkeepers were rarely
bores, he had found from experience. They had seen too
much of the quirks of human nature ever to run dry of
an amusing or sensational anecdote. And that buxom
maid merited a second look. She had signaled her availability in that moment of passing on the stairs. The
decision would be entirely his.

Rutherford was soon settled in the chimney corner, a
pint of ale on the table at his elbow, the coals of the fire
setting his damp breeches to steaming. Three new

arrivals were seated at their ale exchanging loud banter with the innkeeper. The maid had whisked herself in and out of the room a couple of times, entirely for his benefit, Rutherford judged in some amusement, although she preened herself over the ribald comments of the newly arrived trio. He might decide to take his pleasure with her later. There would be no unusual satisfaction in doing so as she was the unsubtle kind of female. But she would at least help pass what promised to be a long and dull night.

His mind went back to that morning. His abrupt leavetaking had been somewhat embarrassing as it had been patently obvious to him that both Lord and Lady Barrie had expected a declaration. Fortunately, he had not seen their daughter before leaving, though doubtless she shared their expectations. She had been treating him with a markedly proprietary air for two or three days past. In fact, right from the start they had all behaved as if he had come as a formal and recognized suitor.

He grinned briefly into his tankard of ale. Life with that particular young lady did not bear contemplation. No beauty. No character. No sweetness of disposition. He pitied the poor man who would finally be ensnared by those three determined persons. His life would not be worth living. And someone would surely be caught. The one desirable attribute the girl had—and for many it would far outweigh all the less attractive ones—was money, and lots of it.

Thank the Lord he did not have to marry for money. He wished he did not have to marry at all. But he had heard nothing else since his nine-and-twentieth birthday had slipped by him eight months before and the dreadful prospect of the thirtieth loomed ahead. It was his duty, it seemed, to plant his seed in some as yet unknown female of suitable background, whom of course he would first have to make his wife. It seemed that a man was likely to pop off at any moment once his thirtieth birthday was behind him. And the best way to protect himself against the imminent danger was to beget some other poor male creature who would be all ready to step into his shoes and his title until he too had the misfortune to find himself in his thirtieth year. It was quite unthinkable to contemplate letting the title pass to a cousin, it seemed, however blameless and worthy he might be.

His parents had been at him, Mama with her quiet smiles and assurances that matrimony was a blessed state, Papa with his reminders that it was not only the title of Rutherford he must safeguard but also his father's of Middleburgh, a dukedom no less. Faith and Hope, his sisters, had added their word—or words would be more accurate, he thought with a grimace. Hope, always an eager matchmaker, had redoubled her efforts during the last year.

And yet again, irrelevantly, he blessed the kindness of fate that had made him, the third child, a boy. Not that he craved the titles, which of course he would not have received had he been a girl, but he would have detested having to go through life as Charity. His mother, he had heard since, had been divided in her feelings at his birth. She was proud and relieved to have produced a son and heir at last, but she did regret the incomplete Biblical trio. They had called him Charles, but he had heard his mother lament the fact that Faith, Hope, and Charles had a decidedly anticlimactic ring to it. A third daughter never did arrive.

His grandmother had been the final straw. He had been in the habit of visiting the dowager duchess at least once every two weeks through all his boyhood and the years since, except when he was at school or university, of course. And he had always enjoyed a good relationship with the old girl, he had thought. She admired backbone in a man, but approved of his sowing his wild oats during his early manhood. He had always been remarkably open with her—far more open than with any other member of his family—about those oats. However, he had realized only within the past eight months that although she recognized the importance of wild oats, she also valued cultivated oats and believed that they were the ones that mattered and must take precedence over the weeds. She had ceased to chuckle over his exploits during those months and had developed the habit of harping on duty.

His duty! He must marry and impregnate his wife on his wedding night, it seemed. His grandmother did not put matters with quite such open vulgarity, of course, but that was what she meant. He had been evasive for months, but just three weeks before he had lost his good humor and pointed out to her in no uncertain terms that there was not a single lady of his acquaintance with whom he could possibly contemplate a life sentence. He would just have to gamble on living a few years longer yet and postponing that comfortable arrival of his heir.

His grandmother had called him a humbug. At least, she had called her needlepoint a humbug, which amounted to the same thing, as the stitchery could have done nothing to offend her.

"Very well, Grandmama," he had said rashly, "you name me an eligible lady and I shall go immediately and look her over. Offer for her too if I don't turn green at the prospect."

"Ella's granddaughter," she had said without a moment's hesitation, speaking of one of her card-playing cronies. "In the country. Coming up for the Season next spring, but bound to be snaffled up in a twinkling, Charles. Father loaded with the blunt. You go down there and forestall the opposition. Good family. Barrie. And just out of the schoolroom. Don't tell me that fact don't set your mouth to watering, m'boy, for I shan't believe you."

"You have not even seen the girl, Grandmama?" he had asked, aghast.

"Don't need to," she had said. "She has everything you could want in a wife, Charles. Haven't heard anything about her being unable to breed. That's all that matters, y'know. You don't need to give up all your high flyers, boy. Always used to tell Middleburgh he might have one for every day of the week as long as he kept up appearances. Didn't want him forever hanging about my skirts, anyway. A devilish nuisance, men. No offense, m'boy. What?'' she said, looking up at him from beneath her eyebrows, her head still bent over her needlepoint. ''Afraid?''

''When do you wish me to leave?'' he had asked, knowing even as he did so that there was no way of reneging on his rash challenge now.

And so he had spent an unspeakable week with the Barries, wishing every moment to be on his way back to London again, but staying for courtesy's sake. But a week was the limit, he had decided the night before after that fiasco with the governess. He would return to Grandmama and insist that he had kept his part of the bargain. He had looked the girl over, found that he did indeed turn green at the prospect of offering for her, and so had come home without doing so.

What a waste of a week, he thought with a yawn, nodding in the direction of the innkeeper and indicating that he wished to have his tankard refilled. The only event that might have made it at all worthwhile would have been a night spent with the gray governess. She had turned out to be even lovelier than he had suspected all week. That hair! He almost regretted that he had not stolen a kiss and drawn her body against his own. He suspected that it was very feminine and very shapely indeed. A night with her would have been rare sport.

However, he had got very little for all his imaginings. Unfortunately, he was afflicted with a conscience that made it impossible for him to take even as much as a kiss from an unwilling wench. Under the circumstances perhaps it was as well that nature had framed him in such a way that he did not often encounter unwillingness. On the contrary. On occasion he had even found himself obliging eager females when he would just as soon not have done so, merely because he did not wish to hurt their feelings. But if a female did say no, he had a lamentable tendency to take her at her word. He had to want her very badly even to try a little further persuasion.

Perhaps it was not an unfortunate trait of character, he decided on second thought. He hated the idea of rape. At an all-male gathering several years before, when he had been very young and considerably more foolish, he had broken a fellow's nose and a quantity of crystal glasses and decanters after the man had recounted with pride for the noisy delight of most of his listeners how he and two other daring blades had held down and ravished a lady's maid as she sat waiting for her mistress in a carriage outside a house where a masquerade ball was in progress. The crowning glory of the tale was the fact that the girl had been virgin and was dismissed three months later for being with child.

Lord Rutherford's hand paused halfway to his mouth. Sure enough, the sounds coming from outside in the cobbled yard could be produced by nothing other than a stagecoach. Very soon now his peace would be shattered by the spilling out of the human contents of that coach. He would finish his ale and retire to the relative quiet of his parlor. It really was going to be a long evening. He would have to avail himself of the services of the maid. Though she was likely to be busy about her chores until late into the night.

He watched the passengers make their noisy entry. Two young sprigs of fashion who had been riding on the roof looked more like drowned rats than the dandies they wished to be taken for. They were both slapping their hats against their legs and shaking their greatcoats, talking and laughing loudly to try to compensate for their less than immaculate appearance. Two females, one thin and one fat. Two males to match. Another man all in black, who looked as if he might be a Methodist preacher. And Miss Moore.

Rutherford's eyebrows rose and he set his tankard down slowly on the table beside him. She did not look around her. She stood quietly a little behind all the other passengers, who were loudly jostling for place and clamoring for rooms. She was clutching a worn valise, her beauty and her form completely swallowed up in gray again. She was turned fully away from him so that there was no chance of her seeing him even out of the corner of her eye. She waited for her turn with the landlord.

He could not hear what she said, even though by the time her turn came most of the other passengers had gone off to their own rooms. But he did hear the landlord's reply quite clearly. There were no rooms left. He was sorry. He sounded far from sorry, Rutherford thought, a different man entirely from the genial and subserviant host who had welcomed a fashionable earl an hour before. She must sleep in the taproom or share Effie's bed. The choice was hers. It was all the same to him. The cost was the same, whichever she chose. Effie was the maid, Rutherford guessed.

She argued. He felt some satisfaction in watching her head come up and in knowing that she was not reacting with that meek, downward glance that she had affected with the Barries. But the show of spirit did her no good. He did not hear what she said. He was sorry, the innkeeper said with an exaggerated and careless shrug. What did she expect him to do? Call out the carpenters and make another room just for her ladyship? She disappeared upstairs after a few minutes trailed by the maid, who first turned and gave him a saucy look. Yes, she was Effie, obviously.

Strange! The woman he would have bedded last night was to share a bed with the female he had intended to make sport with tonight. Why should he feel indignation on behalf of Miss Moore, when he had judged both females desirable enough to lay their heads on the pillow next his own?

The Earl of Rutherford rose to his feet, stretched, and made his way unhurriedly to the staircase.

Jessica was sitting miserably in the taproom, trying to convince herself that she did not look as conspicuous as she felt. There was no separate dining room in the Blue Peacock. There were a few private parlors, she gathered, but of course those were very private. She was forced to take up a position in the common taproom, and there she must stay until it was bedtime. Even then she could expect no privacy or comfort. She must share the untidy and none too clean attic room of the maid, who made no bones about her reluctance to extend such hospitality.

She longed suddenly for her room at Lord Barrie's house. At least it had been her own and only rarely invaded by Lady Barrie come to scold her for some imagined offense or by Sybil intent on wheedling her into doing some task for her. She had not been treated well during the two years of her employment, but at least she had known where she belonged and what to expect. Here she felt conspicuous in her quietness. Her female companion of the coach was seated at an adjoining table, laughing raucously and tipping back a tankard of ale just like the men.

She looked up in some surprise at the sound of a discreet cough beside her. The Earl of Rutherford's valet stood there, looking as immaculate and toplofty as he had looked for the past week as he lorded it over the Barries' servants.

"His lordship 'as begged me to hinform you, ma'am," he said, having the grace to speak quietly, "that 'e would be hobliged to you for joining 'im for dinner in 'is parlor."

Jessica felt the color rise in her cheeks. He was here? And knew that she was here too? And he wished to entertain her? Alone, in a private parlor. He must know the impropriety of the suggestion. Of course, she was merely a governess, a servant. She looked around the room and reminded herself anew of the alternative.

"Thank you," she said, and rose quietly to her feet. She allowed the valet to lead the way across the crowded taproom and up the stairs. Her heart was beating with painful thumps by the time he opened one of the doors on the upper story and stood aside for her to precede him into the room.

The parlor was empty, she saw with great relief. What on earth was he doing at this inn? She had heard nothing the day before about his intention to leave.

It was a comfortable room, not large, but made cozy by the worn carpet on the floor, two shabby armchairs, a table already set for two, a branch of lit candles on the table, and a cheerful fire crackling in the hearth. Jessica crossed to the fireplace and held her hands out to the blaze. She had not realized just how much the cold had contributed to her misery during the day's journey and her short stay in the taproom. The valet had disappeared through a second door.

"Ah, Miss Moore,"the voice of Lord Rutherford said from this inner doorway a few minutes later. "What a happy coincidence that we have chosen the same inn for tonight. I trust you have had a comfortable journey today?"

He looked larger, more overpoweringly masculine in this small room than he had looked at Lord Barrie's. There was a certain haughtiness in his manner that only succeeded in making him look more handsome than usual.

"Yes, I thank you, my lord," she said.

"Liar, Miss Moore." He smiled and advanced farther into the room. "I have traveled on the stagecoach in my time. It is considered one of the necessary experiences of life by young blades, you know. There is no more disagreeable mode of travel. Especially, I would imagine, if one were forced to ride inside, as you must have done. Was the company enlightening?"

"Not especially so," she admitted, unsmiling. "But at least I was out of the rain for the last hour."

"And your accommodations are comfortable, I assume?" he asked politely.

"Yes, quite, I thank you, my lord," she said.

"You are accustomed to sharing a room and a bed with barmaids, then?" he asked, eyebrows raised.

Jessica's lips tightened. "I perceive you are in the habit of asking questions only so that you may contradict the answers," she said. "I have not complained, my lord. My purpose is to reach London as soon as I may. I do not demand luxuries along the way."

"And do you have some bright prospect ahead that makes you rush so, Miss Moore?" he asked. "I was unaware that your departure from your employment with the Barries was imminent."

Jessica did not answer.

He closed the remaining distance between them and stood before her. "Does your presence on the road to London have anything to do with me, Miss Moore?" he asked, hands clasped behind his back.

"My lord?" She looked up at him with wide, blank eyes.

"My lord?" he mimicked. "All innocent incomprehension, my dear? I am asking you if you were dismissed from your employment?"

Jessica's head dropped until one long aristocratic finger came beneath her chin and raised her face very firmly so that she was looking at him again.

"Of what are you accused?" he asked. "As I remember it, we were not even touching when we were so unfortunately disturbed. Not that I would not have had matters otherwise if I had had my way. Surely it must have been obvious to common sense that if we had been in the process of enjoying each other, we would not have been standing in the library, almost respectably clothed."

"In my employment I was not permitted to have any dealings with male guests," Jessica said.

" 'Dealings,' " he repeated. "Standing in the library very properly repulsing the advances of a male guest was construed as having dealings? My poor Miss Moore. I am so dreadfully sorry. I had no idea. Even when I left this morning, I was quite unaware that you had been called to account and sent packing."

Jessica wished he would remove his finger from

beneath her chin. She was finding looking into his eyes
very uncomfortable. "You do not owe me an apology,
my lord," she said. "What happened was not your
fault. I have been in trouble before for leaving my room
after retiring for the night. It was not your fault that I
was in the library when I had no business being downstairs at all."

He looked searchingly into her eyes for a moment but
was prevented from commenting by the arrival of the
innkeeper with their dinner. He released his hold of her
chin and gestured toward the table, where he seated her
with marked courtesy. The landlord too, she noticed,
bowed in her direction after filling her wine glass.

Jessica enjoyed the meal far more than she would
have thought possible. The food was good, though
plain. But it was not that that caused the enjoyment.
She was not, truth to tell, hungry after a day of being
squashed and jostled on the road. But she found the
stiff courtesy of the valet as he served them soothing to
her bruised pride. And she found Lord Rutherford an
interesting and surprisingly charming host. He set
himself to entertain her conversationally and did so,
taking upon himself the whole burden of introducing
and developing various topics.

She realized at the end of the meal that he had succeeded in setting her entirely at her ease. And that was
quite a feat when one considered that she was dining
alone with a man whose attractions had been doing
strange things to her heartbeat for all of a week. And
how improper it was to be sitting thus with him, unchaperoned in the private parlor of an inn! But really,
she thought as she folded her napkin at the end of the
meal, she did not care.

Lord Rutherford had settled back in his chair, one
forearm resting on the table, playing with the stem of
his empty wine glass. He was looking at her in such a
way that she knew that the courtesy a host owed his
guest during a meal was at an end. There would be no

more purely social conversation, she thought with some regret.

"What are your plans, Miss Moore?" he asked.

Jessica smoothed the cloth before her on the table. "I shall move on to other employment," she said with a shrug.

"As what?" he asked. "I do not imagine the Barries have given you a glowing character reference with which to dazzle a future employer."

"No," she admitted after a short pause during which she could think of nothing else to say.

"You cannot be a governess, then," he said quietly, "or a lady's companion. Or a librarian. Or even a lady's maid. Probably not even a scullery maid. Do you have a family to which to return?"

"No," Jessica said after a moment's hesitation.

"I see," he said. "Your options are alarmingly few, are they not, my dear?"

"I am not worried," she said, lifting her chin and looking him in the eye. "Something will turn up."

"Probably," he agreed. "In fact, Miss Moore, I am in a position to offer you employment that is well paid and would place you in a positon of some security and some comfort."

Her eyes widened. She had an alarming feeling of *déjà vu*.

"I do not believe you would regret the decision to become my mistress," the Earl of Rutherford said.

# 3

DURING THE SILENT SECONDS that succeeded Lord Rutherford's words, Jessica mentally rejected the temptation to feign shock or outrage. She was not shocked. Indeed, she found now that the suggestion was out in the open, that she had been half expecting it. Not perhaps the request that she become his mistress. No, she had not given any thought to that. But she had been expecting, at however unconscious a level, that he would invite her to share his bed that night. Why else would he have summoned her to this private parlor? Out of the natural kindness of his heart?

Perhaps the only aspect of the matter that did surprise Jessica was her realization that she had also been weighing the idea in her mind. Would she stay with him? Would she renounce the principles of behavior and morality by which her whole life had been guided thus far for the sake of one night's comfort and pleasure? The alternative filled her with dread. The prospect of climbing the ladder to the attic in order to share the maid's bed was becoming more impossible to contemplate. And doubtless she would have the girl's insolence to contend with, especially after she had spent the evening in a gentleman's private parlor.

Why subject herself to such indignity when she could spend the night in the arms of a man with whom she really wished to stay? She was four and twenty already and had never been closer to a man's embrace than that smacking kiss under the mistletoe and a few somewhat more lingering but very chaste embraces from a childhood sweetheart before he discovered that marriage to her would not be socially wise. She did not want to go through life without discovering what it felt like to be with a man.

Then why not with the man she wished to be close to? The man who had told her only the previous night that he liked to give pleasure as well as to take. There was, of course, all the immorality of lying with a man who was not her husband. But what had morality gained her? A lonely, unfriendly journey to London, where no one awaited her and where there was no prospect of security, that was what.

And he was offering her the chance to make the comfort of this night a long-term arrangement. He wished to make her his mistress. He would take care of her. She would not have to worry about where she was to live, what she was to eat, where she was to find employment. It seemed incredible to Jessica that she could be seriously considering his proposal, but she was nonetheless.

Rutherford was looking across the table at her, a half-smile on his lips. "I find your silence encouraging," he said. "It really would not be a bad life, Miss Moore. I would provide you with a comfortable home, servants, a carriage. All your needs would be supplied. And your duties would not be arduous. Merely to please me. I believe you would not find that difficult to do. And I am vain enough to believe that you would not find the task unpleasant on your own account."

"I wish for honest employment, my lord," Jessica said, but she realized even as she spoke that her protest lacked conviction.

"And being my mistress would be dishonest?" he asked, his eyebrows raised so that he looked again as haughty as he had when he first entered the room.

"I have been brought up to believe so," she said.

"It is easy for the wealthy and secure to talk of

morality, Miss Moore,'' he said. "I hate to bring brutal reality to your attention, my dear, but I believe you are face to face with it. Do you realize that if you refuse my offer it is very likely you will find yourself within the next week facing the choice of walking the streets or starving?''

Jessica had indeed thought of the possibility, though she did not suppose that if matters came to that crisis she would have the courage or the willpower to maintain the stubborn independence that had sustained her through the previous two years.

"Come, Miss Moore," Lord Rutherford said, removing his arm from the table and rising to his feet, "will you be my mistress?''

"Yes, I will, my lord," Jessica heard herself say.

"Splendid!" He smiled, his eyes crinkling at the corners in a manner that quite turned her heart over. He strode around the table and held out a hand for one of hers. "I promise you will not be sorry, Miss Moore. What is your given name?''

"Jessica,'' she said, and she placed her hand in his and rose to her feet. It was a large, strong hand. She felt an inner twinge of panic.

"Jessica," he said, smiling again. "Jess. It suits you. Not in your present guise, of course. Does your hair not pain you, dragged back from your temples so ruthlessly? It is beautiful hair. Let me see it as it was last night.''

He did not wait for her response. He lifted his hands and began to remove the pins that held her hair into its prim bun. His hands were gentle and surprisingly deft. Jessica fixed her eyes on the top button of his waistcoat and stood very still until she felt her hair cascade down around her face and against her back.

"Now you look like a Jess," he said, "and will do so even more when I have clothed you in pretty gowns. Never gray again, my dear. And certainly never that hair knot. You do not have to disguise yourself ever again, Jess Moore.''

His fingers were combing through her hair. Jessica
looked up into his face again. Her father had always
called her Jess. No one else ever had. Indeed, for the
past two years no one had even called her Jessica.

And then he bent his head and kissed her. Very gently
and unthreateningly. His hands were loosely twined in
her hair. Only his lips touched her. But Jessica felt as if
everything inside her changed places with everything
else. This was it, then. She had said yes. She was going
to be his mistress. She was allowing him to call her
familiarly by name, to touch her. She was committed.
She could not now object to anything he chose to do
with her.

And what was more, she thought, as his hands moved
to cup her face and his lips parted over hers, she did not
want to. She knew that soon he must begin to touch her
body. She knew that she would be taken through to the
bedchamber, that he would unclothe her and lay her on
the bed. And she knew that there she would make the
final commitment that would forever remove her from
the ranks of virtuous women, that would forever brand
her fallen.

And she did not care. She wanted his hands on her.
She wanted the unknown rites that would take place in
the bedchamber. She wanted them over and done with
so that she need not be plagued with further doubts.
And she wanted them taking place now, here and now,
because she knew, even without his having said so, that
he would give her pleasure, that the events of the next
minutes would be the most exciting of her whole life.

His hands did move down after a few moments, over
her shoulders, to her full breasts, to her small waist and
the curve of her hips. Jessica's heart beat so painfully
that she thought she must faint.

"What a very effective disguise indeed," he
murmured against her lips, "this gray sack, Jess. You
have the shape of a goddess, my dear."

He spread his hands behind her hips as he looked
down into her eyes and brought her slowly to him. She

bit her lower lip and looked back at him as his hands slid up her back, bringing her fully and intimately against his body.

"I shall have your valise brought down," Rutherford said, smiling warmly into her eyes. "You may go through to the bedchamber, Jess. I shall join you there in—shall we say half an hour's time?"

"Yes, my lord," she said breathlessly, and allowed him to take her by the elbow and lead her to the door of the inner room.

Rutherford looked at his pocket watch. He would give her five more minutes, he decided. He might have made a tactical error in not taking her himself into the bedchamber and undressing her. It was his usual method. They could have sent for her bag in the morning. However, this case was a little different from the usual. Miss Jessica Moore was a virgin, or his guess was very wide of the mark. He had not had a virgin before and, truth to tell, did not know quite how to go about the matter of bedding her. He had deemed it wise to allow her time to prepare herself and clothe herself in that very virginal nightgown she had worn the night before. Time enough to remove it when they were under the bedcovers and he had warmed her up.

He was feeling unusually agitated himself, Rutherford thought, gazing down ruefully at the glass of wine he held in his hands. His third? Fourth? Of course, he was unaccustomed to awaiting his pleasure. And it was quite out of character for him to engage a mistress. He had done it once several years before and had been forced to endure the female long after inclination had made his visits tedious. It is far easier to begin such a relationship than to break it off, he had found.

His offer to Jessica Moore had been quite impulsive. The whole idea had been conceived and put into effect within one hour. Would he regret it? He did not even know if she would make a satisfactory bedfellow, though his brief exploration half an hour before had revealed a body even more feminine and curvaceous than he had suspected. Certainly tonight might not be an enjoyable experience. She would be nervous, awkward. She would have no idea how to please him. And he might hurt her. But even apart from the all-important sexual aspect of their relationship, would he find her an interesting enough companion to make him want to return to her again and again? He had enjoyed their dinner table conversation, but he realized that he had done almost all the talking.

The trouble was, Rutherford thought, putting his empty glass down on the floor beside him, getting to his feet, and removing his coat and waistcoat, he really had not had much choice but to make her his offer. Jessica, he suspected, did not quite realize how serious her predicament was. He had not exaggerated when he had told her that within a week she would be facing starvation or a life as a street prostitute. He owed her his protection. It was because of him that she had lost her situation with the Barries.

And by God, he admitted, removing his neckcloth and undoing the top buttons of his shirt, he wanted her. Finding a luscious beauty hidden behind the disguise of a little gray mouse was enough to stir any man's senses. He would not feel guilt. He was doing the best he could to look after her. He would treat her well. He always treated his women well in bed, always paid them generously afterward. Jess Moore would live like a lady, and he would provide handsomely for her when he finally tired of her. She would not need ever again to be a gray governess.

She was standing at the foot of the bed when he went into the room, brushing her hair and looking just exactly as she had looked in the Barries' library the night before. Rutherford closed the door behind him and allowed his eyes to roam over her. He expected her to look tense. She gazed calmly back at him and laid the brush down on a stool. He closed the distance between them.

"Have I kept you waiting?" he asked. "You look very beautiful, Jess."

He placed his hands on her shoulders and drew her against him. He lowered his mouth to hers. And immediately began the fight to control his desire. There was no virginal shrinking in her. Although his hands held only her shoulders, her body immediately fitted itself to his from firm, full breasts to knees. He cradled her head with one hand and rested the other against the small of her back. He set himself to ignore the demands of his body while he slowly coaxed her mouth into deeper intimacy.

He waited until his tongue had been allowed full and deep possession of her mouth before moving his hands knowingly over her again and lifting her up to carry her to the bed. She watched him as he undressed and climbed into the bed beside her. He had decided not to snuff the candles before doing so.

He wanted her then. He did not wish to wait another moment. He could not remember when the need to mount a woman's body had been quite so urgent. But she was not ready. She was langorous but not aroused. He set himself to arouse her, unbuttoning her nightgown to the waist so that he might touch her warm flesh, stroke her breasts with expert hands and mouth. He slid the linen of her nightgown up her legs so that he might caress her more intimately. She lay on her back, still, her eyes closed, her breathing quickened, her body tensing, and her heart thumping beneath the hand that moved over her left breast.

Now, he thought at last, lowering his head to kiss her deeply once more before moving his weight onto her so that he might enter her body and finally unleash his passion in her. She was looking at him, shaking her head slightly.

"No," she whispered. "No, I cannot. I am sorry. I cannot."

He brushed her lips softly with his own and willed control on himself again. "Relax," he said. "There is no haste. I can wait for you. I know it is your first time. I want it to be good for you."

"No," she said, and her eyes were big with unshed tears suddenly. "I cannot do this, my lord. I thought I could. I truly did. I have reasoned it out with myself and I can see no great wrong with it under the circumstances. But reason is no good against the moral habits of a lifetime, you see. Please, I must leave. I cannot do this."

Rutherford swung his legs over the edge of the bed and sat up with a jerk. He buried his fingers in his hair, his elbows resting on his knees. God, did she know what she was asking? Did she realize how very nearly impossible it was to grant her request? He willed calmness on his body. His mind would not function while the blood pumped so furiously through him.

"I am sorry," she said again from the bed behind him.

"So am I, Jess," he said. "So am I, believe me."

"It is just that I have been so frightened all day," she said. "I do not know what to do, you see. I do not even know why I am going to London. It is because I have to go somewhere and do something, I suppose."

"Yes," he agreed, hoping through words to drown out his physical agony, "I can understand your predicament. I thought I had offered a solution that would be thoroughly satisfactory to both of us."

"I think it might have been," she said, "if it did not feel so very wrong. And I truly do not know what I am to do now. But I must go to the room allotted to me here."

"There really is another alternative for you, Jess," he said, his thumb and one finger rubbing his eyes, concentrating hard on the activity. "I was too selfish to mention it while I thought there was a chance of the other."

"Oh, what?" she asked. She was sitting up behind him. He dared not turn around. Even if she had buttoned up her nightgown again, her hair would be in voluptuous disarray from the pillow and his playing hands.

"I shall take you to someone," he said, "someone in London who will take care of you on my recommendation."

"A brothel?" she asked in a shocked whisper.

Rutherford felt an unexpected wave of amusement at the idea of his grandmother's very respectable establishment being mistaken for a brothel and his grandmother for a procuress.

"No," he said. "An elderly lady of great influence who will find you genteel employment, Jess, despite the lack of a recommendation from your former employers. Her word will be far more respected than theirs, you may be assured.

"Oh, will you?" she cried with such passionate gratitude that he felt sudden guilt for what he had tried to perpetrate against her, and his desire began finally to come under his control. "How very generous you are, my lord. I must leave here and go to my room." She scrambled off the other side of the bed.

Rutherford stood up, raising his eyebrows as he looked around at her and noted her flood of embarrassment. "Get back into bed, Jess," he said. "This is where you are going to sleep tonight. I will not molest you further. You have my word on it, though I do believe there is a lock on the door if you are unconvinced. I shall sleep in the parlor. Perhaps you would do me the honor of breakfasting with me?"

"I cannot stay here," she said, turning to him again now that he had pulled on his breeches.

"Yes," he said. "This you can and will do. You will not spend the night in an attic with the servants. You will sleep in this bed tonight even if I have to break my word and sleep in it with you to hold you here."

The fight had gone out of her, he saw. He picked up his shirt from the floor, made her a mock bow, and withdrew to the parlor, where he spent an uncomfortable and near sleepless night on one of the worn armchairs, feeling less than charitable with the whole of the female sex, devising in his mind wonderful tortures for Miss Jessica Moore, and cursing his own tenderness of conscience that would not allow him any intimacy with a female for which he did not have her full consent.

Moments! Moments only and he would have mounted her and it would have been too late for her sudden attack of moral scruples. He could have taught her to enjoy instead. And she would have enjoyed. He had never failed to delight a woman with that part of his lovemaking. She had already been responding with flattering heat until somehow her mind had gained the ascendancy over her body.

And he would have enjoyed! There was no doubt whatsoever about that. Jessica had excited him more than any other woman he could recall at the moment.

Damnation!

He was certainly never going to have anything to do with virgins again.

Except his wife, he thought with a grimace. Whoever she turned out to be.

Jessica did not sleep much better, though she lay awake in greater comfort than the man in the adjoining room. She was consumed by embarrassment and guilt. Embarrassment at what she had done with Lord Rutherford, what she had allowed him to do. Guilt at what she had done to him. She had agreed to become his mistress, had allowed him to take her to bed, allowed him unimagined intimacies, and then denied him the ultimate one. She had some inkling of the great willpower it had taken him to stop at that particular moment. She also realized full well that perhaps only one man in a thousand would have stopped. And how could she have accused him if he had not?

But he had stopped and then, instead of throwing her out into the inn corridor in her nightgown and hurling her valise after her, he had insisted that she sleep in his

bed for the night while he sat up in one of those shabby
chairs in the parlor. And he had promised to give her an
introduction to a lady in London who would find her
employment. Jessica had her doubts about his ability to
do so, but she appreciated his generosity in being willing
to try.

In fact, strange as it seemed, she felt a certain respect
for the Earl of Rutherford. True, he had tried to seduce
her the night before, and tonight he had made her a very
improper offer of employment and had tried to seal
their contract without delay. But the man was no
ravisher. He took her for a servant, which she was. She
knew that for many gentlemen, women of the servant
class were considered theirs for the having. And yet
Lord Rutherford had been willing to release her without
argument the night before, and he had let her go tonight
even after she had consented both verbally and
physically to allow him his will.

Why had she stopped him? It had not been fear. Not
physical fear anyway. She had wanted him even before
he had come into the bedchamber. The wanting had
become almost a pain as soon as he came to her and
touched her. In fact, she had not waited for him to bring
her against him. She had put herself there, in an
instinctive need to dull the ache of her longing against
his body. And on the bed she had felt no shrinking, no
embarrassment—that came only now, afterward. She
had felt no shock when his hands had found their way
so easily inside and beneath her nightgown. She had
only wanted more, had been aware with an almost
unbearable surge of heat that even that was not enough.
It was not enough that he was against her skin,
caressing, teasing, exploring. She had wanted him
beneath her skin, deep inside her very being.

Why, then, had she stopped him? It seemed now little
short of miraculous that she had been able to do so
when she had wanted him so desperately. But there lay
her answer, she realized. Had she been less excited, less
full of aching pleasure, she probably would have

allowed him to carry the act to its conclusion. It was her very pleasure that had forced her to stop what was happening.

The truth was that becoming a man's mistress, allowing him the full access to her body that her upbringing had taught her she must surrender only to a husband, was totally against all the moral training of her youth. Until this day she had never even dreamed that such an offer as Lord Rutherford's could be a temptation to her. She would rather die than lose her virtue, she would have thought even just yesterday. Yet she had agreed to his offer. Her own future had looked so desperate that she had agreed. Better to become Lord Rutherford's mistress, she had reasoned, than totally to lose her pride by taking the only other alternative open to her.

But, her decison made, Jessica felt the need of punishment, or at least the need to feel that the employment she had agreed to would involve some hard work or some sacrifice. If she had found Lord Rutherford's touch unpleasant, if she had had to contend with fear or embarrassment or a sense of humiliation in bed with him, she probably would have considered that she was earning her keep, doing a difficult job only because she had no alternative, or at least no alternative that she chose to take.

Her conscience would not allow her to do something that she knew was almost the ultimate in sin and enjoy it at the same time. There would be no sacrifice in being the mistress of the Earl of Rutherford, no punishment for the sin involved. It would be wonderful. She would probably enjoy every moment of her life with him.

Jessica was sitting up in the bed, her arms clasped around her knees. She rested her forehead on them. She had saved herself by moments. Although he had still been beside her on the bed, she had sensed that she was about to bear his weight, that he was about to take a husband's privilege. A moment more and she would have known how all the yearning ache of those preceding minutes was to end. There was pain, she had heard. There was tedium and indignity, she had once overheard from two matrons who had not known she was within earshot. But she did not believe any of those things for one moment. Lord Rutherford would be as expert with his body as he was with his hands and his mouth. Probably more so. She had no doubt at all that she had deliberately denied herself what would have been the greatest pleasure of her life.

And for what? For continued life as a governess? As a companion? How very dreary was the prospect for what remained of her life. She slid under the bedcovers, determined yet again to try to sleep. At least she still had her most valuable possession, she thought wryly: her virtue. If she could be said to still have that. And at least she had more hope than she had had all day. Perhaps that elderly lady in London would be able to find her something.

She would not think of it, she decided, until the morning.

Or of Lord Rutherford.

Or of his lovemaking and the consummation she had missed.

Jessica tossed and turned on the bed for what remained of the night.

# 4

THE DOWAGER DUCHESS OF Middleburgh was seated at the escritoire in the morning room of her house in Berkeley Square when her grandson was announced. She was in the process of writing to one of her many old acquaintances scattered throughout the country and farther afield. She peered at him over the spectacles she had affected several years before, though the same grandson was in the habit of telling her that from the windows of her house she would be able to see an ant crawling over the Chinese roof of the pumphouse in the middle of the square if she felt it in her own interest to do so.

"Never tell me you are up and abroad already, Charles, m'boy," she said. "Can't be more than ten o'clock. Must be in love. With the Barrie chit?"

"Quarter past, to be exact," Lord Rutherford said, crossing the room and bending to kiss the wrinkled cheek offered for the purpose. "And no and no."

"You did look her over, though?" she asked sharply. "Not a beauty, I take it. But wealthy, Charles, and of good family. You could do worse."

"I suppose I could," he agreed. "I suppose I could get leg-shackled to a *poor* girl of bad temper and total absence of character. The thing is, Grandmama, that I don't need the blunt. I don't gamble, you know, and have only one expensive habit. And I have quite a sizable income. Papa is as rich as Croesus and you are said to have moneybags stuffed behind every wall in the house. And who else does either of you have to leave it all to but your favorite son and grandson?''

"You are our *only* son and grandson. And don't be impertinent with me," his grandmother said, laying down her pen and blotting her half-finished letter carefully. "Why are you here?"

"I am your grandson," Rutherford said. "And I have just returned from a journey you sent me on. I thought you would be interested to know that the girl will not suit. She turns me decidedly green."

"Nonsense," the duchess said. "You can't expect a gel of good family to jump between the sheets at a snap of the fingers, Charles. Gave you the cold shoulder, did she? Your trouble is, m'boy, that you know only one type of wench and think they must all be the same."

"Grandmama," he protested, "I do not live all my life in the gutter or in the boudoirs of actresses, I would have you know. I have met one or two ladies in my time. You and Mama, Faith and Hope, for example."

"What are we going to do with you, then?" she asked, frowning. "I refuse to die until you have got an heir, Charles. I'm not having anyone emptying out my walls on my death for the sake of what's-his-name. Henry? Theodore? Never can remember which one is next in line. The chinless one, anyway."

"Theodore," he said. "Grandmama, I promise to try my best not to pop off until I have done my duty in the nursery line. In the meantime I have a favor to ask."

"I knew it," she said suspiciously. "You did not rush over here the morning after a long journey because of filial loyalty, Charles."

He grinned. "I want you to help one of my failed oats, Grandmama," he said.

"A wench?" she asked sharply. "And failed, Charles? She's not in the family way? I don't intend to start providing for your bastards, my lad. I always told Middleburgh the same."

"I don't ask you to," he said. "My own purse will

stretch to providing for all two hundred and thirty of them. No, this is a girl after your own heart, Grandmama. She wouldn't have me. Twice. I unleashed all my not inconsiderable charm and skill on her, but she would have none of me. I, of course, consider her remarkably foolish."

"And you want me to help her, Charles? Ring the bell, boy. You will join me for some coffee. Nothing stronger. Too early in the day for you to start drinking. You probably do it for all the rest of the day anyway."

"Coffee will be welcome," he said, settling himself into a chair beside the fire and stretching his boots toward the blaze. "It is deuced cold outside today."

"It often is in November," she said.

"Miss Moore was a governess with the Barries," Rutherford said, "and I somehow caused her to be dismissed. She had rejected me cold, I would have you know, but because she was caught barefoot in the library with me, she was dismissed as a loose woman quite unfit for the charge of the Barrie chit. Oh, she was also wearing a sack of a nightgown and had her hair loose all down her back. And it was midnight or thereabouts."

"Hm," she said. "The chit was asking for it. I should help her to a whipping."

"Nonsense," he said. "She was looking for a book to put her to sleep."

"A man more like," his grandmother said.

"If that were so, she would not have refused my invitation, would she?" he asked reasonably.

"Did you ever consider that perhaps you were the wrong man, Charles?" she asked, peering at him over her spectacles again.

He laughed. "Grandmama," he said, "you will always keep me humble, I'm afraid. I met her on the road two evenings ago and failed again, I am sorry to say. Very sorry! But I feel responsible, you see. I gave her your direction and assured her that you would help her find employment." He smiled disarmingly.

"Did you indeed?" she said. "And as what, pray? As a chambermaid in this house so that you may molest her at your every visit? And I suppose I could expect you to grace me with your company twice daily?"

Rutherford's smile became more rueful. "She is refined, Grandmama," he said, "and virtuous. A lady in everything but fortune, I believe. You must know someone who needs a governess. You know everyone in the kingdom, I sometimes think. But one thing. You must get her away from London. Far away. I really have no wish to meet her again."

The dowager duchess regarded her grandson steadily for a few silent moments. "I begin to like the gel," she commented. "It takes a rare one to discompose someone as jaded as you, m'boy."

"Jaded?" he said, eyebrows raised. "And discomposed, Grandmama? You mistake the matter quite."

"Don't come haughty with me, Charles," she said, quite unperturbed. "If it comes to haughtiness, I can give you lessons. You liked the gel, eh?"

"As I have said, Grandmama," he said, "I could have put her to good use. But she chooses to be an impregnable fortress. I have given up the siege. There are willing females enough."

"Go to it then, lad, but not to be driven in Hyde Park," his grandmother said. "That was a disgusting display."

"I behaved with the utmost respectability, Grandmama," Rutherford protested. "I did not come anywhere near you or even dream of trying to present the, er, female to you. I think you were secretly chagrined that I did not bring her close enough for your inspection. I know better than to do any such thing, my dear."

"About this gel," the duchess said. "She may come here. I shall see what I can do. If I like the look of her, I shall find her something. But barefoot in the library at midnight, Charles! Not at all the thing. She should know better. She is something of a beauty, I take it?"

"A little gray governess actually," Rutherford said with a smile.

"Hm," his grandmother said. "Except when she is barefoot in the library, I gather. Well, and about time, Stebbins. I thought perhaps Cook had had to send to South America for the coffee beans. Now, Charles, let us change the subject. Tell me more about Barrie and his gel."

It was at a somewhat more respectable hour of the following morning that Jessica was shown into the salon that led off the main hallway of the house on Berkeley Square. The hour was almost noon. She had come after some hesitation. Perhaps now she was in London she should not rely on the promised help of the Earl of Rutherford. Berkeley Square was a very exalted location from which to expect help. There seemed every chance that she would suffer the ignominy of being turned away from the door. Besides, she was not sure that she would wish to be beholden to the earl for anything. Perhaps he would use his generosity against her in the future.

That was unfair, though, she realized as soon as the thought had entered her mind. Had he wished to use anything against her, he might have taken advantage of her physical presence in his bed and her verbal agreement to become his mistress at the Blue Peacock Inn. And it was very unlikely that a man of Lord Rutherford's rank and physical appeal would wish to renew his attentions to someone who had repulsed him in quite such a way.

She would have to call at Berkeley Square, she realized finally. She had completed her journey to London on the stagecoach despite Lord Rutherford's almost insistent invitation to ride with him in his carriage. She had refused to allow him to take her to his elderly acquaintance, but had been willing to accept only a written name and address. She had had to spend another night on the road.

Part of her had bitterly regretted her refusal to join the earl in his carriage. He had left before the stage-coach, and from the moment of his departure until her arrival in London she had had to suffer the vicious sarcasm and more open condemnation of her fellow travelers. In fact, the female next to whom she had sat on the previous day had refused to share a seat with "a gen'leman's bit o' fluff."

By the time she had arrived in London her spirits were so low, her confidence so bruised, that she had been rash enough to stay at a respectable hotel. It was not a grand place and not expensive, but it was far beyond her means. She could afford to stay there only one more night, and that was provided she did not eat at all during the day. She had to go to Berkeley Square. And she would have to hope that the Dowager Duchess of Middleburgh would be able to find her an immediate situation.

But she would not beg, she thought, as she stood in the middle of the salon, afraid to approach too near to the fire, although her long walk through the streets of London had thoroughly chilled her, lest she look too forward to the lady when she came. A duchess! She had tried to shut her mind to that fact. Berkeley Square was bad enough.

The door was opened by a footman eventually and a tall, angular lady of exaggeratedly upright bearing swept into the room. Jessica's heart sank. The woman's face was decidedly stern. She looked at Jessica along a thin, pointed nose, for all the world as if she were inspecting a worm and trying to decide if she should have it speared and thrown outside or if she would merely squash it with her foot.

Jessica curtsied and found herself unconsciously resuming the meek manner she had always deemed necessary with the Barries.

"Miss Moore?" the lady said in a voice that matched exactly the expression on her face. "You wished to see me?"

"Yes, your grace," Jessica said, wishing that her voice did not sound quite so thin and breathless. "The Earl of Rutherford said I might come here and beg you to help me find employment." Not at all what she had wanted to say, she thought, annoyed at herself.

"And does the Earl of Rutherford think I am an employment agent?" the duchess asked, eyebrows raised. "If it is work in my scullery you are seeking, child, you must go around to the kitchen door and speak with my housekeeper."

Jessica allowed herself one hurried look up into the stern face. "I have been a governess, your grace," she said. "But I see that Lord Rutherford assumed too much. Please forgive me, ma'am. I would not have come without his assurances that I might."

"My grandson is a presumptuous puppy," the duchess said. "It comes of being the only son of his father and the only grandson of his grandmother. The boy has been spoiled. Thinks he can twist us all around his little finger. And very often succeeds."

Her grandson! She might have known, Jessica thought. The two shared that air of haughtiness. But she felt even more embarrassed than she had already been. He had sent her to his grandmother.

"I—I did not know," she said foolishly. "Please forgive me. I shall not take any more of your time."

"I thought you came for help," the duchess said, sweeping across the room and seating herself with straight back on the edge of a chair by the fireplace. She motioned to a chair opposite hers. "Sit down, gel. Your nose is red. Cold outside, is it? But then it usually is in November. Warm yourself. I shall send for coffee."

"That is very good of you, your grace," Jessica said, taking the offered chair after a moment's hesitation.

She was not a little disconcerted to find herself the object of a silent and intense scrutiny for all of the next minute.

"Well, the boy was right about one thing," the duchess said at last. "You are a gray governess. Did that

Barrie woman insist on such dreary and tasteless garments? Take off your bonnet, child."

Jessica blushed as she obeyed.

The duchess clucked her tongue. "Ruinous on the hair," she said. "Scraping it back like that takes all the natural shine and life out of it, gel. Miss Barrie is not a beauty, I take it?"

"Ma'am?" Jessica's eyes widened in incomprehension at this apparent *non sequitur*.

"The Barrie woman must be a clothhead if she thought to make you uglier than the gel by disguising you like this," her companion continued. "You only look the more intriguing. I don't wonder at Charles's trying to seduce you."

The color flooded into Jessica's cheeks. She stared at the duchess, mesmerized.

"You must have some character," the old lady said. "I do not believe there are many females who have refused an invitation to Rutherford's bed. And you did it twice! I would give a bag of gold to have seen his face when you did so." She chuckled with what sounded like genuine amusement. "Did he turn quite purple?"

Jessica swallowed. "He acted like a gentleman," she said.

The old lady threw back her head and laughed with open amusement. "I don't believe you know what you say, child," she said. "You mean he behaved as a gentleman is supposed to behave. After he had politely requested that you drop your clothes at the side of his bed, of course. But I am embarrassing you, gel. I have always spoken exactly what was on my mind. I was born for a different calling, the duke often used to tell me, except for one essential fact. I had the mind and the tongue but not the inclination. Now then, my dear, who are you?"

"Jessica Moore, your grace," Jessica said.

"My butler told me that this morning and my grandson yesterday," the duchess said patiently. "I wish to know who Jessica Moore is."

"My father was a clergyman," she said. "He was not a wealthy man. When he died, I was forced to seek employment. I have been governess to Lord Barrie's daughter for two years. I worked hard, ma'am, and tried to do a satisfactory job."

"Did you often walk barefoot in the library at midnight?" the old lady asked with a return of the severity she had shown at the start of their interview. "And with your nightgown on and your hair down your back?"

Jessica bit her lip with mortification. Did Lord Rutherford keep nothing from his grandmother? Did the old lady regarding her so closely know that she had lain in bed with him two nights ago, his hands touching even the most secret parts of her?

"I was forbidden to leave my room after bedtime," she said. "I am afraid that I disobeyed on three occasions during the two years."

"And if I recommend you for employment as a governess again," the duchess said, "will I be accused in perhaps a few months' time of recommending a young woman who likes to tempt the male members of the household and then turn the prude?"

Jessica looked jerkily down at the hands clasped in her lap. "I swear you will not, ma'am," she said. "I have learned my lesson, and I am truly sorry for what I did. Your reproof is well deserved."

"Handsomely said," the duchess commented. "And where was your father's parish, gel?"

Jessica named a place in Gloucestershire.

"Your mother died before him?" the older lady asked.

"When I was but two years old," Jessica said.

"In childbed?"

"Yes," Jessica said. "The baby died too. My brother."

"Hm," the old lady said. "These things happen, gel. What will you do if I fail to help you?"

"I do not know, ma'am," Jessica said, closing her eyes briefly against panic.

"Do you have any alternative to walking the streets?"

Jessica hesitated. "I think I will not be reduced to that," she said.

"Charles?" the old lady asked. "He has offered his protection if I fail him?"

"He gave me his card," Jessica admitted, "and told me I might send to him at any time."

"It's not his style to set up a mistress," the duchess said. "But if he offered, he will keep his promise. You could do worse, child."

"I tore up his card before I reached London," Jessica said.

"But you still think you will not have to walk the streets," the duchess mused.

"Yes, ma'am."

"You have somewhere else to go, then, even though you clearly do not wish to go there."

"Yes, ma'am."

"Well," the duchess said briskly, seeming to have come to some decision, "I shall certainly have to do something for you, my dear, or Charles will never let me forget it. You have the look of your grandmother, you know, to quite a remarkable degree."

"Oh, do I?" Jessica said, looking up pleased that the duchess had committed herself to helping her. "Thank you so much, ma'am."

The dowager duchess sat quietly looking at the eager face across from her until it lost its glow and blanched. The eyes in the pale face grew huge.

"You know? You knew my grandmother?" she whispered.

"It is a rough fate for you, is it not, my dear," the duchess said soothingly, "to have been directed to the house of a woman who my grandson claims knows everyone in the kingdom?"

"But I have my father's name," Jessica said. "You cannot possibly have known him."

"No," the duchess admitted, "but it so happens that your grandmother the marchioness was my particular friend. We made our comeout together, you know—a long time ago, my dear. And indeed, the resemblance between you is almost uncanny. I remember well how very upset she was when her only child—they were not as fortunate as we were, you see; their only child was a gel—insisted on marrying a country parson. I even recall the name Moore, my dear. I have a memory full of such apparently unimportant details. Adam was his given name?''

Jessica nodded, feeling numb.

"And I recall how very miserable poor Mirabel was when your mother died in childbed and your father would not allow the marquess to help at all in your upbringing. Yes, I even remember the name Jessica. Your papa allowed you to visit your grandparents only once a year and for only one week?''

Jessica nodded again.

"And then poor Mirabel died herself," the duchess said, "and I heard no more news of you or your father. You did not feel you could turn to your grandfather for help when your father died?''

Jessica shook her head.

"And you don't wish to tell me the reason why," the old lady said after waiting for a moment. "So be it. So now, what do we do with you, grandchild of my dear friend?''

"Please help me find employment," Jessica said. She felt as if she were viewing the duchess and indeed the salon and herself through a long tunnel. She had not intended that anyone but she should ever know more of her identity than her father's name.

"I hardly think it appropriate for the only granddaughter of the Marquess of Heddingly to take employment as a governess," the duchess said, frowning.

"But it is what I wish," Jessica said, leaning forward and staring anxiously across at the older lady. "There is no alternative, your grace. At least, no alternative that I wish to take.''

"Oh, I think there is," the duchess said. "I think it

would be quite appropriate for me to entertain the granddaughter of one of the dear friends of my youth. Up from the country to spend the winter with a lonely old woman. Come to meet society. Not quite as exciting as it would be in the spring during the Season, of course, but not bad even so. There are quite sufficient people here during the winter for you to cut quite a dash.''

Jessica was on her feet. ''Oh, no, ma'am,''' she said. ''No. I could not possibly. Please. I did not come here to beg such favors.''

''Of course you did not,'' the dowager duchess said haughtily. ''No one has held a dueling pistol against my breast to force me to offer my hospitality. I do so quite freely. But you will find that once I have my heart set on anything, it is almost impossible to cross my will. Save yourself a losing fight, my dear, and sit down again. Tell me where I must send for your trunks. You will move in here today, and I shall have a dressmaker and a hairdresser brought to the house this afternoon. We have to rid you of that dreadful gray and that quite horrid hair style. I suspect it will not be difficult to make a beauty of you. And I would say so even if I were not sure from the fact that Charles tried twice to seduce you.''

Jessica blushed and sat down.

The Earl of Rutherford called on his grandmother again during the afternoon of the following day. It was the afternoon of the week when she was known to be at home to callers. His return visit would therefore be less conspicuous, he thought. And realized immediately that if he believed that he was fooling no one but himself. She had known even two days before that his visit was unusually soon after his return from the country. She would know as soon as she saw him today that his interest in Jessica Moore was greater than he had tried to make it appear.

And it irritated him to know that it was so. Why

should he care what happened to the woman? He was not really responsible for her. And he had given her the chance of a secure future. Two chances. She would have lived far more comfortably as his mistress than she had ever lived in her life, he would wager. And when she had refused that life, he had sent her to his grandmother. And Grandmama would not let him down. She would find something for Miss Moore.

Why should he be worried, then, worried to the point of scarcely sleeping the night before and of rushing to Berkeley Square for the second time in three days? Why should he be worried that she would not have gone to his grandmother? He fervently hoped that she had. He had an uncomfortable feeling that he was going to be roaming the streets of London, searching all the favorite haunts of prostitutes for the next several weeks if she had not.

Damn that woman! Rutherford thought as he handed his greatcoat, hat, and gloves to a footman and followed the butler upstairs to his grandmother's drawing room. She had stood before him in the parlor of the Blue Peacock Inn the morning after his sleepless night, the little gray governess all over again, her eyes not once directed at anything but the floor, coolly refusing all his most charming and lordly invitations to ride with him in his carriage. It had been almost impossible to imagine, looking at her, that she was the same woman who had lain hot and aroused in his arms for all too brief and unsatisfactory a period the night before.

Damn her! He hoped she had come and that Grandmama had sent her to a remote corner of Wales or Scotland. Then he could put her out of his mind and seek out more grateful female companionship that night.

"Ah, Charles, m'boy," the duchess said when he was announced, "I have been expecting you. I am in the middle of telling these ladies that I am soon to have company. Young granddaughter of one of the dearest friends of my youth. Coming for the winter. I am going to introduce her to society.''

"You, Grandmama?" Rutherford stared at her in some surprise, his eyebrows raised.

"Lonely in my old age," she said vaguely. "I shall enjoy it.''

It was only later, when the arrival of more visitors led to less generalized conversation that she was able to add for the ears of her grandson only, "Young chit, Charles. Might make a good wife for you, m'boy. I shall expect you to show her some attention.''

Rutherford pulled a face. "So far, Grandmama," he said, "I don't thoroughly approve your idea of eligible females. I am sure that with your connections you will be able to marry her off in a fortnight. Especially if her father has money. Did Miss Moore come yesterday?''

"Eh?" she said vaguely. "Oh, your gray governess, Charless. Yes, yes. I have dealt satisfactorily with that matter.''

"You have found her a situation?" he asked.

"Yes, yes," she said with a dismissive wave of the hand. "Now about this gel, Charles. She will be new to society, you know. I shall be counting on you to bring her into fashion.''

He grimaced. "I suppose that means dancing with her at assemblies, sitting in your box at the opera, and such like," he said. "Well, Grandmama, I suppose one favor deserves another. I shall play the gallant. But only for a few days, mind. If she is from the country, the girl is bound to be a dreadful bore.''

"We shall see," the duchess said, rising to her feet and advancing on a pair of new arrivals, one hand extended graciously.

# 5

JESSICA LOOKED AT HERSELF full-length in the mirror once more. She had dismissed the maid fifteen minutes before. But she still deemed it too early to go downstairs.

What she saw in the glass did not entirely displease her, she had to admit. After two years in unrelieved gray, with her hair constantly pulled back into an unbecoming bun, she felt a certain delight to see herself in a colored gown. The apricot silk fell loosely from beneath her breasts. It was adorned with heavy flounces around the hem. The plain scooped neckline was daringly low, she felt, though both the dowager duchess and the dressmaker had assured her that it was quite conservative. The short puffed sleeves were trimmed with miniature flounces to match the hem. She wore apricot slippers and long white gloves.

And her hair! It had rarely been cut in her life, and then only because she had felt the ends were lifeless and split. Papa had held that a woman was intended to leave her hair long, and she had always respected his opinions. She still could not believe the lightness of her head without all the bulk. Her hair was still not short as the hairdresser had tried to persuade her was all the crack. It was twisted up into a topknot. But the severity was all gone. Soft curls framed her face and trailed along her neck. She really looked quite pretty, she thought privately, for all her four-and-twenty years.

And what an advanced age it was to be making her first appearance in society. And at a ball at that. She had never thought to attend a real grand ball. Indeed, she had been taking dancing lessons for the past five days, brushing up on the steps of the country dances they had performed on the village green at home, learning the more elegant dances, including the scandalous waltz, against which her father had spoken so strongly when he had heard of it.

And what was she doing, Jessica thought, turning away from the mirror again and toying with the brushes on the dressing table, in residence at Berkeley Square with the Dowager Duchess of Middleburgh, friend of her grandmother? And what was she doing allowing the duchess to clothe her and train her in the social skills and organize a social life for her? It was the very life she had refused to allow her own grandfather to provide for her two years before. She had chosen rather to make her own way in life. She had become Sybil Barrie's governess.

She had loved her grandparents while her grand-mother lived. During the one week of each year that she spent with them, she had loved to explore the house with its many treasures and to roam the estate, both on foot and on horseback. And this despite the fact that her grandfather had never had anything good to say about her father. Her grandmother had been a gentle soul who was content to pour out the love of her lonely heart on her one grandchild, whom she saw so seldom.

After Grandmama's death, the visits had been less enjoyable. Grandpapa had been forever criticizing her drab appearance, her love of reading, her serious ideas on life, religion, and politics. He had wanted her to come and live with him so that he could make her into the lady she should be by birth. He had wished to send her to school. She had quarreled quite violently with him two years before her own father's death when he had accused Papa of dreadful things including stealing and then killing her mother. She had refused to visit him after that.

She might have gone to him after her father's death. Although she was of age, she had led a quiet and sheltered life. She was frightened by the prospect of being alone. Her father had left almost nothing beyond a pile of books. But the marquess had come to her and had angered her beyond bearing when he told her his plans for her. They included a Season in London and a dazzling marriage, both of which she had secretly dreamed of for years. But his manner had been irritating. He had not consulted her wishes at all. And he had loudly criticized her poor dead father yet again for holding her back from her birthright until she was already fairly on the shelf.

"It's a good thing I am able to offer a handsome dowry, Jessica," he had said, "or I do not know where we would find the man to take you at your age."

That had been the final straw. "I do not need either your dowry or a husband, Grandpapa," she had said quite firmly. "I am my father's daughter as well as my mother's. I shall make my own way in life without your help."

They had both said a great deal more in voices that had gradually risen in volume and increased in vehemence. But neither had shifted position. In the end the marquess had returned home in high dudgeon, and a frightened Jessica had taken up residence with some friends while the local squire's wife graciously agreed to help her find a situation.

And here she was, Jessica thought now, for all her fine words, doing what her grandfather had wanted her to do all along. She had found it less easy to defy the Dowager Duchess of Middleburgh. That lady did not lose her temper. She merely had a will of iron. Jessica had protested. She could not be so beholden to a stranger. She could not have hospitality and gifts showered on her when she had nothing to offer in exchange. She could not make an appearance in society when nothing in her upbringing had prepared her for such a life. She could not face the Earl of Rutherford if she accepted his grandmother's generosity. This last objection had been stated hesitantly, but in truth it was perhaps the most forceful in Jessica's mind.

The duchess had had an answer for everything. She was not a stranger. The Marchioness of Heddingly had been one of her dearest friends, if not the dearest. Jessica had a great deal to offer in exchange for the little the duchess could give her. She had her youth and her freshness. The duchess was a lonely old woman, who would be eternally grateful for Jessica's company. Jessica had a suspicion that this was quite a bouncer. The "gel" would do very nicely in society for all her lack of formal training. She had a natural refinement of manner. And as for Rutherford—the old lady had made a dismissive gesture—she rarely set eyes on the boy. They certainly did not frequent the same events. It was very unlikely that Jessica would so much as set eyes on him ever again.

Jessica felt somewhat comforted by the last assurance, though not entirely. Why had Lord Rutherford been so certain that his grandmother would help her if he rarely visited in Berkeley Square? And he clearly had been there before her own visit to tell his grandmother of her coming.

However, Jessica thought as she picked up the ivory fan that lay on her bed, it was rather too late to be having second thoughts now. Somehow she had been drawn into the duchess's schemes the week before, and since then she had been wrapped in luxury. The only irksome fact had been having to stay indoors until some presentable clothes could be delivered from the dressmaker's. Indeed, she had not even been allowed out of her room during those afternoons when visitors were expected. She was to make her first appearance, the duchess had decided, on this very evening, when Lord

Chalmers was giving a ball on the occasion of his wife's birthday.

And make her appearance she must, Jessica decided, taking a deep breath and realizing that her heartbeat was becoming painful and was interfering with her breathing. She turned resolutely to leave the room.

He really did not want to be here. Lord Rutherford looked up the staircase to where he could just see the beginning of the receiving line, and down the staircase to where several chattering groups had already gathered behind him. He glanced at Sir Godfrey Hall beside him and marveled at how his friend could always look amiable even in the most trying of circumstances. And this was extremely trying. It was not so much that he objected to being at Chalmers' ball. He supposed it was quite likely that he would have looked in on it anyway, such entertainments being sparse enough at this particular time of the year. What had really set him into a bad temper was having to come at such an hour. He could not remember when he had last been subjected to the tedium of a receiving line.

But he had to be present to lead this new protegée of his grandmother's into the opening set, she had said. It was not enough to assure her that he would sign the chit's card for two separate sets later in the evening. No, he must be there at the start so that she would be seen dancing with him and would be in demand for the rest of the evening. Was the girl so ugly that only such notice by him would induce other men to partner her? He had a premonition that she would be another Sybil Barrie, heaven help him.

But, he thought with a shrug, at least he would not be trapped in the country for a week or more with this particular matrimonial gem. A few days, he had promised his grandmother. He would dance with her twice tonight and lead her in to supper—he had been forced to promise that the second dance he had with her would be the supper dance. He would pay a call on her in Berkeley Square when there were plenty of other people there to take note of the fact. And he would take her for a brisk drive in the park—not such a mark of distinction as it would be in the spring, when there was always such a squeeze that a carriage could scarcely move. But still better than nothing. He would pay his respects at the Middleburgh box if she was taken to the theater.

And that was really about all his grandmother could expect. If that amount of attention did not fire the girl off, then there was little more he could do to help her. She would have to rely on hints dropped about the size of her dowry.

"My heartiest apologies, Godfrey," Rutherford said quietly to his companion. "I would not have dragged you here this early if I had known that there would be enough of a squeeze for us to be kept waiting on the stairs."

"Think nothing of it," his friend replied, smiling and inclining his head in the direction of an acquaintance farther down the staircase. "Being early does have its advantages, you know, Charles. One can find space on the cards of some of the prettier girls before they fill up."

"Hm," Rutherford said. He had never found difficulty in securing a set with even the prettiest girl after midnight if he just smiled at her or her mama in the right way. Perhaps his status as a wealthy, titled bachelor had something to do with the matter.

By the time the two men had made their way along the line ten minutes later, Rutherford was scowling, an expression that paradoxically drew even more female glances his way than usual. He clasped his hands behind his back and surveyed the scene around him, while Sir Godfrey beside him looked more pointedly with the aid of a quizzing glass.

His grandmother was not difficult to find, Rutherford soon discovered. Her tall figure and upright bearing drew one's eyes even without the purple satin gown and turban and ridiculously high plumes. And even from a distance he could see the rouge on her cheeks and lips. She had not yet seen him, or she pretended not to have done so. Probably the latter. No one had sharper eyesight than Grandmama, even without the spectacles.

Rutherford's eyes narrowed on the young person beside her. She was half turned away from him so that he could see only the barest profile of her face. The nose was straight, the chin determined, though not jutting. Pretty hair. It was no decided color, merely a light brown, but it was soft and shiny. Her figure, he guessed, was quite exquisite, though the fashionable gown falling loose from below her bosom hinted at rather than revealed the curves of waist and hips. One leg was slightly bent at the knee, a further hint of shapeliness. Her breasts looked full and high. She was perhaps on the low side of medium height.

Perhaps this would not be such an ordeal after all, he thought, his interest piqued.

"I must go and pay my respects to the dowager," he announced to Sir Godfrey, and began to stroll in her direction.

"Who is the beauty?" his friend asked, falling into step beside him. "Anyone I should meet, Charles?"

"Ah, Charles, m'boy," the dowager duchess said loudly as he approached, "what a surprise. I did not know you frequented *ton* balls."

"Indeed, Grandmama?" he said, eyebrows raised in some surprise. He took the hand she held toward him, executing one of his most elegant bows, and kissed her gloved hand. "I see you are looking quite as ravishing as usual."

"Impertinent boy," she said, rapping him on the sleeve of his brocaded coat with her fan. "Meet my guest, Charles. My grandson, the Earl of Rutherford, my dear. Miss Jessica Moore, Charles."

Strangely, he thought afterward when he had a

chance to think, although he had turned to her and looked appreciatively into her lovely face even as his grandmother still spoke, it was only as she mentioned the girl's name that he was jolted into recognition. His hand was already extending itself, he was already in the motion of bowing. His face was already set into a smile.

He completed his actions, raised her hand to his lips, and murmured, "Hello, Jess," without missing a heartbeat, just as if he had known she would be there, had prepared himself to meet her again. In truth, he was stunned. There was an air of unreality about the moment.

His mind hardly registered the fact that she was very pale when he went into his bow, decidedly flushed when he came out of it, and that almost no sound escaped her as her lips formed the words, "My lord."

"Good evening, Sir Godfrey," the dowager duchess was saying graciously beside them. "How is your father? Recovering? I am delighted to hear it. Do meet my guest, the granddaughter of my dearest friend, who is staying with me for the winter. Jessica, my dear, this is Sir Godfrey Hall. Miss Jessica Moore, sir."

She curtsied to Godfrey and even gave him something that would pass for a smile. She had done neither for him. Rutherford looked at her and then transferred his narrowed gaze to his grandmother. The old fiend. How did she hope to get away with this masquerade? And why was she doing it? To punish him? To have a joke on the *ton*? It was quite a tasteless and certainly an insufferable joke.

She smiled blandly back. "How grand of you to be here so early, Charles," she said. "Do you plan to dance, or are you to spend the evening in the card room?"

"I came to dance, ma'am," he said, his voice icy. "Miss Moore, may I have the honor of signing your card for the opening set and the supper dance? If those dances have not been spoken for already, of course."

There was an awkward pause as she stared at him in

almost open dismay. "No," she said. "I mean no, those
sets have not been reserved. I thank you, my lord."

He looked her straight in the eye before bending his
head in order to scribble his name against the two
dances on her card. He bowed and turned away as
Godfrey—poor fool—was reserving the second set with
her. He clasped his hands behind him and surveyed the
ballroom anew, without seeing anything. He
concentrated on keeping his breathing under control.
He could not recall ever feeling quite so murderously
furious.

He was not given much time in which to either control
his anger or allow it to build. Lord Chalmers was
leading his wife out onto the floor to begin the opening
set. Other sets were beginning to form around them.
Lord Rutherford turned toward Jessica, bowed stiffly,
and held out his arm for her hand.

Jessica was feeling flushed and inwardly excited by
the time the ball was two hours old. Amazingly, she had
been partnered for every set, though she had been fully
prepared to stand on the sidelines with the dowager
duchess for most of the evening as a mere spectator of
the dancing. She had not expected to draw the notice of
any gentleman, unknown as she was.

It was not just gentlemen to whom she had been
presented. The dowager had taken her to meet her
daughter-in-law, the duchess, and her granddaughter,
Lady Bradley. Both were very different from Lord
Rutherford, she noticed. The duchess had graying fair
hair and was comfortably plump. Her daughter was a
younger version of herself though not yet as ample in
figure. Jessica felt deeply mortified at being thus
presented to them. In other, slightly altered circumstances, she would be completely beyond their lowest
notice, their son's and brother's *chère amie*, no less. As
it was, Lady Bradley invited her to attend her *soirée*
three evenings hence.

Jessica also met Lord Rutherford's other sister,

unmarried though she was older than he. Lady Hope looked somewhat like her brother, tall, slim almost to the point of thinness, dark, rather handsome. But she lacked the haughtiness of either her brother or her grandmother. She had a habit, Jessica noticed, of smiling quickly and nervously, her hands fluttering aimlessly.

Lady Hope came to speak to her grandmother and to meet Jessica between the first and second sets and made herself agreeable. Sir Godfrey Hall was forced to interrupt her conversation with Jessica in order to lead the latter onto the floor for the quadrille. Lady Hope smiled at him and curtsied. He smiled warmly back and signed her card for the supper waltz before leading Jessica away.

Had she enjoyed the ball so far? Jessica asked herself when the dowager put that very question to her. The supper dance was next. It was a waltz, and the duchess had assured her that she might dance it though she had not been approved by the hostesses of Almack's. That was a ridiculous custom anyway, the old lady said, and one that certainly need not apply outside the months of the Season and to a lady well past her twentieth birthday.

Had she enjoyed the ball? Yes, of course she had. There was a thoroughly heady feeling of triumph in being at a *ton* event and accepted just as if she were one of their number by everyone present. She had not seen anyone frown her way or whisper behind a hand or a fan. There was satisfaction in knowing that she looked well enough that a whole succession of gentlemen had sought an introduction to her so that they might dance with her. And there was a delightful sense of freedom in being able to dance, to look her partners in the eye, to converse with them, smile at them, laugh with them. Only two weeks before she had been a governess, hemmed in by rules, expected to be seen and not heard outside the confines of the schoolroom.

And yet how could she enjoy herself fully? The

dowager had assured her that Lord Rutherford did not
frequent the same events as she. Was it merely an
unfortunate coincidence that he was in attendance at her
very first social appearance? Or had the duchess lied to
her? Jessica suspected the latter. She did not want to be
in his presence. She had been horribly embarrassed ever
since she had first glimpsed him strolling toward his
grandmother before the dancing started.

She had been unable to relax since, unable to ignore
his tall, elegant presence in the ballroom. How could he
be dressed all in gold and snowy white without looking
to even the slightest degree effeminate? He had not once
left the ballroom even though many other gentlemen
noticeably came and went. She had not seen Sir Godfrey
since the second set. And the Duke of Middleburgh and
Lord Bradley were in the card room, their wives had
explained.

Lord Rutherford had remained, standing beside his
mother much of the time. He had danced with each of
his sisters but with no one else, though even Jessica had
noticed that a great deal of feminine attention was
focused his way. In the few glances she had dared send
his way, she had found that he was not looking at her.
Why did she feel so very observed then, so very
exposed?

What must he think of her? He must consider her a
dreadful opportunist, staying at Berkeley Square as his
grandmother's guest when he had sent her there for
assistance in finding a situation as a governess. No, she
did not need to ask what he thought. Looks had already
spoken loudly enough. He had not said a word during
that first set. Indeed, it would have been difficult to
hold any sustained conversation as it was a country
dance and they were frequently separated by the figures
of the set. But he had looked dictionaries of meaning.

He had not taken his eyes from her throughout the
set, she would swear, and she had found somewhat to
her dismay that she could not withdraw her gaze from
his. And she had read accusation, contempt, fury in his

eyes. She had clamped her teeth tightly together and lifted her chin in an unconscious gesture of defiance. She might be embarrassed, dreadfully so, but she was not going to creep around Lord Rutherford, eyes constantly lowered to the floor, as she had done for two years with the Barries. Those days were over even if she found in the future that she had to go back to being someone's governess.

The dowager duchess was looking at her inquiringly. "Yes, your grace," she said. "I am enjoying myself immensely. How could I not when so many people are quite flattering in their attentions?"

"Here comes Charles to claim your hand for the waltz," the duchess said. "Do have a good time, dear. I have heard that the boy performs the steps with remarkable flair. In my day, of course, we would have thought it a shockingly forward dance. But there is a certain elegance to it, I must confess."

"Miss Moore?" the earl said, stretching out an imperious hand for Jessica's. "My dance, I believe, ma'am."

If he had two ice chips for eyes, Jessica thought, as she laid a hand in his, there would not be enough heat in him to melt them.

"Yes, my lord," she agreed, trying to ignore the voice of the dowager behind her assuring Lord Rutherford that she did the waltz most charmingly.

When he stopped among the other dancers, placed one hand at her waist, and clasped one of hers in the other, and when she lifted her free hand to his very solid shoulder, Jessica had to fight the urge to lower her eyes and hope to escape his notice by meek silence. She raised her eyes and looked into his. They still looked remarkably like ice chips, blue ice chips.

"I totally misjudged you, you know, Jess," he said, his voice as cold as his eyes.

"Did you?" she asked.

"I took you for a meek servant who was quite bewildered and frightened by the prospect of being turned off without a character," he said. "I thought you quite unable to cope with the wide world beyond your schoolroom."

"Did you?" she said. "And was that why you made the offer you did, my lord? Did you hope that I would have been irrevocably compromised and committed to being nothing more than your mistress for the rest of my life before I realized that there were other possibilities for the future?"

His hand tightened at her waist as the orchestra began playing and he led her into the steps of the waltz. He stared at her tight-lipped for the time it took her to count silently in threes and feel the rhythm of the dance. But such concentration was unnecessary, she discovered almost immediately. He was quite as expert as his grandmother had suggested. She could not choose but follow his lead.

"In a word, yes," he said. "And if that was sarcasm in your tone, Jess, I resent it. It is no insult, you know, for such as you to be offered the position of mistress to the Earl of Rutherford. There are many females above the rank of servant who would jump at the chance."

"In that case," Jessica said, "I am glad I resisted, my lord. I think it most unfair to jump a queue, don't you?"

His eyes narrowed. "You are impertinent," he said. "And you have no business in this ballroom. And even less speaking with my mother and my sisters. In fact, I find myself not at all in the mood for dancing. I have a great deal to say to you, Jess, and a ballroom is not quite the place to say it. Come with me. We will find somewhere more private."

He bowed elegantly to her and held out his arm. He even smiled. Jessica did not want to go with him. She did not wish to speak with him. But what could she do? she thought in the split second before she reached up a hand and laid it on his sleeve. He was the Earl of Rutherford, watched at that very moment, no doubt, by almost every lady in the room. And she was a newcomer, whom these people had accepted with remarkable kindness. To refuse to go with him would be to draw attention to herself. To begin some scandal, no doubt. She would be announcing to half the *ton* that she, a mere nobody, had had the effrontery to quarrel with no less a person than Lord Rutherford.

He led her out of the ballroom, along a hallway past several opened doors, all of which revealed rooms that were occupied. Finally he opened a closed door, glanced inside, and led her in. It was in darkness, the only light coming through the unshuttered window. It was some sort of small office, its only furniture a desk and chair and an old chaise longue.

"This," Lord Rutherford announced, closing the door firmly behind them, "will do very nicely. Now, Jess Moore, we will have a full explanation of this masquerade you and her grace have chosen to play."

# 6

"I SHOULD NOT BE here with you unchaperoned," Jessica said, knowing even as the words came out of her mouth what a stupid thing it was to say. "Her grace would not like it."

Lord Rutherford laughed, as she had feared he would. "This is the first I have heard of servants needing chaperonage," he said. "And in light of what happened—or almost happened—between you and me little more than a week ago, I think your protests rather silly. Do you not agree?"

Jessica could think of nothing to say. She crossed the small room and stood staring out into the darkness.

"What story did you tell her grace?" Rutherford asked. "You were utterly destitute a week ago. You were sent to her to beg help in finding employment. And this is the employment you have found? Masquerading as a lady and making all the people here tonight your dupes? I find your appearance and your presence here distasteful, to put the matter lightly. I await your explanation."

"Her grace has been kind enough to take me in for the winter," Jessica said. "I told no lies and used no tricks. Indeed, I begged her to find me employment. If you object to what she has done, my lord, I believe it is to her you should speak and not to me. I do not feel that I owe you an explanation."

"Who are you?" The words exploded into a stunned

silence. "Who is Miss Jessica Moore? I assume that if you had employment as a governess, you are not precisely a nobody. You obviously have some breeding, some education. Your father has some claim to the name of gentleman, I assume. Which fact makes you in the most general application of the term a lady. But there is a difference between being a lady and being of the sort of rank that would gain you admittance to a gathering such as this. You have no business here."

"Her grace apparently disagrees," Jessica said.

"Who is your father?" Rutherford asked. She could see, turning from the window, that his hands were held in fists at his sides.

"My father was a clergyman," she said. "A village clergyman. An *impoverished* village clergyman. He never had the means to send me to school. When he died, I had no choice but to seek employment." Her voice hardly wavered over the lie.

He nodded. "It is as I thought," he said. "My grandmother is growing older and more eccentric every day. Obviously she was taken by your youth and beauty and decided to amuse herself by trying to pass you off as a lady of the highest class. It will not do, Jess. You will be found out. Any gentleman you hope to ensnare as a husband will inquire into your background. He will want more than this mysterious reference to a grandmother who was one of her grace's dearest friends."

"Then you will be able to enjoy my public exposure to ridicule," Jessica said.

He made an impatient gesture with head and hand. "Enough of this impertinence," he said. "I have my grandmother's reputation to consider as well. I cannot tolerate any continuation of this charade. It must end. If you have no alternative, then I will renew my former offer. You may still become my mistress and retain this taste for pretty clothes that you have clearly acquired. That is more the life to which you belong, Jess."

"In your bed," she said.

"When I choose to put you there, yes," he agreed.

"And don't pretend that you would find those occasions distasteful, Jess. We both know different, don't we? But you will not spend the whole of your life in my bed. I will provide you with a home to enjoy. You wil have a carriage in which to travel around almost at will. I will take you to entertainments where it is acceptable for you to appear. Come, I think the time has arrived when you really have little other choice."

"On the contrary," Jessica said. "I find your offer insulting, my lord, when I have already rejected it once and when I am a guest at your grandmother's home and in this house tonight. Very insulting. I believe I shall return to her grace in the ballroom. She will be worried about me."

She lifted her chin, looked him in the eye in the semidarkness, and tried to walk around him to the door. It was a foolish move to make, of course, as she discovered immediately. His hand clamped around her upper arm so that she bit her lower lip with the pain of it.

"Oh no, you don't," he said between his teeth. "I think I will have you learn, Jess Moore, that I am not to be trifled with. Haughty manner and saucy speeches are not suited to a common servant. And that, my dear, is precisely what you are, despite the patronage of a rather foolish old lady. Indeed, there would be many who would call you slut or worse if they knew just one half of what happened between you and me both in and out of a certain bed in a country inn a week ago. Did you not know that unmarried ladies of the *ton* do not lie with men or offer their bodies for free exploration?"

If he hoped to make her blush and cringe, he was not going to succeed, Jessica decided. She glared back into his eyes, only inches from her own. "Do you threaten me, my lord?" she asked. "Am I to expect the story of our night together to become common drawing room gossip if I refuse to repeat that night with you—with a different ending, of course?"

"My patience is wearing very thin," he said. "I do

not need to threaten, Jess. I have never had to resort to using any sort of force to attract women to my bed and would certainly not begin on someone of such impertinent character. But I give you fair warning that I will not allow you to hurt anyone in this masquerade of yours. Do not try to win a rich or distinguished husband for yourself, Jess, or any influential female friend. Be sure that if you do, I shall find out all the details of your background for myself and pass them along to your chosen victims. That is no threat. That is statement of fact. I trust I make myself understood?"

"Oh, eminently so, my lord," Jessica said. "Tell me, pray, am I permitted to seek out a wealthy or influential protector? May I become another man's mistress without your carrying out the dreadful threat to expose my past? Or do you feel that by having lain in your bed and allowed your hands to touch me I have taken your stamp of possession on me? Pray tell me. I do not like nasty surprises. I should hate to have a future protector suddenly discover that my papa was an impoverished country clergyman."

"By God, Jess, you are impertinent," Rutherford said, his iron grip of her arm transferring to his other hand, while she found her free arm subjected to the same treatment. "Have you only just realized how very lovely you are? And how very desirable? Is that it? You have discovered that you need not teach for a pittance when you can make your fortune with your person?"

Jessica smiled broadly into his face. "Yes, that is exactly it," she said. "I may find someone more generous than you, my lord. And then, of course, I may not. Would you care to tell me the exact terms of your offer so that I may make comparisons when the other offers begin to come in? You understand, of course, that your chances will be very small if one of those rich, titled gentlemen should happen to wish to wed me even after you have made your shocking disclosure?"

"You are an unprincipled female of the lowest order, are you not?" he said, his grip tightening so that she winced noticeably. "I wish I had known back at that inn what I know now. I swear I would have carried that act to its completion. Do you believe my grandmother would have allowed you over her doorstep then?"

Jessica was unwise enough to tip back her head and laugh into his face.

She was not laughing a moment later. She was gasping against the onslaught of his mouth, wondering before she grasped the lapels of his brocaded coat and clung if her knees really were going to buckle under her and set her swooning at his feet.

It was a kiss without tenderness. It was meant to be insulting, punishing. One hand splayed behind her head and held it steady against the pressure of his mouth over hers. His tongue plundered her mouth without any pretense of gentle caress. His other hand moved downward over her spine, bringing each part of her body hard against his. Her clinging hands were soon imprisoned between them.

Memory came flooding back: memory of the smell of him, of the taste of him; memory of the ache that his mouth and tongue sent spiraling downward into her throat, through her breasts, and into her womb; memory of a warm bed and the feel of his long, muscled body against hers, of his hands moving, touching, caressing, arousing; memory of those hands against her naked flesh. Her hands loosened their grip on his lapels and slid upward around his neck.

His arms had moved to encircle her body and he held her close, though no longer bruisingly so. He still kissed her as deeply, but his tongue was circling hers, caressing it. Jessica lost touch with time and place.

"Jess," he murmured finally against her ear, "I could teach you to be very good at this, you know. You could be the best, most sought-after courtesan in England after you and I tire of each other. A long time in the future, if ever! You really are suited to nothing else now. You must see that. You have outgrown your days of innocence as a governess. And you can never be a real lady, my dear, however hard you dream. Cinderellas exist only in the pages of storybooks.''

Jessica leaned back against the circle of his arms. Her own were trapped above them so that she was not able to accomplish a very lethal swing. However, her slap did have the element of surprise, and the room was filled for one moment with a very satisfying crack.

"I wish that to be the last time, my lord—the very last," she said, "that you make insulting remarks and suggestions to me. Your assumption that my impoverished background makes me therefore a woman of loose and low morals says a great deal about your own morality. I will not be touched by you again—ever. I trust I have made myself understood?''

He had not moved beyond parting his hands behind her back and dropping them to his sides. He did not say a word or make any attempt to stop her from sweeping past him and out of the room.

It was not wise to gallop one's horse through Hyde Park, Lord Rutherford told himself even as he did just that. Although it was late November and although it was relatively early in the morning, the park was rarely deserted. There was almost sure to be some maid out walking a dog, some tradesman taking a scenic route to his work, or some more fashionable person intent on walking off the cobwebs of the mind acquired the previous night. One was not expected to move at great speed in the park. It was uncivilized to do so. It was also dangerous.

Yet he galloped, the harsh wind of November whipping against his cheeks and causing his eyes to water. Cobwebs of the mind! His brain felt fuller of chain mail.

He did not know quite why he should still feel so furious over the events of the night before. After all, if the woman wished to masquerade as a lady of the *ton*, and if his grandmother chose to aid and abet her for the sake of amusement during the long and often tedious months of winter, it was really none of his concern. He had sent her to Berkeley Square, it was true, but he had done so in good faith, believing that he owed a helpless servant that much assistance in finding a new situation. And he had clearly explained the circumstances to his grandmother, had specifically asked that the woman be sent away from London.

If between them those two women had concocted some mad scheme for the profit of the one and the entertainment of the other, then he should shrug the matter off and forget all about it. At least he felt himself absolved from the promise he had made his grandmother to give the girl his company and help bring her into fashion. Why allow the matter to affect his whole mood, then? He would give it no further thought. Rutherford eased his horse back to a safer canter.

She had been presented to Mama, Faith, and Hope. He had glanced across the ballroom at a time when he was conversing with an acquaintance from the House of Lords, and there she had been with his grandmother, talking to his mother and Faith. Had Grandmama's wits gone totally begging? It was one thing for her to countenance such a trick on the *ton*. It was another to involve her son's family. They would all become the laughingstock when the truth was known. And then at the end of the very next set he had watched Hope approach the dowager and her charge of her own free will and converse with them until Godfrey, bless his heart, had borne Jess away.

It must not be allowed to continue, he decided as he had the night before. There was no point in talking further with Jess and appealing to her sense of decency. Clearly she had none. He must call privately on his grandmother that afternoon and see if he could make her see sense. He did not relish the task. The dowager was notoriously difficult to deal with. She had a will of iron and was not to be turned from any enterprise on which her heart was firmly set. He would just have to hope that she would be satisfied with last night's triumph and uninterested in continuing the experiment.

Good God! he thought with a renewed burst of fury, the woman had been a servant, a little scrap of a gray governess a mere two weeks before. She had been a meek little thing who never raised her eyes in public or uttered a sound. She had certainly known her place when she was with the Barries. And he had been misguided enough to pity her. And less than two weeks ago she had agreed quite coolly to become his mistress and had carried her agreement through to the very brink of fulfillment.

And even then he had pitied her. He had considered her a demure, frightened girl who had felt herself forced into giving up all her principles, but whose character had been strong enough at the last moment to save her and to plunge her into an even worse predicament. He had pitied her and tried yet again to help her.

Had she seen the possibility even then? Had she seen how easy it was to lure a gentleman into making such an offer? If he had desired her when she appeared as she did, clad all in shapeless gray, her hair scraped into its unbecoming bun, what might not be accomplished if she could find some way of improving that appearance and some way of gaining introductions to other wealthy gentlemen? His offer to take her to his grandmother must have seemed like a gift from heaven. It was no wonder that she had refused to be taken but had chosen to go alone!

What story had she spun for his grandmother's benefit? he wondered. It must have been clever indeed. The dowager was no one's fool.

Yes, speak to Grandmama he must. Besides, how could he meekly ignore the woman after the challenge she had flung down the night before? He had never been bested by a woman. Not nearly. And he had no intention of making the encounter of the night before the end of the war. Merely an unimportant skirmish.

He had really thought he was succeeding. He had begun to kiss her in frustration, the need to punish and

insult her the only way he could cope with her stub-
bornness and impudence. But he had felt her almost
instant response. She had not clamped lips and teeth
together as he might have expected. Nor had she
removed her body from his after his one free hand had
brought her against him. He had felt a certain triumph
as soon as her hands came away from his lapels and
moved up to his neck and into his hair. He had not
missed noting that her breasts had then been pressed
more intimately against him.

She had wanted him, he was sure. Even if those
reactions had been feigned in order to take him off his
guard, there had been the very real surge of heat that he
had felt with his hands and his body. He had been careful then to change the quality of his embrace, to woo her
with his body. He had even been weighing in his mind
how comfortable a bed that chaise longue would make
and how safe the unlocked door behind him would be
while he sealed their contract.

The woman obviously had iron-hard control over her
own feelings. He could not have been mistaken about
her response. He had too much experience in such
matters to be easily fooled. But somehow she had
mastered her own desire and had succeeded in dealing
him that stinging slap. That too had never happened to
him before. He had always sworn that the female who
struck him would be struck back twice as hard. And
indeed, it had taken no small measure of control on his
part to let his hands drop to his sides and to allow her to
leave. Instinct had made him long to tip her beneath his
arm and wallop her until she cried for mercy. Alas, he
had discovered that he could no more strike a female
than he could bed an unwilling one.

Physical punishment he could not deal her, then. But
he would not stand meekly by and allow her to make a
fool of him. She had refused to give up her charade. She
had refused his renewed offer of protection. He had
given her every chance. Now there would have to be
punishment of some sort. The woman was to learn that

one did not trifle with the Earl of Rutherford and escape unscathed.

Damnation, but she was a desirable wench, he thought, grinding his teeth as he turned his horse in the direction of home. He could not pretend even to himself that he had been guided solely by his head when he had embraced her the night before. Indeed, he had not really known he was going to kiss her until he was in the process of doing so. And the warmth and moistness of her mouth encompassing his tongue, and the shapeliness of her body pressed against his own had sent his own temperature soaring as well as hers. His sense of triumph had resulted as much from his conviction that she was after all to become his own possession for as long as he chose as it had from the belief that the charade would now come to an end. If he were totally honest with himself, he would admit that he had considered that chaise longue more as a means of fulfilling an almost overwhelming desire than as a way of finalizing a contract.

She was the only woman who had ever resisted him. Oh, not quite, he supposed. There were always those occasions when he sent out tentative lures only to discover that there was no point in expending further energies on a siege. But he had never been rejected on any occasion when he had made a determined effort to attract and even made a definite verbal offer.

And now he had been rejected—three times—by the same female, and a servant at that, a girl past her first bloom and without a penny in the world. And there was probably the attraction, he realized as soon as he had mentally verbalized the facts. He was experiencing the universal human craving for what cannot be had.

She did not wish him ever to touch her again, she had said. What a thoroughly unnecessary admonition! His very sanity might depend on his staying as far away from her as circumstances would allow.

\* \* \*

The Dowager Duchess of Middleburgh bestowed a benign look on her butler. The man had just informed her that her triumph was now finally complete. He had not said those words, actually. He had merely announced in his well-trained confidential tones that were designed to carry no farther than her own ears that the Earl of Rutherford was downstairs in the hall, requesting a private word with her.

"Show him up," she said.

The butler, long trained not to contradict his lady, looked her briefly in the eye to see if she could possibly have missed the detail about the private interview, understood that she had not, made a stiff obeisance, and withdrew himself from the drawing room to carry out orders.

The duchess meanwhile smiled sympathetically at Lord Beasley and Mr. Menteith, who for lack of other entertainment had been thrown into each other's company, and offered them more tea. It was extremely gratifying to know that her charge was too busy to do more than pass the time of day with two such eligible bachelors. Beasley was somewhat too fond of his victuals and the wine bottle, it was true, and consequently was bound together into one large, creaking bundle by heavy stays; it was true too that Menteith was without title, and most of his fabulous wealth had been amassed by his father through trade. But it was a splendid triumph to see them in her drawing room when dear Jessica had so far made only one public appearance.

Jessica had Sir Godfrey Hall sitting on one side of her, engaging her in spirited conversation, and Hope on the other. Miss Menteith was sitting shyly on a stool at her feet, gazing up at the three conversationalists with an almost worshipful attitude. There were some who would have frowned at the girl's visiting with her brother when she would not be brought out until the following spring. But what could one expect of the off-

spring of a gentleman unconventional enough to go into
trade and galling enough to repair the family fortunes
thereby?

"The Earl of Rutherford, your grace," the butler
announced in tones that clearly but silently added, "and
don't blame me for the consequences neither."

"Ah, Charles," the dowager said, advancing on him
with one hand extended, her expression all gracious
innocence. "I have been expecting you, m'boy."

It said something for the boy's experience with life,
she thought approvingly, that he stopped abruptly on
the threshold of the room for only a moment before
recovering himself and advancing into the room to
make his bows to all its occupants. He was unable to
summon a smile, but then modern manners were not
what they had been in her day.

She forced him to accept a cup of tea and limp his
way through a stilted conversation with Beasley and
Menteith for all of five minutes before taking pity on
him finally and laying a hand on his arm.

"Charles and I have some private business to discuss
for a few minutes," she said graciously to the room at
large. "Do, pray, excuse us."

"Certainly, Grandmama," Lady Hope said, while
several of the others gave low assenting murmurs. "Do
come back before leaving, though, Charles. I rely on
you to escort me home as I dismissed my maid when I
arrived. And Mama will certainly be happy to see you.
You have called at the house only twice since returning
from the country, you know."

Lord Rutherford bowed in the direction of his sister,
carefully avoiding the eyes of Jessica, the dowager
noticed with certain amusement, and followed his
grandmother from the room and into a small study.

"Grandmama!" he said, clearly rattled. "You did
not misunderstand my message, I take it?"

"That you wished to see me privately?" she asked. "I
assumed you did not realize there were visitors and
would not wish to appear rude, m'boy."

"You know very well why I asked to see you alone," he said. "It will not do, Grandmama. She has no business in this house. Certainly not as a guest. And certainly not socializing with the likes of Hope and Beasley and Menteith. Your joke is quite distasteful."

"Sit down, m'boy," she said, motioning to a brocaded chair on one side of the desk while she took one on the other side. "You are far too tall to argue with. Puts me at a disadvantage. I assume you refer to Jessica?"

"You know I refer to her, Grandmama," he said. "She is a governess, a servant. And one not even in good standing at present. To my knowledge she has no money, no prospects. Without your mad intervention she would now be walking the streets. And I begin to think that that is where she belongs."

"Oh, I think not," the dowager said with maddening calm. "I do not for a moment believe that you think that, Charles. You think that she belongs in your bed. Can't say I altogether blame you. A pretty and quite delightful little thing."

"If it is in my bed she belongs," Rutherford said, "it is as my whore, Grandmama, paid for the services she renders there and forever kept apart from the sort of company with whom she now mingles in the drawing room. She is there now, for goodness' sake. With Hope. My sister."

"If Hope has not already been contaminated by contact with you," the duchess said soothingly, "I doubt she will be by Jessica, Charles. After all, you have been whoring for ten years and more."

He got abruptly to his feet. "That is an entirely different matter," he said. "I am a gentleman."

"Utter poppycock!" his grandmother said coolly. "Sit down, Charles, and lower your voice, m'boy. Nothing is ever gained by losing one's temper. I thought the gel did very nicely last night, didn't you? She would have been a great success even without your gracious assistance."

"It was a damned trick, Grandmama!" he said, putting his clenched fists down on the desk and leaning across it toward her. He had not obeyed the order to sit down. "You deliberately lured me there last night to witness what dupes the two of you could make of Lord Chalmers and all his guests. All right, you succeeded. But the matter must be left there. Find the woman employment. Let her go. This way, someone is going to get hurt. Probably even her. You are giving her ideas beyond her station."

"Calm yourself, Charles," the dowager said, leaning back in her chair and spreading her hands, palm up. "Actually, we have no quarrel with each other. I happen to agree that Jessica belongs in your bed. But not as your fancy piece. Far too vulgar. As your wife, m'boy. As your countess."

# 7

LORD RUTHERFORD RESTED HIS fists on the desk and stared for a moment into his grandmother's eyes. Then he gave vent to an incredulous bark of laughter.

"You want me to marry Jess Moore?" he said. "The woman who was governess to your last choice of bride for me?"

"I imagine her education and talents were very much wasted in the post," the dowager said. "I think she would make you an eminently suitable bride, Charles. The gel has beauty and breeding. She has character. More important, she has spirit. She will be able to keep you in line after your marrige. And you really must settle down, m'boy. Middleburgh—your grandpapa— had his sidelines, you know, but he was ever discreet. I grant him that. And you are the future Middleburgh, though I wish long life to your father. Won't do for you to settle a mousy wife in the country breeding while you continue to sow your oats in town."

"I agree with you on essential points, Grandmama," Rutherford said. "But how can you possibly suggest that woman as my future duchess? My wife must at least be of the same social class as I."

"Jessica is a lady," his grandmother pointed out.

"Oh, yes," he agreed, "she is somewhat above the rank of scullery maid, I grant you. Her father was a country parson, Grandmama. She admitted as much to

me last night. She even added that he was impoverished
and unable to afford to send her to school."

"Gels also have mothers," the dowager said.

He made an impatient gesture. "Her mother was
probably one of the royal princesses, of course," he
said. "I will not do it, Grandmama. I will not even
consider the matter. And I will not see the woman
again. You may stop trying to throw us into company
together. You will be wasting your efforts."

"Your mama will disapprove of your not spending
Christmas with the family," the dowager said
innocently.

"At Hendon Park?" he asked with a frown. "Of
course I shall be going there. I always do."

"Then you will be seeing Jessica again," she said.

A dull flush colored Rutherford's cheeks. "You are
never taking her there," he said. "To our private family
Christmas, Grandmama?"

"She is my guest for the winter," the dowager said.
"Where else would she go, Charles? And how would I
look back with clear conscience on the memories of my
dear friend, her grandmama, if I left her here?"

"Which fictitious character doubtless has a name, a
home, a history, and a genealogy reaching back at least
five centuries," her grandson said.

"Don't sneer, Charles," she said. "It spoils your
looks. You are quite right, of course." She paused,
looking sharply at him, waiting for the question that did
not come. She nodded briskly. "Now, dear boy." She
rose to her feet and reached for his arm. "We will return
to the drawing room where Hope will be waiting for
you. And you will have the chance to be civil to Jessica.
She was otherwise occupied when you arrived."

"I shall make my bow," he said. "Beyond that I will
not go."

"Just a word of advice for the future," his grand-
mother said, patting his arm. "Jessica is my guest,
Charles, and is to be treated with the proper decorum.
You must not offer her *carte blanche* again, m'boy.

Twice is quite enough. She will begin to find you tedious if you risk a third."

"She told you about last night, then," Rutherford said with some contempt, reaching out and opening the study door. "I might have known that she would go running bearing tales."

"Not by any means," she said. "But I am not quite in my dotage, boy. When a gel disappears with my grandson for almost half an hour and returns with an angry glint in her eye and a mouth that looks quite thoroughly kissed, I do not conclude that they have been discussing Latin literature."

"She refused me again," he said. "She sees that she can gain more from clinging to you, it seems."

"And quite right too," she said. "You should try to eliminate that spiteful inflection from your voice when speaking of such disappointments, Charles. You are a man of close to thirty years, not a spoiled schoolboy, m'dear."

"Sir Godfrey was unable to spend Christmas with us at Hendon Park last year," Lady Hope was telling Jessica. "His father was ill, and he felt obliged to go to his sick bed. But he is to come this year. We often invite close friends, you know, even though it is mainly a family Christmas. I believe you have made an impression on Sir Godfrey, my dear Miss Moore. As you have with several other young men. And that is as it should be. You are very lovely. If I were ten years younger, I should be positively jealous of you."

"You are very kind," Jessica said. "Everyone has been kind. I did not expect to have visitors today after only one appearance in public."

"Oh, there is nothing at all strange about that," her companion said, reaching out and patting Jessica's hand. "Even I, my dear, had my fair share of admirers during my first Season. The fact that Papa is a duke probably had something to do with that, of course. I was never a beauty."

Jessica smiled, but she was not given the chance to frame a reply.

"Oh, you do not need to pity me," the older woman said with a little laugh. "I knew at a very young age that I would never be pretty. Faith was, you see, and when people used to call her pretty and then turn to me and say I was handsome—always with a little pause before the word, my dear—I knew what they meant. I have never allowed the fact to disturb my sleep. I once loved, you know."

"Did you?" Jessica found herself warming almost despite herself to this nervous, talkative woman. All the other guests had taken their leave.

"He was very dashing," Lady Hope said. "And he loved me in return. Now is not that an amazing fact? He was killed in Spain." She gave Jessica a quick smile before her face became serious again. "He was a soldier, you know."

"I am so sorry," Jessica murmured.

"You need not be." She patted Jessica's hand briskly again. "There would have been the devil to pay when he came home to claim me. Papa would not have willingly allowed me to wed a soldier."

"I am still sorry," Jessica said. "You must have suffered."

"Suffering strengthens the mind," the other woman said. "Sir Godfrey would be a good catch for you, Miss Moore. He is a kindly man and only a couple of years older than Charles. About my age, in fact. He will try to fix your interest at Hendon, I would not wonder."

Jessica blushed. "I really am not thinking about marriage at all," she said.

"Oh, nonsense!" said Lady Hope. "We all think of marriage, my dear, whether we like to admit it or not. Usually I pretend that the maiden state suits me very well. But I will confess to you that I would very much like to have met another gentleman to whom I could have given my affection. I would like to have a man to call my own. And a child. Oh, I would like to have just one child, Miss Moore. Now is that not a foolish notion at my age? The child would not know whether to call me Mama or Grandmama.'' She laughed.

"I pray you will have your wish, Lady Hope," Jessica said, smiling.

"Sir Godfrey has been to Greece," Lady Hope said. "He traveled through Russia and even went to Constantinople. Is not that a marvel, now? He could not make the Grand Tour, you see, because of the wars. He will tell you about his travels if you really insist that you are interested. Otherwise, he will not even mention them. He is afraid of boring his listeners. Now is not that a foolish thing?"

The door opened at that moment and the dowager duchess entered with the Earl of Rutherford. Jessica felt as if someone had robbed her of breath. She did not quite know whether she should look at him or pretend that she had not noticed he was in the room. She chose the former.

"Hope?" he said, bowing. "Miss Moore? I trust you are not overtired today after last evening?" He flushed slightly.

"Thank you, no, my lord," she said. And she discovered that they were stranded, looking determinedly into each other's eyes, with an audience of two looking on, and nothing to say. She felt her own color rise.

"Sir Godfrey has invited Miss Moore and me to join him in a visit to Astley's Amphitheater tomorrow, Charles," Lady Hope said, without seeming to realize what an awkward situation she had relieved. "I do believe he intended to ask just Miss Moore, but I was sitting next to her, you see, and he felt obliged to ask me too. Was not that a foolish notion? However, dear Miss Moore would have needed someone to chaperone her, so I daresay it is just as well that he did ask me too. I am certainly old enough to be a quite acceptable chaperone, am I not, Grandmama? And I am most gratified to be asked. It must be all of ten years since I last saw the acrobats.''

"You will enjoy the outing, Miss Moore," Rutherford said stiffly, handing his grandmother to a chair. "The magicians and the clowns were always my favorites when I was a boy."

"You must go along too, Charles," the dowager said. "It does not seem fair that Sir Godfrey should have two ladies all to himself."

"I believe I have a luncheon engagement tomorrow, Grandmama," he said quickly.

"No, dear boy," she said. "That is for the day after. I distinctly recall your telling me so."

"Sir Godfrey did mention that he would ask you to make up numbers," Lady Hope said. "Did he not, Miss Moore?"

Jessica murmured agreement.

"Then it seems that I will have the honor of seeing you again tomorrow, Miss Moore," the earl said, bowing in her direction. "Hope? You are ready to leave? Shall I walk you home or would you like to ride in my curricle?"

"Oh, the curricle, by all means, Charles," she said, getting to her feet after patting Jessica's hands. "I rarely have the chance to ride in one these days. Most people seem to assume that someone of my age should be bundled up inside a closed carriage. Is not that foolish?" She laughed and bent to kiss the dowager's cheek.

Jessica felt that the plum-colored bonnet with the curled pink feather was rather too grand to wear to the circus, but the dowager duchess had assured her that it would do very nicely. And it did match exactly the warm pelisse that she was planning to wear over her pink wool dress. It still seemed strange to her to have a dressing room full of brightly colored, fashionable garments, some for the morning, some for the afternoon, some for informal evening wear, some for formal evening wear. Life had been dull but blessedly uncomplicated when she had used to rise in the morning to don a gray dress and confine her hair into its bun.

She was dawdling, she knew. She should have been downstairs five minutes ago so that she would not have to keep Sir Godfrey waiting when he brought his carriage for her. She was looking forward to going to Astley's, of course she was. It seemed delightfully frivolous to be setting off for an afternoon's entertainment by acrobats, clowns, performing horses, and magicians. She had never seen anything like it. She was not at all sure that Papa would have approved.

But she was not looking forward to the afternoon for all that. She would have thoroughly enjoyed the prospect of going with Sir Godfrey and Lady Hope. She liked them both. Sir Godfrey was an amiable gentleman and had the gift of keeping a conversation alive without either boring his audience with a monologue or demanding too much in the way of speech from them. And she liked Lady Hope, who appeared to have little confidence in either her looks or her charms, though she possessed both.

After having looked at the feathered bonnet for several irresolute minutes, Jessica finally placed it on her head and fastened the ribbons beneath her chin. What if he did think it too grand? What if she must observe him make mental calculations of how much it had cost his grandmother? What if he thought it inappropriate for an afternoon at the amphitheater? She did not owe any explanation whatsoever to the Earl of Rutherford. She did not care what he thought. Indeed, she hoped that he would disapprove.

Jessica had had a dreadful suspicion since the previous afternoon that the dowager duchess was trying to promote a match between her and Lord Rutherford. The realization had taken her completely by surprise. She would not have thought that she would be deemed worthy of the old lady's grandson, despite the fact that

her grandfather was a marquess. After all, her father
had been a clergyman, and she had been brought up in a
country parsonage. And she had been employed for the
last two years as a governess.

But incredible as it seemed, the dowager was
deliberately throwing the two of them together. Jessica
could not believe that Lord Rutherford had voluntarily
come back into the drawing room the afternoon before.
It would have been quite easy for him to send for Lady
Hope without coming to fetch her. And how could his
grandmother have known about his luncheon appoint-
ment—that obviously mythical engagement—when he
had not even mentioned the name of his host? She had
wanted him to accompany Jessica to Astley's.

Should she talk to her hostess about the matter?
Jessica asked herself for surely the twentieth time in as
many hours. Should she explain to her that she did not
wish any but the most unavoidable contact with Lord
Rutherford? But how could she? She was living on the
charity of the duchess. How could she so insult her?

Jessica picked up her reticule and opened it once more
to check its contents. And would it be the plain truth
anyway? Did she truly wish never to see him again? It
was certainly true that she felt great discomfort at the
idea of meeting him, and great embarrassment too. She
could not behave naturally in his presence. Every
faculty was aware of him so that she always found that
she could not look at him and yet could not *not* look at
him either. She wished to behave with easy manners and
easy conversation when he was near and yet found every
movement jerky and every thought and utterance
labored.

And always, always there was awareness of the
intimacies she had shared with him on two occasions.
The greatest liberty of which he should be able to boast
was a kiss on her gloved hand. But he had kissed her
with shocking familiarity, had touched and explored
every part of her with his hands, had lain in a bed with
her. And she had allowed a certain repetition of those

intimacies only two evenings before. Indeed, she had participated with an eagerness that made her cheeks feel uncomfortably hot as she stood inside the door of her room trying to persuade herself that she must go downstairs. She had wanted him quite desperately for a few mad minutes there at Lord Chalmers' ball.

So she could tell herself that she did not ever wish to see him again, that she disliked and despised him. But she would probably never convince herself. She had ordered him never to touch her again and was in despair lest he take her at her word. She dreaded seeing him again in perhaps just a few minutes' time. Yet she had a terror that he would after all have found an excuse not to come. She was horrified at the notion that his grandmother was trying to promote a match between them. Yet her insides performed churning leaps of excitement at the very thought of being Lord Rutherford's bride, his life's companion, his lover.

She would concentrate her attentions all on Sir Godfrey Hall, Jessica decided, opening her door resolutely and striding to the staircase. She would talk to him. She would ask him about Russia and Greece and Constantinople. She would sit by him and look only at him. She would ignore the Earl of Rutherford. She would forget he was even there.

Liar! an unbidden part of her brain commented.

She was choosing to ignore him, Rutherford thought. Apart from a stiff nod of the head and a look that alighted on about the third cape down on his greatcoat, she had cast neither a glance nor a word in his direction. It was really quite a feat of concentration, he decided, since she was sitting directly opposite him in a small carriage, their knees almost touching.

She really was incredibly lovely. Her beauty had been evident even when she was wearing the Barrie disguise and even for that matter when she wore nothing but that shapeless linen nightgown. Dressed fashionably as she had been on the three occasions he had seen her in

London, she was quite breathtaking. He would not have
expected a plum-colored outfit to look becoming on a
young woman, but on Jess it was perfect. That absurd
pink feather curling around from the brim to her chin
helped, of course.

She was talking with some animation to Godfrey and
Hope. He was scarcely aware of the topic since she had
chosen not to involve him in her conversation. She had
clearly set out to entrance Godfrey and was just as
clearly succeeding. Godfrey usually remained amiable
but aloof with ladies, preferring to take his private
pleasures with the mistress he had had under his
protection for all of two years now. It would be ironic
indeed if he should marry Jess when he had never even
considered marriage with the other female. If there
seemed any great chance of such an outcome, he must
warn his friend.

Marriage to Godfrey would be a great coup for her,
though, Rutherford thought, his eyes resting broodingly
on her profile with its straight little nose, flushed cheek,
and arched eyebrow. Fewer than two weeks ago she had
been hoping desperately that it would still be possible to
gain employment somewhere as a governess. Marriage
would have been a possibility only in her wildest
dreams. Now she was living in one of the grand houses
of Berkeley Square, wearing expensive and fashionable
clothes, socializing at this very moment with an earl, the
daughter of a duke, and a baronet. And having every
chance, it seemed, of making their world her own. If she
could but snare herself a distinguished husband, the
matter would be a *fait accompli*.

And it was his grandmother's wish that he become the
bridegroom who would so elevate her. Her wits must
really have gone begging. And she would be a nuisance.
She would be constantly throwing them together here in
London, and there was no knowing what she might try
when they were all together in the cozy atmosphere of
Hendon Park.

He knew what he would want to do with Jess, or to

her, at Hendon Park, Rutherford thought with a flash of the anger that had consumed him for all of the previous evening. And it had nothing to do with marriage or with acting the courteous host, either. Marry her! Make her the Countess of Rutherford, the future Duchess of Middleburgh. Fill her with his children!

Rutherford's jaw tightened. He wanted her. God, he wanted her.

She was looking into his eyes suddenly, appearing rather as if she were thoroughly trapped, as if she had caught herself by surprise. Her eyes widened, drawing him into their dark blue depths.

"Do you not think so, my lord?" she asked somewhat lamely.

"I beg your pardon," he said abruptly. "I confess I must have been daydreaming. I do not know to what you refer."

Sir Godfrey laughed. "Miss Moore agrees with me that I should consider making the usual Grand Tour now that the Continent is safe for travel again," he said. "Italy in particular should not be missed."

"To my certain knowledge, Godfrey," Rutherford said dryly, "you have been considering just such a journey since long before Boney was safely shut away on St. Helena. All you need is for someone to assure you that such an undertaking would not be self-indulgent. It sounds as if you have all the champions you need in Hope and Miss Moore."

"I have always felt it a dreadful injustice that ladies are not encouraged to the same extent as gentlemen to travel," said Lady Hope. "I for one would like nothing better than to see Rome and Florence. Oh, and Naples. We ladies seem to travel beyond our own shores only when we have husbands to take us. Is that not right, Miss Moore?"

"It is because most ladies are such delicate creatures and would suffer from the hardships of the journey," Rutherford said. "You hear only about the beauty of the Sistine Chapel in Rome and the pleasure of the gondolas in Venice and the wonder of the leaning tower in Pisa, Hope, and nothing about the discomfort of the lodgings in France and the vile smell of the canals in Italy and the endless vermin everywhere.''

"I think that is a myth put about by gentlemen in order to persuade us to resign ourselves to our lot," Jessica said. "I am sure that Lady Hope and I could endure the odors and the itching with as much philosophy as you, my lord, if we only had the works of Michelangelo to gaze upon while we scratched.''

Her eyes, looking directly into his own, danced with merriment for one unguarded moment, Rutherford noticed, startled. Then those eyes wavered and dropped to the capes of his greatcoat again, and her face sobered.

"A hit!" declared Lady Hope, clapping her hands. "You have silenced Charles, Miss Moore. He can think of no argument to refute your logic, you see. Unfortunately, that does not mean that you and I may now go and pack our trunks." She laughed.

"Ah, here we are!" Sir Godfrey declared cheerfully as the carriage lurched and slowed down. "Michelangelo may not be available to you, Miss Moore, but the clowns of Astley's will be a worthy substitute, I'll wager. Lady Hope, may I help you to alight, ma'am? It would be a shame for me to bear off Miss Moore and leave you to a mere brother's care, would it not?"

Rutherford's eyes met Jessica's across the width of the carriage. Both sat still until Lady Hope had been helped down the steps. Then Rutherford vaulted out onto the pavement and held out a hand for Jessica's.

"I do beg your pardon," he said quietly as she stepped down in front of him. "I was given a firm command not to touch you again, was I not? It seems that circumstances have made it difficult for me to comply."

She looked up into his eyes, her gloved hand still

firmly clasped within his. "Do we have to do this?" she asked in an undertone. "Can we not at least be civil since it seems that we are to be in company together more than either of us would wish?"

He raised one eyebrow. "Yes, you have done very well in placing yourself quite firmly in the midst of my family, have you not?" he said. "You are to be congratulated, Jess. But have no fear for my manners, my dear. I am, I believe, always civil to ladies and to others of the same gender."

She turned sharply away from him before he could be quite sure if it was tears that suddenly brightened her eyes. He grimaced and held out his arm for her support. How could he have said what he had when the very words refuted his meaning? He felt ashamed of himself and irritated with her for causing him to feel so.

"Please take my arm," he said. "The crowds can sometimes be rough here, I have heard. Astley's attracts spectators of widely varied social status."

"I should be right at home here, then," she said coldly, grasping her pelisse and walking off in pursuit of Sir Godfrey and Lady Hope.

Lord Rutherford was left standing, his arm extended, feeling foolish. He was forced to hurry after her and protect her as best he could with a hand at the small of her back, a gesture that merely made her straighten her spine and walk on.

Damnation take the woman, Rutherford thought. One of these times—just once!—he was going to get the upper hand in an encounter with Jessica Moore.

# 8

THE EARL OF RUTHERFORD did two things that evening that he had not done in years, and one other that he had not done in weeks. He gambled at Boodle's, a club he did not often frequent, though he had been a member for years, and won upward of three hundred pounds. He got drunk at the same club, almost but not quite to the point of incapacity. He even had an embarrassing memory the next morning, which he hoped was merely part of his night's fuddled thoughts, of delivering some sort of monologue and attempting a song. Embarrassing indeed for someone who had disappointed a mama and two doting older sisters by failing to produce one note of music by way of his vocal cords throughout his childhood and boyhood.

And he spent the murky hours between something after midnight and the twilight before dawn in bed with a woman he had no business going to bed with. He had looked in on an old crony on the way home from Boodle's, purely on drunken whim. His way had taken him past the house, and the lights were still blazing in the windows. He walked in on a party that looked as if it should have died a natural death an hour or more before. And he walked off less than half an hour later with Mrs. Prosser on his arm. Rather, he drove off in her carriage, and it was probably he who had been on her arm, he thought later, when he was trying to retrace all his activities of the night.

He could have had Mrs. Prosser years ago. He could name a dozen men who had. She was a widow and had the means and the inclination to remain so. She was willing to tell anyone who was interested enough to listen that she became easily bored with just one man. She had endured Mr. Prosser's unimaginative attentions for three years until the elderly man had had the good grace to bow out of this life and leave her free to indulge her fancies.

Rutherford had always avoided coming to the point with her. She was received by all except the very highest sticklers. He preferred to choose his bedfellows from among those women whom he would not afterward be forced to meet socially. Besides, Mrs. Prosser was an aggressive, voluptuous woman, and Rutherford liked to be totally in charge of what happened between the sheets of any bed he happened to occupy.

However, he thought just before dawn, as he stumbled home, trying to shake the fuzziness from his head and knowing that it was impossible to do—hangovers could not be shaken off at will—one could not expect to act rationally when one was drunk. Mrs. Prosser had taken him home and into her bed, and he supposed that he must have been satisfied with what happened there, because it seemed to him that it had happened more than once, perhaps even more than twice.

His valet hurried into his room, looking only slightly tousled, a few minutes after he had arrived in it. Rutherford was glad. He was sitting on the edge of the bed telling himself to remove his coat and his cravat and yet seemingly unable to lift his hands from their resting place on the bed either side of him.

"Warm water, Jeremy," he said, his nose wrinkling with distaste at the smell of some feminine perfume that clung to him. "Please," he added as an afterthought to the servant's retreating back.

The long-suffering Jeremy tucked his master into bed a short while later, fussed unnecessarily with the heavy velvet curtains that were already tightly drawn across the lightening windows, and tiptoed with theatrical caution from the room.

Rutherford groaned. He remembered now very clearly indeed why he had resolved five or six years ago never to get drunk again. The certain knowledge that he would feel wretched for all of the coming day did nothing to comfort him.

Dammit, he thought, lowering the arm he had flung over his eyes to his nose, he could still smell that woman's perfume. Mrs. Prosser, of all people. She was not at all the sort of woman he found appealing. She had seduced him pure and simple. She had taken advantage of his drunken state. Yet another reason for never getting drunk again! And where was the point of spending half a night making love with a woman when one could not afterward recall whether one had done so once, twice, or three times, or even—horror of horrors —no times at all?

But no, at least he could not be guilty of that humiliation. He could clearly recall her twining her arms around his neck as he was leaving, kissing him lingeringly on the lips, and declaring that she had not spent a more energetic and enjoyable night since she did not know when. Which said nothing about the caliber of his performance, of course, since the woman had meant to flatter, but it was at least an indication that there had been a performance.

Damn the woman! Rutherford thought, heaving himself over onto his side and wincing from the pains that crashed through his head. Damn her to hell and back. She was a nobody, an impudent, opportunistic, conscienceless nobody. And yet she had driven him into conflict with his grandmother; she had forced him into uncharacteristically unmannerly behavior; and she had pushed him into gambling, drinking, and whoring, none of which activities he had undertaken from choice.

Damn Jessica Moore!

He did not believe he was a naturally conceited man.

He had never thought of himself as arrogant. He had a sense of his place in society, yes, but then that was the way of life. Everyone around him had a similar sense, he had always believed. He had always treated servants with courtesy. He had always been charitable to those in need of charity. He had always been courteous and more than generous to his women.

Why, then, did Jess Moore make him feel like an arrogant snob? No, she did not make him *feel* like one. She made him *become* one. Of course he was outraged at her effrontery in trying to pass herself off as a member of the *beau monde*. Anyone of any sense and decency would agree with him. It was she who was in the wrong. Entirely so. There was no question about it. His attitude was perfectly correct. There was nothing cruel, nothing merely snobbish in his disapproval.

Why was it, then, that she made him feel so brutal? Why was it that a few cold words from her could put him instantly in the wrong? His feeling of guilt the afternoon before at Astley's had ruined the first few performances for him. He had been unpardonably rude to her and could not excuse himself even with the assurance that the provocation had been great. By retaliating with words that were so uncharacteristic of him he was merely lowering himself to her level.

Sitting next to her at the circus, Hope at her other side, Godfrey beyond her, he had wanted to take Jess's hand in his again and beg her to forgive him. She sat so rigidly upright next to him that he knew he had made her miserable. She deserved to be miserable, of course, he had told himself. And he had convinced himself; he had not apologized. Thank God, he had not apologized. But he had still felt guilty.

And very aware of her. It would have done him a great deal of good if he had had to endure rejection now and then through his adult years, he supposed. It surely could be only her rejection of him that made him want her so badly. He could not recall ever having had this all-pervading, aching need for one particular woman.

Why should it be so? Really, when it came right down to the physical act of bedding, one female body was very much like another. Why the craving for the one woman who chose not to bed with him?

He had sat beside her, tortured by guilt and desire, until a surprising sound from beside him had caused him to turn his head and look directly at her. She was giggling. Very quietly, it was true, with one hand over her mouth, but her shoulders were shaking and her eyes twinkling. And it was definitely giggles coming from behind her hand, not just polite laughter.

He had turned his head to the performance that had been passing unnoticed before him and saw a group of ragged clowns tripping and falling and stumbling as they rushed around about some urgent errand and constantly collided with one another. It was funny, he supposed. A child would be amused. Jessica Moore was amused.

He turned back to look at her, smiling at her reaction rather than at the antics of the clowns. She was like a child. She would never have been to Astley's before, of course. When she burst into open laughter and turned to him with the human instinct to share delight, he laughed too.

"I wonder they do not hurt themselves," she said. "They collide with such force."

"Doubtless they practice for long hours," he said. "They are all acrobats in their own right."

But she did not even hear his answer. She had turned back to the performance and was clapping with delight.

That was not the part of the afternoon that had really confused his feelings, though, and sent him in frustration and self-hatred on his night's orgy. That had come later, when the trapeze artists had been performing.

She had been amazed, enthralled, and ultimately terrified. His own attention had been caught, too. For the space of a few minutes he had become so involved with the danger of the tricks that he lost his awareness of her. He had stared down almost with incomprehension when her hand had first stolen into his. When it had gripped convulsively and her shoulder pressed against his arm, he had covered the hand lightly with his free one. And his attention had again been effectively drawn from the flying acrobats to the woman beside him. She had watched wide-eyed and with parted lips, gripping his hand, totally unaware of his presence until the act must have reached its climax and she turned suddenly with a gasp and buried her face against his sleeve.

And then looked up at him with round, horrified eyes and down at her hand sandwiched between his two. She had stared at their hands for a stunned moment and then pulled hers away as if from some deadly snake.

"Oh!" she had said and looked back up at him. Her lips had moved but it seemed that she did not know what to say or whom to blame.

"One wishes for one's own comfort that they would work with a safety net, doesn't one?" he had said with a smile, trying to turn the moment into something quite commonplace.

He did not know what she would have said, if anything. Hope had turned to her at that moment in order to make some enthusiastic comment on the acrobats, and she had remained turned away from him for the rest of the afternoon. Somehow she had contrived to be escorted back to the carriage by Godfrey.

Rutherford turned over onto his other side in bed, but much more cautiously than he had done a few minutes before, trying not to alert his headache. Why had he almost held his breath while she clung to him and drew close to him? Why had he been afraid to move a muscle for fear that she would realize what she was doing and withdraw from him, as she had done eventually? Why must he behave as if she were important to him, as if she were someone to be wooed and won with patience and tact? She was a governess masquerading as a grand lady. A servant. A country parson's daughter. A female appealing enough to be invited to his bed, shrugged off and forgotten if she declined.

Not a woman to watch as if there were nothing else around him to see, to absorb all of his attention as if there were nothing else worth paying attention to. Not a woman whose unconscious touch was to be so cherished that he must hold himself still and breathless for fear of losing it. Not a woman to so torment his mind and his body that he must go out at night trying to free himself through the entertainment of cards, the oblivion of drink, and the drug of sexual satiation.

And now this morning, Rutherford thought with a sigh, kicking the blankets off his body and turning onto his back again, she was causing him even greater torment than she had the day before. Drinking had brought him a hangover but no oblivion. Sex, for the first time in his memory, had left him feeling soiled, nauseated, and quite unsatisfied. He had an ugly suspicion that the sort of desire Jess had aroused in him could be satisfied by no one else except Jess. And if that fact was not about to ruin his hitherto quite satisfactory life, he was a fortunate man indeed.

Who exactly was Jessica Moore? he wondered yet again. Strange to be so obsessed by a woman one scarcely knew at all. Girls have mothers too, his grandmother had said. Who had her mother been? And who had the parson been before becoming a clergyman?

It seemed that further encounters with Jess were going to be inevitable. He would dare swear she would be at Faith's *soirée* during the coming evening. If meet her he must, he might as well talk to her too. Find out more about her. But whether he wished to find out good things or bad he did not know. Further reason to spurn her or some hitherto unsuspected reason to see her as more of a social equal.

"*Not as your fancy piece,*" his grandmother had said. "*As your wife.*"

Rutherford swung his legs over the side of the bed,

drew himself cautiously to a sitting position, groaned, and rose to his feet. Riding would probably bounce his head right off his shoulders, he thought, moving slowly into his dressing room to find riding clothes with which to cover his nakedness. But it seemed to be the only alternative to lying sleepless on his bed. He certainly would not be able to support the exertion of walking.

The Bradley *soirée* did not involve either dancing or card playing. Such activities were frequent enough at evening parties to become tedious, Lady Bradley told her grandmother and Jessica as she was welcoming them to her drawing room. Consequently, there was music in the music room for those who were interested, provided by a hired pianist, violinist, and harpist, though guests were encouraged to contribute their talents too. And there was conversation in the drawing room for those who wished to discuss politics or art or literature. Or even the weather and the state of the participants' health, she added with a laugh.

"Hope is beckoning you, Miss Moore," she told Jessica. "She is with Sir Godfrey Hall and Lord Graves. Would you care to join them? Grandmama, Mama has directed me to fetch you to her the moment you arrive."

Lady Hope was indeed gesturing to Jessica from across the room. And Sir Godfrey rose to his feet, bowed, and smiled amiably at her as she approached. Jessica scurried across to them in some relief. She felt decidedly self-conscious about attending a party given by Lord Rutherford's sister. Of the earl himself there was no sign. Surely she would not be fortunate enough to find that he would not attend at all.

"We have been telling Lord Graves about our afternoon at Astley's Amphitheater, dear Miss Moore," Lady Hope said. "And I do believe he is laughing at our childish delight in all the splendid acts. Do come and lend your voice to ours."

"I protest," Lord Graves said, also rising to bow to Jessica. "I merely smile at your delight, ma'am. I must confess a weakness for magicians myself. Do tell us your preference, Miss Moore."

Jessica took the offered seat. "I suppose the trapeze artists are the most spectacular," she said. "But just too agonizing to watch." She blushed at the memory of how she had not watched that final leap.

"You should have been sitting next to Sir Godfrey," Lady Hope said. "He talked to me the whole time and calmed my nerves wonderfully well. I declare he does not have a nerve in his body at all. And I daresay he would have preferred to sit next to you too as it was you he invited first. Foolish of me to sit between you. I would have done just as well next to Charles."

"My dear ma'am." Sir Godfrey looked somewhat taken aback. "I invited both you and Miss Moore to accompany me to Astley's. And indeed, I must say that I found your very sensible conversation calmed my nerves during the trapeze act."

"Well, is not that a foolish thing?" Lady Hope said with a laugh. "Lord Graves, would you be so good as to escort me to the music room? I really do love harp music, and one gets to hear it so rarely."

Lord Graves jumped to his feet and held out his arm to her. She flashed a smile at Sir Godfrey and Jessica.

"I do hope you do not think me rag-mannered to leave you to each other's company," she said. "But I am sure you will not mind."

Jessica could not decide whether she was more amused or dismayed at being left thus. Lady Hope seemed to have convinced herself that she and Sir Godfrey would make a good match and was making every effort to throw them into company together. She decided on amusement when Sir Godfrey smiled comfortably at her.

"I can see that you are having the same thoughts as I, Miss Moore," he said. "Lady Hope has been trying to marry me off for the past five years or more. It seems that you are her latest candidate. I hope you will not be embarrassed by her attempts. I find them amusing and somewhat endearing. Shall we be friends so that we may be comfortable together even when she is at her least subtle?''

Jessica laughed. "I thank you for your plain speaking, sir," she said. "And yes, of course, I had noticed and was hoping desperately that you had not. I am told, sir, that you have fascinating stories to tell about your travels if you are sufficiently assured that your audience is interested. Will you share some of them with me?"

"My dear ma'am," he said with a smile, "are you quite sure? I find that people who prose on about their experiences on the Continent can be dreadfully boring. Everyone seems to feel that a year or two spent abroad qualifies him to describe with perfect accuracy the national character of the Italians or the French or whoever it happens to be."

"Yes, I am quite sure," Jessica assured him. "Now do tell me, sir, how do you see the national character of the Russians?"

They both laughed.

But through her laughter Jessica became aware of a prickling sensation down her spine. She knew even before she turned her head rather jerkily in the direction of the door that Lord Rutherford was there. He was standing rather indolently in the doorway, looking quite splendid, she thought, in dark blue velvet coat, silver silk knee breeches, and white linen and lace. His narrowed eyes were directed at her. She turned her head abruptly back to her companion and immediately regretted the rather gauche action. But it was too late to turn back and incline her head or smile easily.

"How would you like a description of some of the more spectacular sights of Greece?" Sir Godfrey was asking with a grin. "And incidentally, have you seen the Elgin marbles? They are well worth a visit, though I do believe lady visitors are somewhat frowned upon. It is felt that so much naked stone might have a corrupting influence on them. You would need to be well armed

with vinaigrette and eau de cologne and handkerchiefs
and whatever else you ladies need to ward off the
vapors."

"Never!" Jessica said. "I would not be so poor-
spirited, sir. All I would need is a stout gentlemanly arm
on which to lean. But yes, all the famous sights,
please."

They smiled at each other, and Jessica rested an
elbow on her knee and her chin in her hand and prepared to focus all her attention on her companion.

"Godfrey. Miss Moore." Lord Rutherford's voice
sounded somewhat bored. He bowed stiffly from the
waist. "I hope I am not interrupting a private *tête-à-
tête*?"

"To tell the truth, you are, Charles," Sir Godfrey
said with a grin as Jessica shook her head in some
embarrassment. "I was about to mesmerize Miss Moore
with an account of my travels in Greece, and you have
come along to spoil all. Since you have heard it all at
least twice before, I am bound to have you yawning
behind your hand in no more than two minutes."

"When have I ever displayed such bad manners?" his
friend asked, drawing up a chair and seating himself. "I
shall be merely envious that I do not have a similar topic
with which to entice Miss Moore's admiration."

She blushed. He was looking at her quite intently and
with a quite unreadable expression on his face. "Have
you not made the Grand Tour, my lord?" she asked.

"Alas, no," he said. "The Continent has rarely been
free of war since I left off leading strings. My travels
have all been confined to these shores, ma'am."

Jessica turned her attention back to Sir Godfrey, who
had apparently decided to talk about the less serious
aspects of his travels. He kept her amused for the next
half hour with comical details about the difficulties of
travel and accommodations and language in the part of
the world to which his tour had taken him. Other guests
who joined their group added to the anecdotes. She

found herself almost unaware of the silent presence of
Lord Rutherford at her side.

Almost. But not quite, of course. In fact, not at all,
she was forced to admit to herself at last. Much as she
was growing to like Sir Godfrey Hall, amusing as his
stories and those of other members of the group were,
there was always Lord Rutherford. She found herself
eventually wanting to leap to her feet and turn and run
for air. It was hard to shake the memory of the afternoon before, the memory that had kept her awake
through much of the night.

She still turned alternately hot and cold at the
realization that she must have voluntarily placed her
hand in his when her attention was so engrossed by the
trapeze artists. And if there was some doubt about that,
there was certainly none about the fact that she had
hidden her face against his sleeve when she was so afraid
that one of the leaping figures would fall to his death
from the trapeze.

She had turned to Lord Rutherford for comfort, like
a small child. He had not repulsed her—indeed, his free
hand had been covering the one she clasped when she
had looked to see what she was doing. How he must
have been laughing at her, though. How naive and
childish he must think her. Or how conniving. Would he
think that she was trying to attract him? But why would
he think so? He had already offered her *carte blanche*
on two separate occasions.

And now he sat next to her, their arms almost
touching, this man who had wished to be her protector,
her lover. And the man whose presence could instantly
interfere with her heartbeat, her power to think.

"Are you tired of sitting in the same place for so long,
Miss Moore?" he was asking her now. "Would you like
me to accompany you to the music room?"

"Thank you," she said, looking at him for the first
time in half an hour, though they had sat so close during
all that time. "That would be pleasant." But she had

spoken before her mind had had time to function, she realized even as she got to her feet and laid a hand on Lord Rutherford's sleeve. The muscles of his arm were firm beneath her hand. It was the arm that had held her close on more than one occasion. She felt as if she were suffocating.

"Faith and Aubrey always make an effort to seek out the best musical talent," he was saying conversationally. "I am sure that this trio is worth listening to."

"Yes," she said. "I was hoping not to miss it altogether."

They stood in the doorway to the music room for a few moments while Lord Rutherford located two vacant chairs at quite the other side of the room. He guided her quietly toward them, and they sat side by side until the music came to an end fifteen minutes later. For the first time Jessica did not feel oppressed by his nearness. She sensed that he was quite engrossed by the music.

"Do you play an instrument, my lord?" she asked when the polite applause had died down and while one of the guests took the place of the pianist on the stool.

"The violin," he said shortly. "And you, Jess? I imagine that such an accomplished governess must have all sorts of hidden talents."

Jessica's jaw tightened. "I play the pianoforte," she said.

"And might I ask how the daughter of an impoverished country parson—your own words, Jess— can have had the opportunity to practice on such an instrument?" he asked.

"We had a harpsichord," she said, turning to look fixedly at the young lady who was about to play on the pianoforte. "My mother brought it on her marriage."

"Ah," he said with a half-smile, "the royal princess."

"My lord?" Jessica frowned up at him, but he merely shook his head and looked away from her.

"Perhaps I can prevail upon you to play for the company when Miss Lacey has finished," he said.

Jessica looked up at him in alarm. "Oh, no, my lord," she said. "I am out of practice, and I do not pretend to any extraordinary talent even when I am not."

He turned his head and looked very deliberately into her eyes. "I would have expected you to jump at the opportunity to place yourself even more firmly in the public eye," he said. "You seem to be doing quite famously so far."

Jessica would not look away. "Have you brought me here to quarrel with me, my lord?" she asked. She was whispering, for the pianist had begun her recital. "If so, I must beg to be excused and return to the drawing room."

"To Godfrey?" he whispered back. "Save your smiles and your wiles, if you know what is good for you, Jess. He will not marry you, you know."

"Will he not?" she hissed. "Am I to expect another offer to become a mistress, then?"

He smiled, if such a sneering expression could be called a smile. "It is hardly likely," he said. "I believe he is perfectly comfortable with the female who has held that position for the past two years and more."

"In that case," Jessica said, leaning toward him so that her face was only inches away from his own, "I would say he is due for a change, would not you, my lord? I count my chances quite favorable."

She had the satisfaction of seeing his eyes spark with fury before his expression was suddenly transformed to blandness. He smiled and inclined his head toward a turbaned matron one row ahead of them who had turned and directed an indignant lorgnette their way.

Jessica sat silent and stiffbacked through the lengthy recital that followed. She could not have said afterward whether the performance was worthy of such an occasion or not. She was too preoccupied with feeling

# 9

"IF YOU WILL EXCUSE me, my lord." The pianoforte recital had finally ended, and Lady Bradley had announced that supper was being served. Jessica rose firmly to her feet.

"Are you hungry?" Lord Rutherford asked. "Then I shall escort you. But do not think to escape so easily, Jess. I wish to talk to you."

"Why?" she asked. She turned to smile at other guests who were trying to pass her, and moved closer to her chair. "I really do not believe we have anything to say to each other, my lord. If you wish to appeal to me once again to leave your grandmother's house and seek employment, the answer is no. I intend to accept her hospitality until—well, until other arrangements to my liking can be made. And if you wish to renew your request that I become your mistress, the answer is still no."

"Sit down," he said, and Jessica complied without thinking. The guests around them were slowly leaving the room, presumably in search of supper.

"I want to know who you are," he said. "Whether we like it or not, Jess, you and I seem fated to be thrown into company together, and the situation can only get worse over Christmas. Let me know with whom I deal. Tell me more about yourself."

"What do you wish to know, my lord?" Jessica

straightened her shoulders. She could feel anger beginning to ball inside her stomach.

"Who was your father?" he asked. "He was an impoverished country parson, you say. Where did he come from? Was he a younger son of someone of consequence? Many of our clergymen are."

Jessica forced her hands to remain relaxed and unclasped in her lap. "He was the twentieth son of a duke, actually," she said. "My grandfather was not wealthy to begin with and did not possess many titles apart from his dukedom. You can imagine that there was not much left for a twentieth son."

"Sometimes," Rutherford said through his teeth, turning to drape an arm along the back of her chair, which she was not touching, "I could readily throttle you, Jess Moore. Does not a civil question deserve a civil answer?"

"Yes, it does," she readily conceded. "An arrogant one does not."

"Arrogant?" He raised his eyebrows.

"It astonishes you, does it not," she asked, "and impresses you too to find that you are capable of condescending to talk to such as I? Of course, you would readily do other things with me that would involve no condescension at all. They would merely be your rights as a gentleman. But conversing with me? In respectable company? So you try to discover if perhaps it is unexceptionable to do so, after all. If the Reverend Adam Moore of Glouchestershire would just turn out to be the impoverished son of a baron or a viscount, then all is well. Suddenly his daughter is no longer a pariah."

The room was empty. The silence around them seemed loud for a few seconds.

"You do not help yourself," Rutherford said. "If you have a legitimate claim to be in this sort of company, why not say so?"

Jessica smiled. "But you are the only person who has questioned that claim, my lord," she said. "And I do not feel the necessity to justify my existence to you. My mother, by the way, was a scullery maid at the home of the local squire. My father did not deal in social snobbery."

"And you have inherited your tongue from her," he said, something that was almost a smile curling his lips for a moment. "The harpsichord was a wedding gift from a grateful employer, I suppose?"

Jessica inclined her head and was surprised to see a grin on his face when she looked up again.

"Three minutes," he said. "Your hand was in mine for all of three minutes, Jess. It quite distracted my attention from the trapeze artists, you know."

She blushed but would not break eye contact with him.

"Would the same thing have happened if you had been sitting beside Godfrey?" he asked.

"I have no way of knowing, my lord," Jessica said, very much on her dignity. "The action was quite involuntary."

He laughed and picked up her hand, which was lying in her lap. He turned it over and ran a finger over the lines in her palm. "I wonder what your plan is," he said. "Marriage to a rich and titled gentleman, Jess? One who will treat you as a lady?"

"Yes," she said, watching the long, slim finger on her palm, feeling her whole arm sizzle to life from the tickling sensation of its movements. "Though I could live without the wealth and the title."

"Could you?" he asked, his eyes narrowing as he lifted them to look into hers. "What an enigma you are, Jess. I never know quite when you are lying and when telling the truth. You are becoming something of an obsession with me. Did you know that?"

"No," she whispered.

"And do you care?" he asked. "And will you admit to sharing that obsession?"

"No." She looked away from him.

"I think you do, Jess," he said, his free hand taking her chin and turning her face back to his. "You are neither a gray governess nor a demure young maiden, my dear. You are a woman of unusual passions. You know that you and I are destined to end up together, don't you?"

"In bed?" she asked. "I think not, my lord. You are incapable of ravishing a woman, a fact of which I have had happy proof. Yet there is no other way that you will gain what you want of me."

"You think you will not one day come to me and offer yourself to me?" he asked. His eyes were on her lips.

"Not until hell turns to ice," she said. "One's desires are not the most important forces of life, my lord, not when they are divorced from all more tender feelings."

"Love," he said with a scornful little laugh. "Never tell me you believe in love, Jess? You a romantic? I would not have thought it. I see you as a very practical young lady, an opportunist, no less."

"Let me go, my lord," she said. "Everyone must be served with supper already." She was suffocatingly aware of the hand that still held hers, the other hand beneath her chin, his face only inches from her own. She was fighting the humiliating urge to lean forward and close the gap between their mouths.

He did it for her. "You see?" he said, his lips already touching hers. "You talk of love in one breath and food in the next. Bodily appetites, Jess. They figure very large in your thinking."

And his mouth opened over hers, his tongue tracing a tantalizingly light course around her lips so that sensation vibrated through her.

"Children, children! The proprieties, please!" The dowager duchess's voice was booming enough to set the pair into jolting apart. Yet it was a brightly cheerful voice. Rutherford's eyes sought Jessica's for one moment, and he raised the hand that he still held to his lips before turning to greet his grandmother and mother.

"Miss Moore and I have been discussing our various

musical talents," he said, rising lazily to his feet. "Are we too late for supper? I believe Faith can consider the evening a resounding success, Mama."

"I told you they would be in here *tête-à-tête*, Marianne," the dowager said. "Your mama was becoming convinced that you had left altogether, Charles. But I assured her that if we could just find Jessica, you would not be far away." She tapped him on the sleeve with her fan.

"I am so pleased you could come, Miss Moore," the Duchess of Middleburgh said. "You do look lovely in that particular shade of pink, my dear. Of course, someone with your figure would look delightful even in a sack, I daresay. I have always had to fight against fat, alas. Come along to the supper room while there is still food left. Charles is always indifferent to food and sometimes forgets that his companions are not necessarily so."

"Exactly what I was discovering, Mama," Rutherford said with a bow. "You go along. I want to have a look at this violin while the artist is still at supper. It has quite a superior tone."

"Jeremy." Lord Rutherford slapped down the third ruined starched neckcloth onto the dressing table before him. "My damned fingers are all thumbs today. Come and work one of your miracles."

The valet, busy brushing invisible lint from the green superfine coat that he was all ready to help his master into, crossed the room in some surprise. It was only on the most gala of occasions that he was ever called upon to perform his art's supreme creation: a well-tied neckcloth.

"Hif your lordship would 'old your 'ead still for one minute," he scolded a few moments later, "hit would be done and over with."

"Sorry," his lordship muttered meekly, holding his head poker still. He was nervous. By God, he was nervous! He would not be surprised to find that if he held out his hands, they would be shaking. Lord Rutherford smoothed his hands over his waistcoat and turned to reach his arms into the sleeves of the coat Jeremy was holding out for him. He would not put the matter to the test.

Well, it would all be over within the next hour or so, he consoled himself. And it was after all something he had never done before. And if it was something that every man intended to do only once in his life, he supposed he had some right to be nervous. Even if she was an ex-governess, a social nobody.

It was his own idea, he was convinced of that. He had not been browbeaten into it by his grandmother. She had been quite annoying the night before, it was true, but his mind had been made up even before she appeared on the scene. Or almost, anyway.

She had not followed his mother and Jess to the supper room. She had seated herself in the music room, occupying the chair on which Jess had sat, while he crossed to the abandoned violin and picked it up to inspect it. He had hoped that she would go away. A fond hope where Grandmama was concerned!

"And when might I expect you to call to pay your addresses, Charles?" she had asked archly.

He had run his thumb experimentally across the strings of the violin. Why pretend to misunderstand her? Her meaning was pretty obvious.

"Tell me more about her, Grandmama," he had said without looking up. "Who is she?"

"My dear boy," the dowager had said, "you must know far more about Jessica than I do. Every time you are in company with her you seem to get very close to her indeed. You were not offering her *carte blanche* again just now, were you? Very poor form, m'boy. Only marriage will do under the present circumstances. She is my guest, you know, and has been received by your sister."

"And is the granddaughter of the dearest friend of your youth," Rutherford had said, lifting the violin to his chin and drawing the bow across its strings. "Is that true, by the way? I find it hard to penetrate the tissue of lies that both you and Jess seem bent on throwing my way."

"Of course it is true," she said carelessly. "But of course you will not believe me. You owe her marriage, Charles. You have been with her unchaperoned for a quite scandalous length of time this evening, and both your mama and I have witnessed your holding her hand and kissing her. On the lips, no less."

"Tomorrow," he had said, laying the violin down at last and looking at his grandmother for the first time. "If you will engage to be at home tomorrow afternoon, Grandmama, I shall call to make my offer."

"Oh, splendid, Charles!" she had cried, getting to her feet and clasping her fan to her bosom. "I really did not think it would be quite this easy, m'boy, I must confess. But you will not be sorry. Jessica is the ideal wife for you, princess's daughter or barmaid's daughter notwithstanding. She will be at home tomorrow. You have my word on it."

But it was not she who had trapped him into doing it. Perhaps he would not have gone quite as soon as today, but sooner or later he would have been preparing himself for this same errand. He had known as he sat beside Jess in the music room that his words to her were quite true. He was obsessed by her. They were fated to end up together. It had been equally obvious to him that the time when she might perhaps have been persuaded to become his mistress was well past. Jessica Moore might not have a legitimate claim to move among the *haute ton*, but she was there now and seemed to have been accepted with remarkably little inquiry.

No, he had decided as he took her hand in his and ached to gather her completely to himself, if he wanted Jess—and he did want her, had to have her, in fact— then he must marry her. The thought should have shocked him, repulsed him. Even the thought of her resident in his grandmother's house had offended his notions of proper behavior just a few days before. But the idea came with ease and little resistance from his rational mind.

She was, after all, accepted by society. It seemed that she was not completely beyond the pale of his social milieu. It seemed likely that her father had been able to lay claim to membership of at least the lower gentry. She was educated and accomplished. Her total absence of dowry would matter not at all to him. He already had more money than one man should fairly expect in a lifetime. And she was refined. And beautiful. And very desirable. Achingly so. He did not believe he could go on living with any degree of comfort until he could somehow make her his own.

And the more he thought about it, the more he realized that it would not be enough after all to establish her in some quiet dwelling where he could visit her and enjoy her at his leisure. There would be something missing from his pleasure. He wanted Jess in his own home. He wanted to be able to take her about with him, show her off to the people of his world, take her home with him at night, or return there to her and make love to her to his heart's content without that tedious necessity of rising at dawn to return to the respectability of his own establishment.

Yes, he had decided he would marry Jess. And he had little understanding of why he should be nervous about going to make his offer to her. She wanted him too. She had admitted as much both in words and in action. And it would be a very advantageous marriage for her even if she did not. Yet he was nervous. Jess was the one woman he had ever found to be unpredictable. Their encounters never progressed quite the way he expected. He had the quite unreasonable fear that she might reject him.

Jeremy helped his master into his heavy greatcoat and handed him his beaver hat and cane. Lord Rutherford hesitated for only a moment before striding out of his room and down the branched marble staircase that led to the tiled hall below. One thing he must not do was betray any of his nervousness or uncertainty. Jess Moore had already wounded his masculine pride on several occasions. He must at least show confidence in claiming her as his bride.

"It is a great pity you are too unwell to join me in a walk, my dear Miss Moore," Lady Hope said. "It is such a beautiful day. Cold, but crisp, you know. However, I suppose Grandmama knows best, even if you do protest that you feel perfectly healthy."

"Jessica is unused to an active social life," the dowager said from the fireside chair in her own drawing room. "Often one can be exhausted without realizing the fact, and it is just at such times that exercise like walks and drives can bring on a chill. We would not want anyone to be poorly over Christmas, now would we?"

"Certainly not, Grandmama," Lady Hope said. "My dear Miss Moore." She patted the hands of the young lady sitting next to her. "How annoyed I was to see that Charles had taken you away to the music room last evening. Sometimes my brother has no more sense than a small child. And just at a time when Sir Godfrey so clearly wished to converse with you. And I thought myself so clever to take Lord Graves out of the way. I mean to have a talk with Charles."

"But I really did wish to hear the musicians," Jessica said. "It was unfortunate that we heard only part of one of their performances. Miss Lacey played before supper."

"However," Lady Hope said cheerfully, "Mama was sensible enough to bring you to join our table for supper. And did you notice how deftly I brought the conversation around to the Elgin marbles, Miss Moore? Sir Godfrey was clearly grateful for the opportunity to offer to take you to see them."

Jessica smiled. "He had talked of them earlier in the evening," she said. "Though he did warn me that it is not considered quite the thing for ladies to go."

"Pooh," Lady Hope said. "We are not such poor-spirited creatures, are we? Why, Grandmama has been to see them and professed herself quite impressed."

"Gentlemen like to see us as poor wilting females, who do not even realize the fact that they possess more flesh than what we see on their hands and faces," the dowager said. "If you wish to impress when you make this visit, Hope and Jessica, you must appear suitably shocked to discover that indeed there is considerably more."

"I shall be sure to engage Lord Graves in constant conversation," Lady Hope said. "You will enjoy having Sir Godfrey explain everthing to you, Miss Moore. He is very clearly taken with you, you know."

Jessica laughed. "And yet it was to you he first issued the invitation, Lady Hope," she pointed out.

"But of course, dear." Her companion patted her hand again. "He had to make sure that you would be properly chaperoned before he could invite you. And we are old friends, you know. He would feel that he must invite me."

Jessica smiled and said no more. Gentlemen could be left in an unenviable predicament, she felt, if they must always ask a chaperone first. What if the real object of their invitation then said no?

"Ah," the dowager said as the door opened to admit her butler. "Who is having the audacity to call on me this afternoon? Everyone knows this is not my day for visitors."

"The Earl of Rutherford, ma'am," that austere individual said, bowing woodenly before standing aside to admit the guest.

"Ah, Charles, m'boy," the dowager said, offering her cheek as he strode across the room. "What a surprise. To what do we owe this pleasure?"

"Hope. Miss Moore." Lord Rutherford did not feel

one whit the less nervous now that he was there. And he would have felt far more comfortable if his grandmother had not chosen to put on this great pretence. "I trust you are both well?"

"Oh, perfectly, Charles," his sister said. "I must tell you that Faith was most gratified that you came to her *soirée* last night and stayed the whole evening. I do believe Lady Sarah was not displeased either."

"Lady Sarah?" Rutherford frowned his incomprehension as he seated himself.

"You were in conversation with her for all of an hour, I dare wager, after supper," his sister said archly. "I do believe she has been angling for you since last Season, Charles."

"Lady Sarah!" he said with a frown. "The chit was in her first Season last year, for God's sake, Hope. She is a mere babe. She talked to me for the whole hour last evening about her lapdogs, I do believe. At least, that is what she was talking about every time I brought my attention back to her."

"Charles!" Lady Hope admonished him. "I am quite sure you cannot be as indifferent to the charms of all ladies as you pretend to be. It would be most unfair when all the young ladies are far from indifferent to you."

"Cut line, Hope, will you?" Rutherford said. "Or I shall start making insinuations about you and Graves. You seemed to be together for much of last evening."

"Don't be absurd, Charles," she said. "What would Lord Graves see in an aging spinster like me? I was merely trying to keep him out of Sir Godfrey's way, you see, so that he would be free to speak with Miss Moore. But you had to come along and assume that she wished to listen to the music."

"My apologies!" Rutherford said, his eyes straying for the first time to Jessica, who sat with her eyes downcast. She was pleating the wool of her dress between her fingers.

"Hope, my love." The dowager duchess rose to her

feet, a determined look on her face. "Every year I face
the same problems as Christmas approaches. Which of
my clothes should I have my maid pack away to take
with me? And what gifts will be suitable for each
member of the family? It must be advancing age. I never
used to give a thought to either matter. Come to my
sitting room and help me."

"Me, Grandmama?" Lady Hope viewed her
grandmother in some amazement. "You know you will
never take advice from anyone."

"Age, my dear," the dowager insisted. "I begin to
think I will have to change my habits. My brain is not as
firm as it used to be."

A moment later she was ushering Lady Hope out of
the drawing room. "We will not be long, dear," she
said to Jessica. "Entertain Charles for me until we
return, will you?"

Jessica stared at the closed door in some dismay.
Then she turned suspicious eyes on the man sitting
quietly across the room from her.

"Why have we been left alone?" she asked. "That
was quite deliberate, was it not? Is there something
going on that I do not know of?"

"It seems so," he said. He was sitting perfectly
relaxed. He was even half smiling at her. "I wondered if
Grandmama would prepare you. It seems that she has
not."

"Prepare me?" Jessica was on her feet. She felt
instant alarm.

"I am here to make you an offer," Lord Rutherford
said.

"An offer?" Jessica stared at him, her hands
clenched at her sides.

He held up a hand as she drew breath to speak again.
"Of marriage, of course," he said. "Did you think it
was *carte blanche* again, Jess? I would not repeat that
suggestion again, my dear. And you must know that
Grandmama would not conspire with me in such a case.
It must be marriage between you and me." He got to his

feet to face her. He smiled full at her. "Will you do me the honor?"

Jessica was staring at him incredulously. "Marry you?" she said. "You wish me to marry you? How positively absurd! Of course I will not marry you."

He raised his eyebrows and strolled toward her. "Is your answer a considered one?" he asked. "Did I not express myself well enough, Jess? Was it an arrogant proposal? Do you wish me to go down on my knees? I will, you know. And I am very serious."

"Why?" she asked. He could see that her knuckles were white, her hands balled into fists at her sides. "Why do you wish to marry me, my lord?"

"I told you last night that I am obsessed with you, Jess," he said. "We are meant for each other. I do not believe I can do without you any longer."

Jessica laughed, though there was no amusement on her face. "It must be a poweful obsession indeed, my lord," she said, "if you are willing to marry me in order to get me into your bed."

"But you feel it too, Jess." He reached out a hand and took one of hers. He held it palm up, uncurling the suddenly nerveless fingers with his other hand. "We want each other. I believe we need each other. We must marry. There is no other choice."

"Despite the fact that my mother was a scullery maid?" she asked. Her head was thrown back, her expression scornful.

He smiled, trying to keep the uncertainty out of his expression. "I do not believe that story," he said. "But yes, even despite that fact, Jess."

"Then finally we have one thing in common," Jessica said. "We are each willing to ignore the social credentials of the other. I reject your offer, my lord, despite the fact that your father is a duke."

"Why, Jess?" He was holding her hand firmly sand-wiched between his own.

"I will not be anyone's whore," she said. She was staring straight into his eyes so that he could not look away. "Even with the respectability of a wedding ring. I am a person, Lord Rutherford, a whole person. I am not just a body to be used for a gentleman's bedtime pleasure. Thank you, but no."

He searched her eyes, her hand still clasped between his. Then he stood back abruptly, dropping her hand, and bowed stiffly.

"I shall wish you good day, then, ma'am," he said. "Please accept my apologies for taking your time."

And he was gone.

# 10

THEY WERE TO LEAVE for Hendon Park in just a few days' time. Jessica was not sure whether to be glad or sorry. She was glad that perhaps at last her future would be settled once and for all. Sorry because she was almost sure to see the Earl of Rutherford again. At least, he seemed not to have sent word to anyone that he did not intend to join his family for Christmas.

Jessica had allowed the dowager to send a letter to her grandfather. She should have written to him herself, of course. If she wanted his help—and she did—then it was only right that she be the one to write to him. Besides, it was time to patch up their quarrel. He was her only living relative, and she his. They had been fond of each other all through her childhood and girlhood. It was absurd to break all connection with each other over a stupid matter of pride. And he was not getting any younger. Perhaps the opportunity to mend their differences would not be open to her for much longer. And how would she ever forgive herself if she let the chance forever pass her by?

More than anything she needed his help. The Dowager Duchess of Middleburgh continued to shower new clothes and gifts on her and continued to extend her full hospitality. To a young lady who had been brought up to be proudly independent, it was an increasing embarrassment to accept such charity from a lady on whom she had no claim of kinship. She must let her grandfather support her, either with an allowance in her present abode or in his own home in the country.

She should have written herself. But how could she begin to explain herself to him? How strike the right note of humility without sounding servile? She had given in to cowardice when her hostess, with her usual iron-willed insistence, declared that the letter would be much better coming from her. Jessica did not kow what had been in that letter except that the marquess had been invited to Hendon Park for Christmas.

There had been no reply yet. Would he come? She did not know. Her grandfather had never been given much to traveling. For this particular occasion perhaps he might. Perhaps he still loved her enough. But surely some reply would come there even if he did not arrive in person. Somehow by Christmas she would be independent again, or at least independent of all except her own family. It was something to look forward to.

And now more than ever it was imperative that she be free of her obligation to the dowager duchess. The last few weeks had been dreadfully hard to live through. It was true that she had not set eyes on the Earl of Rutherford since he had left her abruptly after his insulting offer of marriage—and neither had anyone else, it seemed. At least she had been spared that embarrassment. But she had had to face the severe disappointment of his grandmother—the same woman who was paying for her very keep.

She had returned to the drawing room with Lady Hope quite soon after Lord Rutherford's departure, but she had kept her surprise at finding Jessica the room's only occupant well concealed until her granddaughter had taken her leave. It had not taken her long after that to discover the truth.

She had been very kind. Jessica had to admit that. There was no accusation of ingratitude, no suggestion that she was no longer welcome at Berkeley Square. Quite the contrary, in fact. When Jessica, in great distress, had insisted that she must leave, whether her hostess was willing to find her a situation or not, that lady had shown uncharacteristic gentleness, patting her on the shoulder and telling her that she was a goose if she thought their friendship must come to an end merely because Jessica had had the good sense to reject "that puppy."

But she clearly was disappointed, Jessica knew. Although she rarely spoke with open kindness either to or about him, it was very clear that the dowager doted on her grandson and wished dearly that he would settle down with a wife and family. And she had wanted that wife to be Jessica. She had not pried. She had merely assumed that Rutherford had presented himself as if he were God's answer to a maiden's prayer and had offended Jessica's pride.

"Spoiled," she had said, handing Jessica her own lace handkerchief with which to dry her eyes. "Charles has always been surrounded with women ready to jump at his every bidding. Too many females in the family and not enough males. Middleburgh is no earthly good—always buried in his library or ensconced at one of his clubs. Dear Charles has grown up with the belief that he has merely to snap his fingers and a female will come running. He is too handsome for his own good too, of course. This will do him good, Jessica, m'dear. Just what he needs."

But Jessica knew that she did not mean it. She was beginning to know her hostess rather well, and the severe outer appearance hid deep feelings. Jessica knew every time a visitor was announced that the dowager looked up expecting it to be Lord Rutherford. She knew when the old lady looked around her at any gathering that she was looking for his tall, distinctive figure. And she sensed that her hostess's enthusiasm for the various gentlemen who came to call on her and take her walking and driving was somewhat forced.

Strange as the idea seemed, Jessica became more and more convinced that the Dowager Duchess of Middleburgh had grown to love her and had wished to gift her with what was most precious in her life: her grandson, the Earl of Rutherford.

Jessica did not know where he had gone and did not care, provided only that he stayed there. She did not wish to see him ever again. And she did not like to explore the reason for her reluctance. It was embarrassment merely, she would have assured herself. How can one face and be civil to a man whose marriage proposal one had rejected out of hand? It was intense dislike. The man had had only one use for her ever since he had set eyes on her. At least his offers to make her his mistress were an honest acknowledgement of that fact.

His offer of marriage was pure insult. He was desperate enough to possess her that he would even marry her to get what he wanted. Clearly he valued marriage very little. It meant nothing to him but the acquisition of an elusive bedfellow. What would he do when he grew tired of her? Presumably by that time she would have presented him with a male heir and she could be respectably housed on one of his country estates. There would be nothing to hold him after his passion cooled, of course. Unless he discovered something of her background. He would probably be suitably impressed to discover that Papa had been the youngest son of a baronet and Mama the daughter of a marquess.

Jessica was not necessarily in search of a love match. She knew that if she was to marry within her social class, she would probably marry and be married for any of several reasons. Her grandfather would wish her to ally herself to wealth and rank. She would wish also to like and respect her prospective husband. He would offer for her probably because of her relationship to the Marquess of Heddingly. She would hope also that she would be respected for her modest education and accomplishments.

She would not be married solely because she had a desirable body. And she would not marry a man for whom she felt only physical attraction. No matter how powerful that attraction was. She would never marry the Earl of Rutherford.

Her relief at not seeing him probably stemmed as much from this undesirable attraction as from embarrassment or dislike. When he was there, when she saw him, she was aware of nothing and of no one else. He was tall and athletic and of course impossibly handsome, as his grandmother had pointed out. And there was even a certain integrity in his character that drew her against her will. She knew that no matter what the circumstances, her person would somehow be safe with Lord Rutherford. There was the memory of the night at the inn, when he had entertained her with charming conversation during dinner and afterward insisted that she take his bed.

And always there were the memories of his kisses, of his touch, and the certain knowledge that he would be a lover who could make her forget all her scruples and even her very self if she would let him. And when she was with him, when he touched her, she always came perilously close to giving herself up to his care. To relax into his desire, to give herself to him body and soul, to forget that the person that was Jessica Moore mattered not at all to him, to forget that the future would hold nothing for them except a waning of passion and a long boredom: it was very hard to hold firm against all these urges when she saw him.

She was glad that he had made his offer the way he had. He had been so relaxed, so smilingly confident that she would swoon at his feet with gratitude for the great honor he had done her, so arrogant. Oh, yes, he had quite correctly labeled his own attitude. It had been relatively easy to refuse him. Anger had carried her through. And pride.

But oh, it had been difficult when he took her hand and uncurled her fingers not to lean forward to rest her forehead against his chest. And difficult not to call to him in panic when he strode from the room. Or to run after him down the stairs.

She wanted him, ached for him even when she could not see him. How much more dreadful it would be if she had to meet him as frequently as she had for the days preceding his offer. And how impossibly difficult it would be to see him at Hendon Park after all this time. To be in the privileged company of his family for that most intimate of seasons, Christmas.

Perhaps he would not come, Jessica sometimes thought, when she allowed herself to think of him consciously at all. But that possibility was so dreadful that she would always crowd it out of her mind and think of other more pleasant matters.

She had made several friends, young ladies whom she met frequently at various social functions, gentlemen of various ages, some of whom singled her out for a lone evening of gallantry only, some of whom became regular visitors at Berkeley Square and occasional escorts on the walks and drives that were becoming almost daily occurrences.

There was Sir Godfrey Hall, of course, but he was an easy, amiable friend merely. Jessica enjoyed his company and noted with amusement that whenever she saw him she almost invariably saw Lady Hope too, the latter trying with something less than subtlety to throw the two of them together. Yet it seemed that whenever Sir Godfrey offered to escort her anywhere, he had always asked Lady Hope first. There was Lord Graves, an older man of solid substance and little humor, whom she suspected of the intention to begin to court her seriously. There was Lord Beasley, who liked to show off his high-perch phaeton, a dangerous vehicle for winter conditions and for a man of his bulk, Jessica always felt, as she clung, smiling and apparently relaxed, to the seat beside him. And Mr. Menteith frequently sat beside her at assemblies or danced with her.

It would not be difficult, Jessica concluded, to acquire a husband for herself before the end of the coming Season. Despite her age, she seemed quite able to attract the notice of eligible gentlemen. And even if the fact that she was the guest of the Dowager Duchess of Middleburgh was part of the attraction, it could not be the whole matter, for the dowager had never substantiated that very vague explanation that Jessica was the granddaughter of a dear friend of hers. No one knew that she was the only granddaughter of a very wealthy marquess.

She would wait and see what Grandpapa would do about the dowager's letter. Perhaps she would go home with him and be content to live quietly in the country. Perhaps she would allow him to arrange a marriage for her or wait for one of the gentlemen she knew to offer for her. Perhaps she would be able to find something to do that would take her mind off the dreadful obsession she had with the Earl of Rutherford.

Lord Rutherford rested one booted leg against the velvet upholstery of the seat opposite him in his traveling carriage. He shifted his position and tried to find a more comfortable resting place for his back. Four days of travel, even inside a comfortable coach, were beginning to feel like protracted torture. He would have far preferred to ride the distance on horseback, or at least part of it. But good manners dictated that he stay with his companion. It was some relief to see the countryside begin to grow familiar and to know that there was only one tollgate between them and London. They would stay at his town house for the night before proceeding the short distance south to Hendon Park to join the rest of the family.

"We should be home in good time for dinner, sir," he said. "You will doubtless be as relieved as I to see the end of this journey."

"Never could stand traveling," the Marquess of Heddingly grumbled. "Roads full of potholes. Beds in inns full of fleas. Other places just as full of fools as the places one has just left behind. It always seemed pointless trouble to me."

"My grandmother will be delighted to see you, I

know," Lord Rutherford said. "And of course there
will be mutual delight when you are reunited with Miss
Moore."

"Headstrong girl," the marquess said. "Too much
like her grandfather, I suppose. We never could agree
on anything for more than five minutes together. I am
glad to hear she has finally come to her senses,
anyway."

"And she will have a secure future," Rutherford
said. "Of that I can assure you, sir. She will not want
for any luxury or any care as my wife."

"It is just as well," Lord Heddingly said, turning to
look keenly from beneath bushy white eyebrows at his
companion. "It is perfectly clear that you must marry
the girl, Rutherford, as you have admitted yourself. But
no great harm is done, I believe. I could not have chosen
a more eligible husband for the girl myself."

"Thank you, sir," his companion said. "I would
have been very careful, of course, not to compromise
your granddaughter had I realized who she was. But she
has never been willing to tell me. One is not always so
careful of the honor of a governess."

"Typical of Jessica," the marquess said. "She
probably don't even realize that she is bound to marry
you. Will she have you without fuss, do you think?
Does she care for you?"

"I have reason to believe that she does," Rutherford
said after a pause. "But she is stubborn, sir, if you will
pardon me for saying so. She will not take kindly to
being told what she must do."

"Hm," the marquess said. "Leave her to me, my
boy. Though Jessica has never been known to do as I
say merely because I have said it."

"My grandmother will perhaps be my best
advocate," Lord Rutherford said. "I believe Miss
Moore is fond of her."

"And so she should be," the marquess said, "taken
in off the street as she was. Dratted girl. She would
probably have gone to the poorhouse sooner than come

to me for help. I hope you will be firm with her when she is your wife, Rutherford. I do not believe that fool of a father of hers ever once gave the girl a good thrashing. Would probably do her the world of good even now."

Lord Rutherford did not reply. He turned his attention to the window to view the final tollgate at which the carriage had already stopped. He felt a wave of amusement although he did not allow his expression to show it. He was quite sure that if he ever did persuade Jess to marry him, he would feel regular urges to pinion her beneath his arm and wallop her until she was too sore to sit down. He was equally sure that if he ever tried it, she would be sitting down in comfort long before his eyes recovered from their rainbow colored bruises.

But would she ever marry him? That was the key question. And he was far from confident even though his discoveries of the past few weeks had made it quite imperative that she do so. Confronting her with his new knowledge would only make her so much more stubborn and contemptuous, he did not doubt. He had a powerful ally in her grandfather, but it seemed that she could defy him too in a grand manner when she chose to do so.

And to think that he had once labeled Jess Moore as a little mouse, a gray governess, Rutherford thought with a grimace of wry humor as the carriage lurched into motion again.

Granddaughter of the Marquess of Heddingly, indeed! The only direct descendant of that legendary aristocrat, a man rarely seen but fabled to be enormously wealthy and very influential in the affairs of his country despite his physical retirement on his country estate. Jess was his granddaughter! And rather than submit to allowing the marquess to bring her out and arrange some sort of brilliant match for her, she had taken a situation as governess with those unspeakable Barries and become the colorless, demure creature he had first encountered. It was almost unbelievable.

It had taken him an irritatingly long time to find out the truth. All he had known for certain—and indeed he had not been thoroughly sure of even that—was that her father, one Adam Moore, had been a country parson in the county of Gloucestershire. Who could possibly have guessed that there would be two Adam Moores with parishes in that county and that he would have the misfortune to investigate the wrong one first? However, he had finally been brought face to face with the incredible truth. And he had taken himself off to call on the Marquess of Heddingly.

He was not quite sure why he had rushed away from London after her rejection without telling anyone he was leaving and without taking even the indispensable Jeremy with him. He knew he was going in search of her background, but why he did so he had not stopped to consider. She had refused him in a very definite manner. There seemed no possible way he could persuade her to reconsider. Indeed, he had not even wanted to change her mind when he left. He had been more furious than he could remember being for a long time. Had she had to treat his offer with such open contempt? Did she not understand what an effort of nerve it cost a man to propose marriage to the woman of his choice?

Perhaps he had been hoping to find that the worst of the stories she had told about herself were true. He did not know. He could not remember. Perhaps it would have soothed him to know for certain that he had narrowly missed allying himself to someone quite unsuitable for the rank of countess. Perhaps he had no clear motive at all. Perhaps there had just been the unconscious need to keep some contact with her.

He had certainly not dreamed of finding a very powerful reason for going back to her and insisting that she reconsider. When he recalled his relationship with Jess in light of his meeting with her grandfather—the attempted seduction in the Barries' library, the very nearly consummated seduction at the inn, the unchaste embrace and renewed offer of *carte blanche* at Lord

Chalmers' ball—he shuddered with embarrassment. He had never before dreamed of doing more than kiss the fingertips of an unmarried lady of her rank. He had had Jessica Moore in bed, his hands roaming and exploring every inch of her body! He had been within moments of violating that body.

She would have to marry him. Surely even a lady of her stubborn independence must see that. She had been hopelessly dishonored, her reputation compromised beyond repair. The only way out for her was to wed her would-be seducer. Once her grandfather arrived at Hendon, once he had talked to her, once everyone knew her real identity, she would realize for herself that she had absolutely no choice in the matter. Even if she hated him, even if she was repulsed by him, she must marry him.

But it was not as bad as that. She did not hate him, Rutherford convinced himself. She was certainly not repulsed by him. It was just that their relationship had made a very poor start, a purely physical start, and she was convinced that he saw her as a sexual object only. Her pride was hurt. But she wanted him as badly as he wanted her. She just needed to be persuaded that marriage to him was the answer.

He just wished that there were someone more tactful than he to do the persuading. Somehow he did not seem to have the gift of talking to Jess. He was always so conscious of her, of his great need for her, that he could not possibly act naturally with her. Always he seemed like two persons, the one taking the most disastrous approaches to communicating with her, the other standing back and watching in dismay.

Unfortunately, he did not believe there was any more tactful advocate of his cause. Obviously her grandfather was not the man. The marquess himself admitted that he and Jess had never been able to agree on anything for any length of time. And she had rebelled in no uncertain manner the last time he had tried to order her life. And Rutherford was not convinced that even his grandmother would be able to change Jess's mind once it was made up. The dowager might have a will of iron, but he suspected that perhaps she had met her match in Jess.

Lord Rutherford sighed as he gazed about him with some satisfaction at the buildings of London. Jess. How would he ever get her out of his blood if she refused him this time? He might have agreed with her a few weeks before that his need for her was a purely physical thing, that if he could once bed her a few times, the obsession would disappear and she would become merely a woman to be used until all pleasure gave way to boredom. But it was not so. How absurd ever to have thought it.

Jess was part of his very being. He did not know her very well. She had never allowed him close enough to the person that she was. But he knew one thing. The one goal of his life, the one activity that could make it worth living, was to reach beyond the self-imposed barriers and learn to know her as well as he knew himself. He wanted her in his bed, yes. Nothing had changed that desire. But that would not be enough. Not nearly enough. He wanted Jess in his home, in his life. In his heart.

If he had discovered one thing during his long and tedious travels of the previous few weeks, he had discovered that. He loved Jessica Moore.

"We will be home in ten minutes, sir," he said, turning to his silent traveling companion with a smile, "and I do believe we will have time for a rest before dinner. I am sure you could use one."

"Damn the rest," the marquess said. "A hot bath and a good stiff drink will go a much farther way to restoring me, Rutherford. I shall spend long enough in my bed, doubtless, in the coming years unless I have the good fortune to pop off suddenly."

# 11

LADY HOPE WAS LOOKING almost pretty, Jessica decided. And it was strange really, because that lady was not dressed up in any of the finery that she usually wore when Jessica saw her. She was wearing a warm woolen dress, which had obviously seen better days. And even that was not wholly visible behind a large paint-streaked bibbed apron. Her dark hair, usually schooled into a tidy and smooth chignon, was less than immaculate, stray wisps having escaped from their bonds all over her head. Her cheeks were glowing with color.

The two ladies were relaxing on the window bench of the nursery at Hendon Park, favorite country seat of the Duke of Middleburgh. Lady Hope had been on all fours on the floor, one shrieking nephew on her back, a cousin's infant yelling to be allowed up as well, when Jessica had come to visit. The game of horsy had come to an abrupt end despite Jessica's laughter and protests. Lady Hope had scrambled to her feet, apologizing for her loss of dignity, her less than immaculate appearance, and the paint that her young niece had daubed her with earlier as they had tried to reproduce the scene from the window.

And now she was trying to appear dignified as she perched beside Jessica, ignoring the pleas of niece and nephews and other young relatives to come and play.

"I daresay I would quickly tire of playing with the

little dears if I had some of my own,'' she said.
''Foolish, is it not, my dear Miss Moore, to enjoy
romping with the youngsters at my age?''

''Not at all,'' Jessica assured her. ''I am sure they all
look forward vastly to seeing you, Lady Hope. I believe
too many times children see all too little of their parents
or other adult members of their family until they are old
enough to join them at adult entertainments.''

''Just look at that child!'' Lady Hope said with an
indulgent smile. ''No, no, Robbie, my love, it is not
gentlemanly to pull your sister's hair. You see? Now
you have made her angry. Don't slap, dear. Yes, I know
he pulled your hair, but it is not ladylike to retaliate.
There. Robbie will apologize, will you not, my love?''

''Mm.'' Jessica drew in a deep breath and closed her
eyes. ''I do believe a person can smell those mince pies
all over the house. Christmas does have a special smell
all its own.''

''I do wonder where Charles is,'' Lady Hope said.
''Only two days to Christmas and not a word from him.
Mama will be very upset if he does not come, not to
mention the rest of us. We have never had Christmas
without our all being present. I remember how empty it
seemed the first year without Grandpapa, though I was
a mere girl at the time.''

''Perhaps he will come yet,'' Jessica said, schooling
her voice to casualness. ''Surely he would have let her
grace know if he were not coming at all.''

Lady Hope sighed. ''I do wish Charles would marry
soon,'' she said. ''My youngest niece is four years old
already, and I am quite sure that Faith does not intend
to have any more. It is high time Charles set up his
nursery. He will be thirty on his next birthday. He just
does not seem to be interested in any of the young ladies
of the *ton*. It is said—though I should not repeat such
gossip to someone of your years, Miss Moore—that he
is too busy with his high flyers to be interested in more
refined ladies. I do hope someone of exceptional beauty

and breeding will appear next spring. Someone to catch his eye."

Jessica said nothing. The thought of Lord Rutherford paying court to a lovely girl fresh from the schoolroom made her feel slightly ill.

"I suppose I could have had children of my own if I had not been so fussy," Lady Hope said rather wistfully.

Jessica looked her inquiry.

"I have loved, you see," Lady Hope said, flashing her rather nervous smile. "And love is not always good for a person, Miss Moore. It leaves one dissatisfied with lesser feelings. You would not dream to look at me now, would you, that I had numerous offers even up to my thirtieth year? Of course, I daresay most if not all of them came because of who I am. Anyone can see that I was never a beauty. Not like Faith. But some very eligible gentlemen offered, for all that. And I refused them all. I loved my Bevin even when it was useless to do so—he had been long dead. Sometimes one regrets the lost opportunities. I would have liked to have a child."

"Yet you are still not old," Jessica said gently.

Lady Hope seemed to come out of a reverie and laughed heartily. "Oh, my dear," she said, "I am very firmly on the shelf and gathering dust. Two and thirty years old, you know, and no beauty to begin with. No matter." She patted Jessica on the knee. "I take pleasure these days in watching other people make good matches and produce children for Aunt Hope to play with. I was so glad to see Sir Godfrey arrive yesterday. I was afraid that with Charles away, he would not come. Not that he had anywhere else to go, of course, with his father away in Scotland with his sister. I thought perhaps you would be out walking with him, my dear Miss Moore."

"It is snowing," Jessica reminded her.

"And so it is." Her companion turned to look out of

the window. "I hope not too hard to block the roads.
Then Charles will never be able to come. Someone has
arrived, though." She leaned closer to the window.
"The carriage has moved away. I could not see if it was
familiar. Oh, I do hope it is Charles."

Jessica sat very quiet and tense, quite unable to decide
if she shared Lady Hope's sentiment or if she should
pray hard that the snow would form into twenty-foot
drifts so that no horse or vehicle would be able to move
for a month.

"Oh, delightful, Annie!" Lady Hope exclaimed.
"You have written your name, dear, and not a letter
missing. How very clever you are. And now you are
going to write 'Mama'? Indeed, dear, are you able to do
that? Yes, certainly I will watch you."

Jessica held her breath. Had it been Lord Rutherford
arriving? How soon would they know?

She had not long to wait. A mere few minutes later
the door to the nursery opened to admit the animated
figure of Lady Bradley.

"Oh, here you are, Miss Moore," she said. "So
exciting, my dear. Grandmama is quite beside herself.
Guess who has arrived?" She did not wait for an
answer. "The Marquess of Heddingly. Your
grandpapa! And we had no idea. Why did you not tell
us? Aubrey has had the honor of meeting him once
before. Such a distinguished gentleman. And he has
traveled all this way to see you, Miss Moore, and to
spend Christmas with us. But just listen to me prattle
on. Go down immediately. He is in the blue salon with
Grandmama. Oh, I am so excited for you, my dear."
She caught Jessica as the latter reached the door and
hugged her warmly.

Jessica's mind was in a daze. She had been half
expecting a reply to her hostess's letter some time over
Christmas. Indeed, until a week or so ago, she had been
wondering if her grandfather would make the journey
to Hendon Park for Christmas. But only now did she
realize how very unprepared she was to meet him again.

More than two years had passed since they had met last, and that parting had been a bitter one.

She did not stop to go to her room to tidy herself. She passed her hand over her hair as she ran lightly down the stairs to make sure that her curls were not too wayward, and smoothed out the creases of her dress. She would be cool. Affectionate but cool. She would show him that she loved him but could live very well without him.

Jessica paused outside the doors leading into the salon, schooled her features into bright welcome, took a deep breath, and nodded to the liveried footman who was waiting to open the door for her.

The first person she saw when she entered the room was the Earl of Rutherford, standing with his back to the fire, his hands clasped behind his back, looking grim and surely more handsome than she remembered him to be. She could feel the color draining from her face. There has been some mistake, she thought, some trick.

But at almost the same moment she was aware of her grandfather rising from a winged chair, the dowager beside him, smiling with benevolent triumph. Her grandfather looked very familiar though she had not seen him for so long. A little more stooped, perhaps. But Grandpapa nevertheless. Her very own. The only relative of her very own.

"Grandpapa," she said, holding on to her dignity, smiling politely, and advancing on him with both hands outstretched.

"Well, Jessica," he said gruffly, "you have led me a merry dance, my girl. I was beginning to think I would not see you again this side of the grave."

"Oh, Grandpapa," she said, her outstretched hands reaching up suddenly to encircle his neck as she hurled herself against him, wondering for one startled moment who it was that was sobbing so loudly.

It was a humbling experience, the Earl of Rutherford considered, to find himself so totally ignored. He had been away from her for three weeks, living and

breathing Jess Moore, scarce able to live through the
days until he would see her again, until he could try once
more to persuade her to be his wife. And it looked for
all the world as if she in the meanwhile had forgotten his
very existence.

There had been that moment, of course, when she
had entered the blue salon and seen only him. There had
been no unawareness of his existence, no indifference in
her face for that brief spell. He had been about to start
forward to catch her before she swooned. But it had
lasted only a moment. She had soon been distracted.
And there had been nothing like that first look in the
whole day since. And who could say now what it had
meant? Acute embarrassment at coming face to face
with him again most probably.

He watched her now covertly from across the drawing
room, sitting close beside Heddingly, her arm linked
through his, her cheeks flushed, her eyes bright with
happiness. They were in conversation with Faith and
Aubrey. It was impossible to hear the topic on which
they talked. The room was crowded to overflowing with
his own family and aunts, uncles, cousins, and cousins'
children galore, in addition to special guests like the
marquess, Jess, and Godfrey. The week of Christmas
was the one time of the year when the nursery brood
were allowed to spill downstairs on numerous
occasions. No one minded. It all added to that special
atmosphere of the season.

He was happy for her. Remembering how she had
appeared to him during that week at Lord Barrie's, he
could imagine how very lonely her life had been for the
past two years with no family of her own around her. It
was hard for him to picture life without family. His was
always there to exasperate him, to criticize him, to interfere in his affairs, to love him. Above all, he supposed,
to give him a sense of his own identity. Jess had been
without that for more than two years.

The scene in the blue salon had been very affecting. It
was the only time he had ever seen Jess completely out

of control of herself. Her face had crumpled as she hurled herself into old Heddingly's arms, and she had sobbed there loud and long before the marquess had given over kissing her hair, patting her back, and blinking his eyes fiercely and had drawn a large square of linen from a pocket and put it into one of her hands.

His grandmother had also been blowing her nose, Rutherford recalled, her face severe, muttering about the drafts at Hendon that always succeeded in giving her a cold over Christmas. And he had had to clasp his hands behind his back until his knuckles almost cracked and regard his boots with particular concentration to keep from showing his own emotion.

She had stopped eventually and availed herself of the handkerchief. And she had sat on a sofa beside Heddingly, as she did now, his hand firmly clasped in hers, her eyes wide on his face, almost as if she believed that if she lost touch with him and stopped seeing him he would disappear again.

Not a look in his direction.

"We have Charles to thank for your grandpapa's arrival, my dear Jessica," his grandmother had said during the conversation that ensued. "The marquess had decided that he did not own a traveling carriage fit for the journey. A letter would have had to suffice until the weather grew warmer. But Charles brought him."

She had looked at him then. Through him, rather. He had had the impression that she did not see him at all.

"Thank you, my lord," she had said before turning and smiling with warm affection at the old man again, laying her cheek against his shoulder for a moment.

No questions of how it had come about that he had gone to her grandfather. No queries about his health, about his whereabouts for the past three weeks. No polite wishes that his morning's journey had been a pleasant one. No sign of any gladness to see him. Or of displeasure in seeing him. No reaction at all.

"Charles." Hope was tapping his arm. "Claude has asked you twice already if you wish to play a game of billiards. You look as if you might be a million miles away."

The cousin in question laughed. "There must be a female in it," he said. "And where have you been for the last three weeks anyway, Charles? Is she to appear in London during the coming Season?"

The group around him all joined in the laughter.

"My lips are sealed," he said, grinning. "You don't think I would confide in you, Claude, do you, you puppy? An older cousin has to have some secrets. And I thought you had learned long ago not to humiliate yourself by challenging me to a game of billiards. It seems I have to refresh your memory. Are you coming, Godfrey?" He got to his feet.

"I shall stay to keep your sister company," Sir Godfrey replied. "I know that I would be drawn into challenging you too. And I know just as surely that you would crush me as you always do. You run along, and I shall stay here and hold on to my self-esteem."

Lord Rutherford put his arm across the shoulders of a tall, thin young lad who had been hovering in the vicinity of his group for several minutes.

"Are you coming too, Julius?" he asked. "Have you really grown a foot since last year, or is it just my imagination? Can I interest you in a game of billiards?"

Young Julius was beaming with pride as he left the room with his idol's hand still resting casually on his shoulder.

"I understand that the pond is to be scraped off tomorrow for the children to skate on," Sir Godfrey said. "And you are to accompany them, Lady Hope?"

"Oh," she said, flashing him an apologetic smile, "skating at Christmas time has always been traditional, Sir Godfrey, when there is ice. We are not always so fortunate, of course. We all go, you know. The distinctions between children and adults become somewhat blurred at this time of year."

"And is a mere family friend permitted to join the fun?" he asked.

"You, sir?" she asked. "But of course, if you wish to do so. You must not feel obliged to, of course. We will all understand perfectly if you choose to behave in a more dignified manner than the rest of us."

"How could I resist?" he said. "I do not believe I could even count the years since I last wore a pair of skates."

"You will not be the only person outside the family to be there," Lady Hope said, smiling slyly at her companion. "Dear Miss Moore is also to come."

"Is she, indeed?" he said, looking at her with a twinkle in his eye. "Then I shall certainly have to attend, shall I not, Lady Hope?"

"Is it not delightful to see her so happy?" she said, gazing fondly across the room at Jessica. "And she kept so quiet about the Marquess of Heddingly's being her grandfather."

"I suppose it would be a happy occasion to be reunited with the sole remaining member of one's family after longer than two years," Sir Godfrey agreed.

"And so pretty she looks with her fair hair and delicate complexion," Lady Hope continued.

"Indeed, yes," he said, "though sometimes I believe I prefer a dark beauty. Dark hair can be more striking."

"Perhaps," she agreed absently. "Would you not say that happiness has made Miss Moore look years younger, sir? Tonight she could pass for a girl in her first Season, I declare."

"My feelings exactly, ma'am," he said, a tremor of something very like amusement in his voice. "I suppose I must be feeling the effects of my age. I do believe my attention is usually caught these days by ladies of more mature years."

"Yes," she said, "and that is just as well. Miss Moore is four and twenty, after all. Have you told her about your horses, sir?"

"My horses?" He raised his eyebrows.

"Is she aware that you own one of the best stables of racing horses in the country?" she asked. "I am sure Miss Moore would be vastly impressed."

"I do not believe the chance to mention them has arisen in my conversations with her," he admitted. "No matter. There is always time. But what about you, ma'am? I begin to think you are not as interested in them as you have always appeared to be. You have been promising these five years past to visit my stables with your brother, but I have yet to see you there."

"Oh, me," she said with a self-deprecating laugh. "I am sure you do not wish to be encumbered with the likes of me at your stables when you must be forever busy with the horses."

"I have grooms and stable hands and jockeys to tend my horses for me," he said with a smile. "Really, Lady Hope, I am just a lazy owner who happens to have a shrewd eye for a good horse and a large enough purse to indulge my whims. I would not have invited you, you know, if I did not wish you to come."

"That is very civil of you, I am sure, sir," she said. "Perhaps when the weather improves I can accompany Miss Moore on a visit."

"A good idea," he said. "She seems to be a suitable chaperone."

Lady Hope appeared to miss this last comment. A whole flock of little children had descended on her demanding good night kisses. A nurse stood in the doorway, a firm look on her face. Evidently even the persuasions of the Duke of Middleburgh himself would not have shaken her decision that it was high time all those in her care were tucked up in their beds.

Jessica was brushing her hair absently before her mirror. She had dismissed her maid for the night several minutes before. What a very eventful day it had been! She still could scarcely believe that her grandfather had actually come—all the way to London in the middle of winter, merely to see her, the granddaughter who had defied him and rejected his care two years before. And he had not scolded all day. He had been content to let her hang on his arm, and had even patted her hand frequently with what she could only interpret as affection.

She had not realized until this day how starved she was for love. Not that she could complain. The Dowager Duchess of Middleburgh had shown her quite remarkable kindness since her arrival in London, and for no real reason at all except that she had been a friend of Grandmama's. But Jessica had not been able to quite relax. She had been so very aware of the fact that she was living entirely on the charity of a near stranger.

Now she had Grandpapa, and everything was going to work out well for her. They had not had any sort of personal talk during the day. They had not been alone together at all. She did not know what he would suggest, whether he would stay with her in London perhaps until the Season and continue with his plans of a few years before, or whether he would take her back home with him after Christmas. At the moment she did not care. It was enough to relax her stubborn independence for just a little while and let someone else decide her future for her.

Jessica turned from the mirror and climbed into the high bed. She pulled the covers around her although she did not lie down. The fire was still burning in the grate. But it was going to be a cold night. She must warm up the bed before the fire burned itself out.

The Earl of Rutherford had brought Grandpapa. He had been gone for three weeks, and he had returned with her grandfather. Why? What had he been doing all that time? It seemed very clear to Jessica that after all he must have gone in search of her identity. And he had discovered the truth. But why? She had refused him. Why would he still show any interest in her? Had he been hoping to find some dreadfully low or even scandalous background so that he could return to

London and expose her to the *ton*? Yet he had said that he wished to marry her even if her mother had been a scullery maid.

It had been a happy day. She could not deny that. The happiest she had known since before Papa had died. But, oh, it had been a wretchedly unhappy day too. How was she to spend a week longer in this house when Lord Rutherford would be there too? He was there now, sleeping in his own bedchamber. She did not know where that was. Perhaps not far off.

Jessica rested her forehead on her raised knees. Did he know, could he possibly have guessed, how achingly aware of him she had been all day, from the moment of her entry into the blue salon that morning? Could he have any inkling at all of the fact that when she had wept in Grandpapa's arms, she had done so as much because he had come back as because Grandpapa had come? She had not realized that even herself at the time. She had tried to tell herself that she was dismayed he had returned. She had tried to pretend that he was not there.

But she had known when she was forced to look at him at last. The dowager had told her that it was Lord Rutherford who had brought her grandfather, and she had been forced to look at him and acknowledge the fact. He had been standing there before the fire exactly as he had when she had entered, the same stony expression on his face. There was no sign of gladness for her happiness, no sign that he had done what he had done for her sake. He had barely acknowledged her thanks.

She had wanted to jump up at the dowager's words, throw her arms around him, and share her joy with him. But he had looked like a man made of stone. And all day he had ignored her. He had talked with almost everyone else in the house, had appeared progressively more cheerful as the day wore on, had talked with and teased the children, whose favorite he clearly was as much as Lady Hope was. But she might have been a hundred miles away.

How perverse of her to have expected or even wanted some sign from him, she thought. What did she expect? That he still wanted her? She had convinced herself and told him in no uncertain terms that she had no interest in being wanted merely. Did she expect that he would treat her with more respect, deeper regard, knowing who she really was? She would despise such a change in his behavior.

So what did she want?

Jessica turned her head to rest her cheek on her knees. She wanted his love. How very, very foolish! What had she ever done to earn the love of the Earl of Rutherford? And what had he ever done to make her crave his love? He was a man for whom the satisfaction of physical appetites was the most important thing in life. A man to despise.

Or was he? He had respected her wishes on more than one occasion, although she knew that on one of those occasions she had asked more of his self-control than any woman had a right to ask of a man. He had charm and knew how to set one at ease in conversation. There was some kindness in him. How many gentlemen would give up their bed to a mere governess? Especially when that governess did have a bed of sorts to go to? And he was dearly loved by a family of which Jessica was growing increasingly fond. There must be good in him when she had seen how anxious all his family had been lest he not appear for Christmas.

It was stupid to pretend. Of course she felt a strong physical attraction to Lord Rutherford. She would be almost unnatural not to do so. He was extraordinarily handsome, and she had moreover tasted his kisses and caresses. Yes, of course she wished to be in his bed again but without any of the moral scruples this time to prevent her from knowing the deepest caress of all. Of course she wanted all that. Her body ached and throbbed at that very moment for his touch.

But it was not just that. Oh, of course it was not just that. She wanted Lord Rutherford. All of him. Everything that made him the person he was. She wanted him to talk and talk to her, as he had at dinner at the inn. She wanted to share her thoughts and emotions with him as she had done unconsciously at Astley's. She wanted to laugh and be teased by him, as his nephews and nieces and cousins had been that day. She wanted to know him.

Could one love someone one did not really know very well at all? If not, what other name could she use to describe this feeling that was washing over her, that would not let her go? This feeling she had not been free of since that night at the inn?

And how foolish to love a man whose offer of protection she had refused twice, and whose marriage proposal she had rejected with some contempt. How very foolish to be depressed because he had shown no interest in her for a whole day. How ridiculous to have felt in the drawing room earlier in the evening that half the candles must have been snuffed merely because he had left the room talking and laughing with a couple of his cousins.

She must live out the week somehow, Jessica decided. And then she must studiously avoid him whatever Grandpapa's decision was about where they would live. She must put him out of her mind, out of her life. She must encourage one of her present suitors. Or allow Grandpapa to find her an eligible husband.

That was what she would do. She would concentrate on being a docile and obedient granddaughter. Had she done so two years before, she would probably be contentedly married by now and even perhaps have a baby of her own. She would have been immune to these painful and dreadful excesses of emotion.

What was he doing now? she wondered as she slid down in the bed to lie staring at the canopy over her head, picked out by the flickering of the flames in the hearth. Was he asleep? Had he spared even a single thought for her? Did he still find her desirable?

Jessica closed her eyes. Enough! she scolded herself. Tomorrow perhaps she would be able to have some private time with Grandpapa, and she would find out what was to be arranged for her future.

# 12

TO THE DELIGHT OF all members of the younger generation, and some of the adults too, the ice on the large pond north of the house was declared solid enough for skating the following morning. By luncheon time a contingent of servants had cleared the snow off the surface, and the ice was smooth and clear, shining invitingly in the watery sunlight. The same servants carried out two large boxes of skates of all sizes that had accumulated over the years.

"We all skate almost as well as we walk and ride," Lady Bradley explained to Jessica as they walked side by side out to the pond. They were slightly behind the main party of exuberant children, and adults trying to appear more dignified. "Hope and Charles and I, of course, had numerous opportunities as children to skate here. And even our cousins have been fortunate. If the weather is not cold enough at Christmas, Mama usually invites them all out here again in January. Of course, it is always a disappointment if there is no snow or ice at Christmas."

"I have tried skating only once, I am afraid," Jessica said. "It was on the village pond when I was quite a child. I seem to remember spending more time sliding around on my posterior than impressing the villagers on my skates. They were very much too large for me as I recall."

Lady Bradley laughed. "That was probably the whole

problem," she said. "It is essential to have the right size skates laced to your boots so that they feel almost part of your feet. But you really must not be too shy to try today. There will be plenty of skaters willing to help you along until you get your balance."

Jessica felt even more dubious when they arrived at the pond to find that several of the children were already dashing all over the surface of the ice as if moving on blades at high speed were the most natural way in the world to move around.

Lady Hope was looking brightly animated, seated on a makeshift bench, strapping skates to her boots and trying at the same time to help the efforts of two small children. Her cheeks were already flushed from the brisk air.

"Ah, you have decided to try after all, Miss Moore," she called. "I was sure your refusal at breakfast time was mere temporary cowardice. You will find it easy once you try, I do assure you. Penelope and Rupert both learned to skate last year, but they have convinced themselves that they no longer know how. I am going to show them how wrong they are. Come on, children."

She took a child's hand in each of her own, helped them down from the bank onto the surface of the ice, and skated slowly across its surface, encouraging the wobbly-legged younsters with a continuous and cheerful monologue.

"Here," Lady Bradley said, returning to where Jessica stood. She had one arm linked through her husband's. "Aubrey has volunteered to be your instructor, Miss Moore. I do assure you that he is as solid as a rock on the ice and will not let you fall."

"I think perhaps for this afternoon I shall watch," Jessica said.

"Nonsense, Miss Moore!" Lord Bradley immediately stooped over one of the boxes of skates and drew out a likely pair, his eyes moving critically from the skates to Jessica's feet. "Try these. You will be considered a poor creature indeed among this family if you cannot skate. I know. It was one of the first things I had to learn when I married Faith. There is nothing to it really once you have sensed the correct balance over your skates.''

Jessica was far from convinced as he stooped in front of her and began to strap the skates to her boots. She was about to make a dreadful cake of herself. The children would surely consider the show more entertaining than the clowns at Astley's. And the adults! How foolish she would appear. Lord Rutherford was out there, skating very expertly with a young female cousin of his, even twirling with her and skating backward as well as forward.

"Well," she said, smiling bleakly up at her teacher after he had strapped on his own skates, "I do hope you are as rocklike as Lady Bradley claims, my lord."

He was a very solid and dignified man, one whom she had rarely seen smile or heard speak a frivolous word. But as she took his hand and allowed him to help her to her feet, she was very glad of that solidity. Even before he stepped down onto the ice and helped her after, she felt as if her ankles would not be able to cope with balancing her weight above the flimsy blades.

But really, she discovered after a couple of minutes during which her eyes did not leave her boots, the thing was perhaps possible after all. It was true that Lord Bradley was probably supporting every last ounce of her weight, but she was beginning to feel some exhilaration. She was actually skating! She dared to look up for a moment at all the twirling figures, huddled warm inside their fur-lined cloaks and hoods, scarves covering necks and mouths.

"Oh dear," she said. "I really should not have looked up. I thought I was doing quite well until I did."

Lord Bradley laughed. "It is a humbling experience, is it not," he said, "to find that one performs some skill less well than even the smallest child? I would not worry about it, Miss Moore. You will do well with practice. You are relaxed. Many people tense up as soon as they step on ice. Then of course when they fall, which they inevitably do, they fall very heavily. I hate even to remember some of the bruises I sported during the first winter of my marriage to Faith.''

Jessica laughed.

"Let us try an experiment," he said. "Link one of your arms firmly through mine. Right. That will do. Now let us see if you can skate along with me. Quite sedately, ma'am, as if we were strolling through Hyde Park on a spring afternoon. I shall not let you fall.''

And without the total support of one of his strong arms beneath each of hers, Jessica found that the thing was still possible. When her skates did suddenly move too fast and threatened to leave the rest of her behind, the arm through which her own was linked tightened with reassuring firmness and she regained her balance with only a slight loss of dignity.

"How well you are doing, my dear Miss Moore," the cheerful voice of Lady Hope called as she and Sir Godfrey came skating effortlessly up to them. Her cheeks beneath the fur-lined hood of her blue cape were glowing brighter than ever. A few strands of dark hair had blown loose about her face.

"I am afraid I owe all my prowess to the steadiness of Lord Bradley," Jessica said ruefully.

"I am quite sure you would do equally well with a little support from any partner," Lady Hope said. "All you need is confidence, my dear. Sir Godfrey, I am sure you would enjoy taking a turn about the ice with Miss Moore. Do so, please. Do not mind me. I have promised to play with the children.''

"And I have just been congratulating myself on capturing the best skater on the ice for my partner," Sir Godfrey said, relinquishing her hand. "You are quite wasted on the children, ma'am.''

"Oh, is not that a foolish thing?" she said. "Your flattery is quite outrageous, sir. What would you want with twirling about the ice with someone like me? Aubrey, if we can arrange the children in two long lines, each clasping the waist of the one in front, we could have a very enjoyable race—you at the head of one line and me at the head of the other.''

Lord Bradley groaned. "Try Charles with your mad schemes, Hope, please," he said. "I intend persuading Faith to skate sedately around the perimeter with me, as befits a couple approaching middle age. She thinks she is of an age to retire from skating altogether, of course. I intend to disabuse her.''

Jessica found her arm being transferred very carefully to Sir Godfrey's.

"Come then, Miss Moore," he said, smiling cheerfully down at her. "Lady Hope thinks she has very subtly thrown us together in company again. She will eventually be most disappointed, will she not, when she discovers that we do not have a tendre for each other at all?''

Jessica skated gingerly at his side. He was not nearly as large and solid as Lord Bradley. "You mean you do not?" she asked. "I am shattered, sir.''

"No, you are not," he said. "I believe Miss Jessica Moore has eyes for only one gentleman, and he, alas, is not I. Perhaps it is just as well that my feelings too are otherwise engaged.''

Jessica looked up at him quite startled, completely forgetting that every jot of her attention needed to be focused on her skating. One foot shot out from under her, she turned to try to grasp her partner's arm with her free hand, her feet became hopelessly tangled up with each other, and somehow she found herself sprawled ignominiously face-down on the ice.

Pain was lost for the moment in embarrassment. Some female close to her shrieked. Several children laughed. Sir Godfrey apologized.

"My dear Miss Moore," he was saying. "Are you hurt, ma'am? How could I have let you fall like that? I am most dreadfully sorry.''

Jessica pushed herself to her knees and brushed ineffectually at the snow that clung to her cloak. "I am all right," she said in a daze. "How foolish of me."

She took a firm grasp of the arm held out to her and pulled herself somehow to her feet with its help. She clung with both hands.

"Oh, thank you," she said, looking up into the rather amused face of the Earl of Rutherford.

"Oh, but you have hurt yourself," he said, the amusement fading. He pulled his glove off his free hand with his teeth, reached into a pocket for a handkerchief, and stuffed in the glove in its place. "You have cut your mouth."

She was totally his captive. The death grip she had on one of his arms was the only thing that ensured her survival, she was sure. Several people skated up to them to exclaim and commiserate. Sir Godfrey hovered, delivering abject apologies until Lord Rutherford sent him off to deputize for him in Lady Hope's race. He dabbed the handkerchief gently against Jessica's lips. She was shocked to see it come away red. Her mouth was only just beginning to throb.

"Come," he said, "we will go and sit on the bench for a while. No, don't look so terrified." The amusement was back in his eyes for a moment. "I promise you will not fall again. I shall pick you up and carry you if you wish, but it would be a most ignoble end to an heroic first skating lesson, do you not think?"

They were seated on the rickety bench a minute later, Lord Rutherford again turning his attention and his handkerchief to Jessica's mouth. She reached for the handkerchief in some embarrassment, but he tightened his grip on it.

"There is no mirror here," he said. "Let me do it. What did you do, do you remember? Did you bang your lip on the ice or bite it as you fell? A foolish question. You are quite incapable of answering at the moment. Let me see."

He took the handkerchief away and she felt a gentle thumb at either side of her mouth pulling down her lower lip.

"It is not as bad as it could be," he said. "You have not bitten the inside of your mouth. You may have a fat lip for a day or so, Jess, but I do believe you will be able to enjoy your Christmas dinner tomorrow."

His eyes were on her mouth. Uncomfortable feelings were churning Jessica's insides, completely distracting her mind from the throbbing lip. She felt no better at all when he looked up into her eyes and grinned.

"Do you have any other injuries?" he asked. "Two scraped knees, for example?"

"No!" Jessica said very firmly. "I am quite all right, I do assure you, my lord. This is all very humiliating."

"And certainly not the memory to leave with the whole houseful of guests," he agreed. "Come. You will skate with me."

"No," she said sharply. "No, I think I have entertained everyone quite sufficiently for one day, my lord. I shall go back to the house. I wish to talk to my grandfather."

"If you leave now, Jess," he said, "you will never find the courage to return to the ice, you know."

"I do not feel I shall consider the lack the great tragedy of my life," she said.

"Coward!" he accused, grinning. "You were doing quite nicely with Aubrey. Godfrey, of course, is a careless creature who probably became so absorbed in conversation that he forgot he was your sole prop and staff. Trust me. I will not let you fall."

It was the charge of cowardice that did it, probably. Jessica rose to the challenge even as she realized that the word had been deliberately thrown out to goad her. She got to her feet and wobbled slightly even before he jumped up and drew one arm firmly through his.

"Try this," he said when he had lifted her down to the ice. A few lone skaters were twirling around. The main bulk of children and some of the adults were in a dense and noisy group at the far end of the ice, the race presumably over. "We will pretend we are waltzing. You may put your hand firmly on my shoulder. Grasp one of my capes if you will feel safer. Your other hand quite firmly in mine. And my other hand at your waist like this. Now, have you ever felt safer in your life?''

Many, many times, Jessica thought, her face upturned to his, drowning in his eyes. Oh yes, at almost any other moment of her life that anyone would care to name she had felt considerably safer than she did at this moment.

"One problem," he said. "We cannot possibly waltz without music, can we? I would hum a tune, Jess, but I am afraid you would not even recognize my efforts as music. You will have to do it.''

"Hum a tune?" she asked, incredulous.

"A waltz tune," he said. "Any one, Jess. Anything that goes one, two, three, one, two, three.''

"How foolish!" she said, glad of her cold-reddened cheeks that must mask the blush she could feel hiding beneath.

"Coward, Jess?" he asked with one eyebrow raised, and she found herself humming a waltz tune that she remembered from Lord Chalmers's ball.

"Mm, lovely," he said, smiling down at her and skating slowly backward in time to the music, drawing her with him. "But we will have to make one adjustment for your safety. Clasp both hands around my neck, Jess, and I shall set one on either side of your waist. Ah, much better, is it not? The music again, please, ma'am.''

She wanted to cry. How very stupid to want to cry. She felt so safe. It was her hold of him and his of her that kept her on her feet, of course, but she felt light, as if she skimmed over the ice of her own volition. They moved very slowly, but the hissing of their skates on the ice gave an impression of speed. His eyes held hers as she hummed her tune almost without realizing that she still did so. For the space of perhaps two minutes nothing and no one existed outside the circle of their arms.

And finally the music trailed away. The lump in her

throat that made her want to cry had also made the music wobble.

"Out of breath already?" he asked, tightening his hands at her waist and bringing them to a stop. "But you did very well, Jess. If you just had the confidence, you could skate on your own, you know. But not today. Your lip looks sore. My mother will have some salve for it, doubtless. Come, I will help you off with your skates."

He lifted her effortlessly and set her feet on the bank.

"You played a cruel trick on me, Jess Moore," he said as he knelt before her, despite her protests, to remove her skates.

"Did I?" she asked.

"Did I?" he mimicked. "Why did you not tell me? I should have known right from the start, you know."

"Would it have made a difference?" she asked.

He looked at her intently as he straightened up and tossed her skates into one of the boxes. "Of course it would have made a difference," he said.

"I was afraid you would say that," she said.

"It is Christmas, Jess," he said, smiling and passing one hand briefly beneath her upturned chin. "For today and tomorrow let us not quarrel. I should not have referred to the matter at all. I am sorry. We will do battle again the next day if we must. Agreed?"

"I have nothing to battle with you about, my lord," she said.

"Agreed, Jess?" he insisted.

"Agreed," she said grudgingly.

It was not until the following day, the afternoon of Christmas Day, that Jessica finally succeeded in being alone with her grandfather. The morning had been taken up with all the excitement of watching the children open their gifts in the morning room, as was traditional, exchanging gifts with one's immediate family, and entertaining the servants to cider and cakes while they too were presented with gifts by the duke and duchess.

Her grandfather was tired, Jessica could see when luncheon was over. He readily agreed to her suggestion that she accompany him to his sitting room so that they might talk quietly. She resisted Lady Hope's invitation to join a smaller group than the day before for skating.

"You really should give Sir Godfrey a chance to redeem himself, you know, my dear Miss Moore," she had said. "I believe he is dreadfully upset for allowing you to fall yesterday. And I must say, my dear, that I was most vexed that Charles rushed to your assistance the way he did. I am sure Sir Godfrey would have been only too glad to help you to your feet and spend more time in your company. Sometimes I suspect that Charles lacks all sensibility."

"Well, Jessica," the marquess said, lowering himself heavily into a chair beside the fire in his sitting room, "are you happy, my love?"

"Yes, I am," she said, perching on the arm of his chair and smoothing back some wisps of his white hair, "now that you are here, Grandpapa. You cannot know how lonely Christmas can be without any members of one's family present."

"Can I not?" he said gruffly. "Each year you have been without me, I have also been without you, you know."

"Yes, that is true," she said, bending to kiss the top of his head briefly. "How foolish we have been, have we not?"

"We?" he said ominously.

Jessica laughed. "Come now, Grandpapa," she said, "admit the truth. You can be every bit as stubborn as I can at times. I believe both of us place pride before love far more than we should."

"Well," he said, patting one of her knees with a gnarled hand, "since it is Christmas, I shall agree with you, girl. We cannot quarrel at this season, can we?"

"Absolutely not," she agreed. "And perhaps we can make every day Christmas from now on. I do love you, Grandpapa. I do not know if I have ever told you that."

"I am glad you have come to your senses finally, anyway, Jessica," the marquess said. "The dowager duchess was a particular friend of your grandmother's, you know. The connection with her grandson will be even more eligible than I could have hoped for you."

Jessica's hand, which had been playing with his hair, became very still. "My connection with the Earl of Rutherford?" she said.

"You are fortunate, my love," he said. "Rank and wealth on the one hand seldom go together with looks and character. I shall be delighted to see you well settled before I meet my end."

"There is to be no connection between the Earl of Rutherford and me, Grandpapa," Jessica said. She found that her voice was shaking.

"Of course there is," he said. "I gather you have refused him already, Jessica. It is never a bad idea to do that once, you know. Your grandmother did it to me. It merely piques a man's interest. But you must have Rutherford, of course. There is no question about that."

"I beg your pardon, sir," Jessica said, sitting upright on the arm of the chair, "but I believe there is every question about the matter."

"Sometimes you can be very exasperating, Jessica," the marquess said. "What possible objection could there be to Rutherford? He is an earl and heir to a dukedom. He has property, wealth, character."

"He is a rake!" Jessica said.

"Jessica," her grandfather said, making an effort to sound patient, "if you are looking to find yourself a husband who has never kept a mistress or a high flyer, my girl, you are likely to be looking until your dying day. Besides, it don't mean he will continue the same habits. You are pretty and lively enough to keep his interest if you set your mind to it. I was never unfaithful to your grandmother, you know, after our marriage."

"When I refused the Earl of Rutherford," Jessica said, "I meant my refusal for all time. I was not hoping to entice him to renew his attentions with increased ardor. I do not want him as a husband, and I will not have him." She was on her feet by this time, her hands clenched at her sides.

"You have no choice, foolish girl." The marquess had abandoned his attempts to deal patiently and rationally with the situation. "You have been compromised. That employer of yours—Beattie? Bering?—saw the two of you in his library. You spent the night at the same inn together. To his credit, of course, Rutherford did not know who you were on either occasion, but it will not do for the granddaughter of the Marquess of Heddingly. Not at all. Marry the man you must, Jessica, and quickly too, whether you like him or not."

"What?" Jessica said, hands on hips. "I am to marry a man I despise, spend the rest of my life with him, become his possession, all because he mistook me for a servant and treated me accordingly? Besides, Grandpapa, who is to know of those incidents if neither you nor the Earl of Rutherford tells anyone? Of course I will not marry him. And I think it highly unlikely anyway that he will renew his offer."

"Of course he will renew his offer," the marquess barked. "He already has my permission to do so, Jessica. We have already agreed on a marriage settlement."

"Oh!" Jessica moved toward him, her hands still on her hips, her eyes blazing. "So I have become an object of barter between you and Lord Rutherford, have I? Not at all a person with feelings and opinions to be consulted. Merchandise merely. If you have offered a large dowry, Grandpapa, you are remarkably foolish. The Earl of Rutherford would have paid you to get me into his bed. He offered twice, you know. Did he tell you that?"

"He thought you a servant," the marquess said. "Of course he told me. All the more reason why you must accept him. And enough of this nonsense, Jessica. I will hear no more on the matter. This time, my girl, we will have your future all tied up right and tight. You have had your flight of rebellion. Time now to settle down."

"Do you know?" Jessica said. She had turned away from him and crossed the room to the window, where she stood drumming her fingers on the windowsill. "I thought things were different this time. I really thought you had grown to love me. I thought I mattered to you as a person."

"Tush, girl!" her grandfather said impatiently. "Since when does a grandfather's concern to marry his girl well and secure her future and her reputation show lack of love? Of course I love you, girl. Would I be here otherwise?"

"Then don't," she said, turning back to him to reveal eyes brimming with tears. "Don't do this to me, Grandpapa. Please. I have been of age for several years and have the right to make my own choice of a future. I hoped to spend some of that future with you. I have even planned to allow you to order my life and find a husband for me if you wish. But not the Earl of Rutherford. Please, anyone but him. I cannot agree to it. Yet I don't want to quarrel with you. I need your love so much, Grandpapa. Please!"

"There," he blustered, patting the arm of the chair beside him. "Come back here, girl, and stop your silliness. Of course I love you. Always have. There have been three women very precious to my life, Jessica, and you are the only one left. Now don't go trying my patience when I am tired and irritable after a busy morning. Have you ever heard such a whooping and screeching of children in all your life?"

Jessica laughed. "You loved every moment of it, Grandpapa," she said, "especially when that tiny tot climbed into your lap and demanded that you read a story from her new book."

"The one with the hair bow as large as her head?" He chuckled. "She reminded me of you, Jessica. When your Mama brought you to visit when you could scarcely walk and had scarcely any hair, you had two scarlet bows, one on each side of your bald head. I never did find out what held them there."

They both laughed, and Jessica laid her cheek against the top of his head.

"Let me help you to your bedchamber, Grandpapa," she said. "You really should have a sleep. Oh, I know you are not old enough yet to give in to afternoon naps. But Christmas is a busy time, you see, and I am going to tiptoe along to my room and have a sleep too. I shall just have to hope that no one shames me by finding out. You will not tell, will you? If you do, you know, I shall tell on you."

"You're a good girl, Jessica," he said, pulling himself to his feet and leaning on her arm. "Stubborn and chuckleheaded as they come, but a good girl. All you need is a gentleman of strong character to settle you down."

"Well," she said, squeezing his hand, "let us agree not to pursue that topic any further for the time being, shall we, Grandpapa?"

# 13

THE EARL OF RUTHERFORD was not eager to see the end of Christmas Day, but inevitably it came. It had been a day teeming with activity: opening gifts and holding a party for the servants in the morning; skating with most of the children and some of the more energetic adults in the afternoon; playing billiards and cards with the men while the ladies rested before dinner; romping at children's games in the evening until their bedtime; playing a high-spirited game of charades for the rest of the evening. It had been the usual Christmas Day. The only part that ever varied was the skating. The weather was not always kind enough to permit it.

He always enjoyed the day. One grumbled, of course, assuring one's parents each autumn that really one had far better activities with which to fill the festive season. But inevitably one came, not because one was necessarily weak-willed or because one did not have anything else to do, but because Christmas simply would not be Christmas if one were anywhere else or engaged in any other activities. On what other day of the year would one join in a spirited game of blindman's buff with hosts of giggling children and very young adults, completely oblivious of one's dignity, and actually enjoy oneself?

Yet it was not just the sheer exuberant enjoyment of the day that made him sorry to see it at an end, Lord Rutherford thought, unconsciously moving closer to the

fire in his dressing room as he pulled off his shirt. It was
that tomorrow he must act. He must do something
about Jess.

He wanted to, of course. He was very eager to offer
for her again, arrange for an early marriage, and begin
to live out the blissful remainder of his life with her. In
some ways the delay of the past two days had been
torture. Yet in another way he had welcomed the excuse
of Christmas to hold back and postpone the inevitable
moment. She was not going to take kindly to his
proposal. He just had a very strong intuition that she
would not.

He had not spent a great deal of time in her company.
Quite deliberately he had kept apart from her most of
the time. He did not wish to invite any quarrel between
them, and he did not wish her to feel that she was being
pursued so closely by him that she could not relax and
enjoy the season and the recent arrival of her grandfather.

So apart from that one spell on the ice, when he had
not been able to resist rushing to her assistance after she
fell, he had contented himself with watching from afar.
He had denied himself the pleasure of taking her in to
meals, and this evening he had resisted the temptation to
let her catch him at blindman's buff.

But he had enjoyed watching her. She seemed to
enjoy the company of all his family, especially Hope,
who was making something of a fool of herself trying to
throw Godfrey and Jess together. Fortunately, he could
see quite clearly that those two felt no dangerous
attraction for each other. He might have been ready to
do murder otherwise. But Hope clearly could not see it.
Anyone would have thought that by her age she would
have realized that she had no talent whatsoever at
matchmaking. She had even scolded him for taking Jess
away from Godfrey out on the ice. It was far more likely
that Godfrey was interested in her than in Jess. They
certainly spent a great deal of time in company together.

Interestingly enough, too, he had heard from a cousin

since arriving at Hendon Park that Godfrey had put an
end to that long-standing affair of his. Had he shed the
mistress in preparation for taking a wife? Godfrey
himself had said nothing about the matter in the past
few days. That in itself might be significant.

Well, tomorrow, Rutherford thought, he would pay
his addresses to Miss Jessica Moore. She would not
refuse him, surely. It was merely his extreme eagerness
to marry her that made him nervous. She had no reason
to refuse him. Indeed, the Marquess of Heddingly must
have already pointed out to her the utter necessity of
accepting him. She really had no choice at all. Even if
she detested him, she must marry him. And she did not
detest him. He even had good reason to believe that he
could teach her to love him.

There had been that short spell on the ice, for
example. The pull of attraction between them had been
almost suffocatingly strong. He could not have felt it so
powerfully while she felt nothing. He knew she had not
felt nothing. When she had skated with him, she had
been as incapable of looking away from him as he from
her. Her eyes had been dreamy. She had been in a world
of her own. No, that was wrong. *They* had been in a
world of their own. Together. She could not have
looked at him like that and felt nothing.

If he could only approach this meeting with her, then,
with care, there was no reason at all why this time
tomorrow night he should not be the happiest of men.
He settled into bed and clasped his hands behind his
head. He would announce their betrothal at dinner
tomorrow night before any members of the family
started to disperse to their own homes. Rather, he
would have his father make the announcement. They
would marry in the spring, during the Season, when
London was crowded with fashionable people. He
wanted to show Jess off to all the world. The thought
surprised him rather. He would have expected that once
he did decide to marry, he would dread a large and very
public wedding.

How should he approach tomorrow's meeting, though? With confidence? Yes, he decided, but he must be certain that he did not give the impression of arrogance. With common sense, certainly. He must point out to her all the advantages of a marriage between them and all the necessity of it. She must be made to realize that really she did not have a choice.

Yet he must almost make it seem as if she did have a choice. He must show some vulnerability. The thought was not a pleasant one. It was not in his nature to admit any personal weakness to himself or anyone else. He had been brought up to think that manliness and unyielding strength were one and the same thing. But he must show Jess that he cared, that she mattered to him. She must be made to see that he wanted her as a bride, that his life would somehow be incomplete, meaningless even, without her.

Yes, he must, more than anything else, be sure to tell her that he loved her. It would not be so difficult an ordeal after all, perhaps. For weeks he had been wanting to tell Jess just that. Tomorrow he would have the opportunity. And how could he not tell her with his every look as well as with his words? Once he was alone with her, it would be impossible to hide the truth even if he wished to do so.

And he certainly did not wish any such thing.


"What a poor-spirited family we have become," Lady Hope was complaining the following morning at the breakfast table. "Charles, I thought at least you of all people would not have refused to accompany the children sledding."

"They have nurses and governesses and such to take them, Hope," he pointed out, folding his napkin and laying it beside his plate.

"But there is the exercise," his sister insisted. "And you know we have always had enormous fun out on the hills, Charles."

"I prefer to leave it to the children now that I am

entering my dotage," he said firmly. "There is a two-mile tramp before one even reaches the hills, Hope."

"Well," she said, "it seems that I am the only one with any youthful spirit remaining. Very well. I shall go alone."

"If a nonmember of the family is permitted to make one of the party," Sir Godfrey said, "I should be delighted to make the trek, Lady Hope."

"Well, how very gracious of you, sir," she said. "The children will be very grateful. It adds enormously to their fun, you know, to have some of us there with them. Especially if we should fall off a sled into the snow. That would complete their joy for the day."

"I could probably arrange to supply that fun too, ma'am," he said, "without even trying."

Those who still remained at the breakfast table laughed.

"And I am quite sure that dear Miss Moore would enjoy the outing too," Lady Hope said. "I believe she felt somewhat embarrassed while skating, though there was absolutely no need to do so. But anyone can sit on a sled and slide down a hill. I shall go immediately to ask her. She is breakfasting in Lord Heddingly's sitting room. He is somewhat tired from the excitement of yesterday, I daresay."

Lord Rutherford drew breath to reply, but Sir Godfrey forestalled him.

"I do not doubt that Miss Moore would enjoy the outing," he said, "but I am sure that her grandfather would enjoy her company too. Let us leave them to each other and the warmth of the house, shall we, Lady Hope?"

Rutherford could almost have laughed at the expression on her face.

"Well, certainly, sir, if you really think it would be better to do so," she said. "We will be back before luncheon, anyway, and there will still be a great part of the day left, I suppose. If you would really prefer to stay yourself, sir, you must not feel obliged to accompany me, you know. I shall be quite happy with the children.''

"Ah, but I wish to accompany you, Lady Hope," Sir Godfrey said, rising to his feet decisively and holding out a hand to help her.

Rutherford's lips twitched. It seemed entirely possible that there would be two family betrothals to celebrate that evening. If Godfrey could but convince Hope that he really wished to address himself to her and not to Jess, that was.

Lord Rutherford would probably have enjoyed listening to the conversation between his sister and his friend as they walked the two miles to the snow-covered hills to the south, surrounded by running and yelling children, two nurses and a governess, and two gardeners pulling along behind them a string of wooden sleds.

After various comments on the weather and the personalities of the children and young people around them, Lady Hope steered the conversation determinedly to Jessica. Sir Godfrey followed her lead with some amusement for a few minutes before drawing her to a halt and turning to face her.

"Lady Hope," he said, "may we put an end to this topic by agreeing that Miss Moore is indeed a beautiful and accomplished young lady who will make some fortunate man a good wife?"

She looked somewhat taken aback. "I beg your pardon, sir," she said. "I did not realize that I had embarrassed or offended you by talking about her."

"You have done neither, I assure you," he said, a twinkle in his eye. "But much as I esteem the young lady, I must admit to some boredom at finding her so frequently the topic of conversation between you and me."

"Oh," she said.

"Why do you not tell me about Lady Hope?" he asked, patting her hand on his arm and beginning to stroll onward again. "Have you finally recovered from your sad loss, my dear? And are you now ready to continue with the rest of your life?"

"Do you speak of Bevin?" she asked. "But that was long in the past, sir, and we were never officially betrothed, you know. I daresay Papa would not have easily given his consent, anyway. The matter was of no great significance."

"On the contrary, my dear," he said, "the passing of Lieutenant Harris has been very much the most significant event in your life. I have wondered many times if you would ever recover from it. You loved him very dearly, did you not?"

Her eyes looked suspiciously bright as she darted a glance and her nervous smile up at him. "Yes," she said. "Foolish, is it not, for a spinster of my age to have ever felt such emotion?"

"It is not foolish at all," he said gently. "I have found myself several times over the past several years almost envying the late lieutenant. And is not that foolish?"

For once Lady Hope seemed lost for words. She looked up at him, incomprehension in her face.

"I have waited for years," he said, "and am prepared to wait for as many more if I must. But I do feel the natural human need for hope, you know." He grinned. "And the pun was intentional. Rather clever, don't you think?"

She was still staring up at him. They had stopped walking again.

"Is there a chance, my dear," he asked, smiling almost apologetically down at her, "that if I remain patiently your friend for long enough, one day you will find yourself able to feel enough affection for me to put your safekeeping in my hands? I will never expect you to stop cherishing Lieutenant Harris in your memories."

"You have a tendre for Miss Moore," she said.

He shook his head.

"She is young and beautiful," she protested. "She

would make you an admirable wife, Sir Godfrey. What would you want with an old spinster like me?"

He smiled. "I could answer that," he said, "but I would not wish to embarrass you, my dear. I have been your faithful admirer for years, Lady Hope. My life will be complete if the day ever dawns on which I may call you my wife."

Her eyes widened. "Me?" she said foolishly. "Me, sir? Your wife?"

He nodded.

"And I have always thought you so wonderful that I must find you an equally wonderful wife," she said.

He laughed and took both her hands in his. "That has been the only tiresome part of my association with you," he said, "though amusing too, I must admit. You have been making a particularly vicious siege on my heart with Miss Moore, though, have you not?"

"Oh, Miss Moore!" she said, pulling one hand away from his and covering her mouth with it. "She will be so disappointed."

"How flattering to think so," he said with a grin. "But it is not so, you know. Have you not noticed, my dear, that it is Charles and Miss Moore?"

"Charles?" she said, her eyes blank. "And Miss Moore?"

He nodded. "Is there any chance for me, my dear?" he asked.

She swallowed quite visibly. "I am two and thirty," she said.

"Are you?" he said. "I am relieved to say that I can still say the same. In two weeks' time I will have to add one number to the total."

"It may be too late for me to give you heirs," she said, her cheeks reddening to a deeper color than could be attributed to the cold.

"If I had to choose between a girl who would give me ten children and you with none, there would be no choice at all," he said. "It is you I love, my dear.

Besides, I see no reason for its being too late. And I believe that motherhood is an experience you really should have if you possibly can. You are wonderful with children.''

"Everyone will laugh," she said, "at a woman of my age marrying and talking of having children.''

"I believe everyone in your family will laugh with great delight," he said. "At least, I hope they will be delighted at your choice of me. I hope they will think me worthy. And we can keep secret our plan to have children, if you so choose.''

"Aunt Hope. Aunt Hope.'' They were both suddenly distracted by the row of children standing at the bottom of the distant hill, all chanting in unison.

Lady Hope beamed at them and waved her hand vigorously. "Coming, children," she called.

But Sir Godfrey caught at her hands again before she could move. "Is the answer yes?" he asked. "Or is there at least a chance that if I wait longer. . . ?"

Her hands suddenly squeezed his with quite unlady-like force. "I am so glad we are going sledding," she said. "I would not know else how to contain my emotions, sir. Of course, I will marry you if you are quite, quite sure that you really wish to marry me. I have always envied the young lady who would eventually capture your heart. And you need not fear that I will still harbor a love for Bevin. I did love him dearly, and of course I shall always treasure his memory. But a dead love cannot sustain one through life, sir. It has been a full year or perhaps more since my heart has felt empty again. And I have been afraid to put you there in his place, for really I never did dream that you would ever wish to be there.''

"For the rest of my life, if you please, Hope, my dear," he said, "as you will surely be in mine.'' He brushed the backs of his fingers lightly across her cheek and smiled down at her.

"Aunt Hope. Aunt Hope. Aunt Hope.'' The chanting became unrelenting.

"Coming!" she called back, beaming ahead of her and reaching for Sir Godfrey's arm. "They will not be content for us to merely push them from the top, you know. We will have to ride. And we must fall off at least once, preferably in the part where the snow is thickest. They will be most disappointed if we fail to do so."

Sir Godfrey smiled fondly down at her beaming face. "What a very kind lady I am going to have as a wife," he said. And then into her ear as they drew closer to the children, who were dragging the sleds uphill, having seen that she was coming at last, "I love you."

"Oh," she said, looking up at him with sparkling, excited eyes before gathering her fur-lined cape in her hands and hastening up the hill in the wake of the children.

Jessica had hoped that she would not have to venture downstairs at all during the morning. Her grandfather was tired after all the traveling he had done before Christmas and after the excitement of the day before. She had persuaded him to keep to his rooms until luncheon. What was more natural in the world than for her to stay with him?

For the rest of the day she hoped to be able to stay very near him or the dowager duchess or Lady Hope or anyone safe. She must not, whatever she did, put herself in the position where Lord Rutherford could have a private word with her. She found it difficult to believe that he really did intend renewing his offer for her. Yet her grandfather said it was true. But she was not going to give the earl a chance to do any such thing, she had decided.

Yet even before luncheon it was impossible for Jessica to put her resolve into effect. Her grandfather wished to know if a certain book was kept in the duke's library. Nothing else would do. Jessica suggested the titles of several books she had in her room, but quite in vain. She must go downstairs and see if that one volume was there.

How could she say no? she thought in some despair as she crept stealthily down the staircase, first past the floor on which most of the living apartments were situated and on down to the hall and the library. Even though she was convinced that Grandpapa would be asleep again before she returned to his room, she could not have denied his request.

She drew a sigh of relief as a footman opened the door into the library for her and she discovered that it was empty. And although the door to the morning room had been open and a hum of voices coming from inside, she did not believe that she had been spotted. If she could just find the book quickly and be as fortunate on her way back upstairs!

Jessica knew, even as she descended the library ladder, the book she wanted clasped in her hand, that she was not to be that fortunate. Her back was to the door when it opened. The person entering could have been any one of a dozen or more people. But she knew without turning just who it was. And she knew by the way the door closed quietly but firmly behind him that he had seen her come in and had come deliberately to talk to her. She drew a deep breath and returned both feet to the floor.

"Good morning, Jess," the Earl of Rutherford said.

"Good morning, my lord," she said, turning and smiling brightly—too brightly, she thought immediately with some annoyance. She held up the book. "I am on an errand for Grandpapa." She moved purposefully toward him and the door.

"Let him wait for it a while," he said, smiling at her and taking the book from her suddenly nerveless fingers when she was close enough. "May I talk to you, Jess?"

"Grandpapa is waiting," she said. "He has nothing else with which to occupy his time."

"Stay and talk with me, Jess," he said.

If he just would not smile! she thought. A smile did wonders for his face. It did not make it exactly more handsome, but it made him look kindly and far more human. She preferred his arrogant look. It was easier to withstand. She said nothing.

"I made a mess of things rather the last time I talked to you about marriage," he said. "I am hoping I can do somewhat better this time."

"Oh, no!" Jessica put both hands up defensively before her. "Please say no more, my lord. I told you on that occasion that I have no wish to marry you. Nothing has changed since then."

"But why not?" he asked. "What is the problem, Jess?"

She was shaking her head. "We would not suit," she said. "You are not the sort of man with whom I would feel comfortable. I . . . I cannot accept, my lord."

He frowned. "What have I done that is so dreadful in your sight?" he asked. "From the first I have shown a preference for you. I have never forced you into anything against your will. I offered you marriage even before I knew who you were, so you cannot accuse me of snobbery. I know you are not averse to my person."

"That is unimportant," she said. "There are many qualities one looks for in a husband beyond that."

"And you can find nothing else in me to esteem, Jess?" he asked.

She shook her head but said nothing. She was gazing at him almost imploringly.

"Am I so lacking in all admirable qualities?" he said harshly. "I had not thought myself quite so depraved. Perhaps your standards are just too high, madam."

"Perhaps they are," she said very quietly.

He looked at her in exasperation for a few silent moments. "You realize that it makes no difference whatsoever, don't you?" he asked. "You must marry me whether you admire me or not. Perhaps it is fortunate that at least my caresses please you, Jess."

"I will not marry you," she said calmly.

He laughed unpleasantly. "You did not hear me," he said. "You have no choice, my dear, any more than I have. Do you think I enjoy the thought of marrying a woman who despises me, who cannot see one trace of goodness in me? And a woman, moreover, who has deceived me and thereby trapped me into having to marry her? Oh, I know you did not deliberately do that, Jess, but you did it nonetheless."

"You need not fear," she said, her voice flat. "I will not marry you."

Two very heavy hands clamped onto her shoulders suddenly, and she found herself looking into two very intense blue eyes. "You are still a virgin," he said, "but do you realize by what narrow a margin, my girl? You and I have done together everything else that a husband does with his wife except that and indeed a great deal more than a wife of any great sensibility would ever dream of doing. You have lain in bed with me, Jess. Your body holds only one secret from me. In this society that you have shown some eagerness to be a part of young ladies do not offer even their lips to a man unless they are prepared to marry him. You have been compromised, Jess. Hopelessly and irretrievably compromised. You must marry me."

"I will not marry you," she said. Her breath was coming fast, but she looked steadfastly back into his eyes. She would not cringe before him.

He shook her roughly before releasing her and turning his back on her. "There are certain things that one does, whether one likes them or not," he said. "Marrying a lady one has compromised is one of them. It seems you have been shut away from proper behavior for too long to know what is what, Jess. Marry me you must. You will find that your grandfather will be as adamant as I. I shall discuss the matter further with him. I am more likely to get satisfactory results."

"Do so," she said. "Perhaps you would also like to marry my grandfather. It might be a more satisfactory marriage."

He spun around again, his face such a mask of fury that Jessica took an involuntary step backward. His hands opened and closed into fists at his side.

"By God, Jess," he said, "you had better learn to curb your tongue before we are wed. I am very like to strike you if you speak to me in that way ever again, and then you will have yet another evil aspect of my character to throw in my teeth. I have tried to be pleasant to you. I have tried to make a friend of you. I have tried to show you in the last few days that marriage to me will not be such a bad bargain after all. It seems you are determined to cast me in the role of villain. But it would be in your own interests to try to alter your vision, my dear. I would imagine it is a dreadful thing indeed to hate one's husband. And I will be your husband."

"Fortunately, my lord," she said with as much calm as she could muster, "I live in England, where one may expect to have one's freedom upheld in a court of law, and I am of age. I will not be married merely because I have a desirable body or merely because I have transgressed a rule of a society that I have lived without all my life. I am a person, Lord Rutherford, and when I marry—if I marry—it will be to a man who believes that he cannot live a complete life without that person—all of it. All of me. Call me a hopeless romantic if you wish. Yes, that is what I am. I will not marry because I must. I will marry only when I will."

He was staring at her with wide-open eyes, the harsh, arrogant look completely gone. Jessica picked up the book very deliberately from the table where he had laid it, stepped past him, and left the room. When she turned to shut the door quietly behind her, it was to find that he had not moved.

# 14

LORD RUTHERFORD STOOD FOR a long time in the same spot after Jessica had left the library, his eyes closed, his hands clenched loosely at his sides. She would not marry a man who wanted her for her physical attractions merely, she had said, or one who offered only because she had broken society's rules. She would marry only the man who could assure her that he wanted all of her, her whole person. She would marry only a man who loved her.

Had he failed, could he possibly have failed to show her that he was such a man? Could he possibly have given the impression that he wanted her only for one of the first two reasons? Surely not. He loved her so very deeply, had been so obsessed by his need of her for weeks, that surely he must have made that fact obvious to her. She could not have failed to understand. She had rejected him because she did not want him, did not love him, not because she misunderstood. Surely.

Had he told her that he loved her? Lord Rutherford cast his mind back over his confused memories of their interview. No, he had not used that exact word. He could be almost sure of that. It was not a word he was accustomed to using. He would be self-conscious using it. He would certainly remember if he had told her that he loved her.

What had he said, then? He must have said something

that would have conveyed the same message to her. He recalled admitting to her that he had made a mess of the last proposal. That was when he had planned to tell her that at that time he had still been largely unaware himself of the fact that his whole happiness depended upon her accepting his hand. That was when he was to have told her how much he had come to esteem her, how much he longed to get to know her fully. That was when he might have told her he loved her if he could have summoned the courage to use that exact word.

But he had not said any of those things. She had stopped him. She had told him they would not suit. She had told him that there was nothing in him that she could esteem. He could not recall her exact words, but that was what she had meant. He had felt almost blinded with hurt. To be told by anyone that one is worthless is painful. To be told that by someone one loves is almost unbearable.

What had he done? How had he reacted? Had he become angry immediately? He knew he had become angry. He had even threatened to strike her. But no, he had not lost his temper right away. He might as well have, though. He had turned high-handed, pointing out to her with bull-headed arrogance that she had no choice but to marry him. If anything could be more calculated to make Jess Moore quite immovably determined never to marry him, it was just such an argument. And he had used it to the full!

What a fool. What an utter fool! Lord Rutherford took a long and uncomfortable look at himself through the eyes of Jessica and shuddered. Had he ever once in their whole acquaintance asked her what she wanted? As a governess she must wish for the unexpected delight of a night spent in his bed. As a dismissed employee she must receive with gratitude his flattering offer of employment as his mistress. As a young guest of questionable social status in the home of his grandmother she must accept with alacrity his condescending offer of

marriage. As the compromised young granddaughter of
a marquess she must rush with relief to the haven of his
arms away from the jaws of scandal.

Oh, yes, he had never done anything to Jess against
her wishes. He had said something like that to her a few
minutes before, had he not? So self-righteous! He could
even say with some truth that he had frequently acted
with her own interests in mind. But had he ever thought
of asking her—and waiting to listen to her response—
what she wanted of life? Must he always be telling and
assuming? It was the habit of a lifetime to behave as the
lord and master, he supposed.

And now he had lost his final chance with Jess. There
could be no more. She had made it very clear to him on
two occasions that she wanted none of him, and this
time he must respect her wishes. It was the only way he
could prove his love for her. It was still true that
according to all the rules of society she must marry him,
and without delay too. But really, what did society's
rules amount to in this case? Who would expose Jess's
terrible indiscretion to the *ton*? Grandmama? The
Marquess of Heddingly? No one else knew.

The Barries when they arrived during the spring could
create some nasty gossip, he supposed. But it would not
matter. Jess would not care. He really believed that she
would not care. Or if she did, she would still consider
the gossip preferable to marriage to him.

The Earl of Rutherford winced.

He must go away. He must talk to her grandfather,
explain that they were not to marry and that no pressure
must be put on Jess to change her mind. And then he
must leave. She must be free to do with her life what she
decided to do, with the help of her grandfather. He
must stay away from her.

Perhaps in a year's time, or two . . . But Lord
Rutherford turned decisively toward the door of the
library. No, not even then. He had always lamented the
fact that he had been unable to travel abroad when he
was a young man. He would go now. During the spring.

And he would stay away for two or three years. Long enough certainly for them both to forget. He would stay away and keep temptation at arm's length.

He would leave the following day, Rutherford decided as he left the library. He would have liked to saddle a horse and gallop back to London at that very moment. He could be back long before dark if he did so. But he could not leave the day after Christmas. The whole family would be upset. Everyone would know that something must have happened. And some might begin guessing. He did not want that to happen. He did not want anything to cause possible embarrassment to Jess.

"Jessica, my dear girl, do come along to my sitting room with me," the Dowager Duchess of Middleburgh said, laying a hand on Jessica's arm after luncheon. "The trouble with the members of this family is that they forget I am an old woman and unable to stand the noise and constant motion of their merrymaking. What I need is an hour of peace and quiet with someone sensible to converse with."

It seemed reasonable to Jessica. She was in the habit of thinking of the dowager as indefatigable. But then, of course, the elderly lady usually lived a fairly quiet life in the house on Berkeley Square. Jessica did not have the heart to say no. She had spent so much time with her grandfather in the last few days that she had almost neglected the lady who had been so kind to her since her arrival in town.

But truth to tell, she did not feel like being sociable to anyone. She wanted to be alone. She wanted to get away altogether. She could not remember ever feeling so miserable.

"Of course, your grace," she said. "I shall run to my room for my embroidery."

"Yes, do that, dear," the dowager said.

But Jessica was not to get much needlework done.

She had barely drawn her needle through her work when her companion began to speak.

"Now what is troubling you, my dear?" she asked. "Is it Charles again? I would guess it must be, judging from the look on his face and the look on yours at luncheon."

Jessica darted her a troubled look. "I have refused him again," she said.

"Oh dear," the dowager said. "I was afraid this would happen. Patience was never the dear boy's greatest virtue. I suppose he came thundering back with Heddingly, full of the conviction that as the grand-daughter of a marquess you must marry him. What the dear boy would not have realized, of course, is that you have known of the connection all your life. It is a new idea only to him."

"Grandpapa shares the idea," Jessica said. "He gave Lord Rutherford his blessing."

"Yes." the dowager sighed. "He would. I remember wondering when Mirabel accepted his offer all those years ago just how she would manage such a very prickly character. She seemed to do quite well. But tell me, my dear, did you have to refuse?"

"Yes." Jessica threaded her needle through her embroidery and set it aside. She stopped even pretending to work at it. "Yes, I had to, your grace. I am sorry."

"You do not have to be sorry for me," her companion said. "After all, Jessica, you are the one who would have to live with the dear boy for the rest of his life. Forgive me for prying, but are you quite sure that you could not do it? It has always seemed to me that you have something of a tendre for Charles."

Jessica bit her lip. "I love him," she said so low that the dowager leaned forward somewhat in her chair. "But I could not live with him, no."

"His high-handed tactics have wounded your pride?" the old lady said.

"It is not just that," Jessica said. "I think if I did not love him I might be able to do it, ma'am. But how can I marry a man who offers for me only because it is the proper thing to do? I should feel all my life that I was a millstone around his neck."

"Gracious!" the dowager said. "The boy has never told you that that is his only reason, has he? What nonsense! He has been hankering after you ever since he first set eyes on you, m'dear."

"I know," Jessica said miserably. "Sometimes I think it would have been better if I had allowed him his will when I first knew him—pardon me, your grace. Then none of all this would have happened. He would have been satisfied. And perhaps I would have been too."

"What a very confused young lady you are, to be sure," the dowager said briskly. "I am not at all certain you understand the situation, my dear. But be that as it may, you have refused Charles again. I suppose he ripped up at you and said all sorts of rash things."

"It was a nasty interview," Jessica admitted. "Oh, ma'am, please, please help me. I must go away from here. I cannot stay, a guest of his family. I cannot face him every time I go beyond my room. Please help me."

"Poor dear." Her companion crossed the room and patted her on the shoulder. "You must remember that you are here on account of me and not on account of Charles at all. No one will think you are out of place here merely because you have refused him. But if you feel you must go, then of course you must. The marquess must take you back to London. Will he stay at Berkeley Square, do you think? Or will he insist on staying at a hotel?"

"No," Jessica said, shaking her head. "Grandpapa must not know I am leaving. Oh, please. He gave me a thundering scold when I went back to his room this morning and told me that I must reconsider. He will not even listen to any other idea. I cannot talk to him. I know what he is like when he once gets an idea into his head. The same thing happened two years ago. Please, I cannot face Grandpapa again.''

"Well," the dowager said, scratching her head and returning to her seat, "what are we to do with you, child? I shall have to take you back to London myself tomorrow. We shall resume our quiet life, Jessica, until the marquess comes to his senses. Or failing that, we will start making plans for the Season. I shall find you so many eligible suitors, m'dear, that your only trouble will be to choose among them.''

"No," Jessica said. "You are most kind, ma'am, and I cannot begin to thank you for all you have done for me. But I cannot continue to be beholden to you. Do you not see? I must return to my old way of life if only I can. Can you help me, ma'am? Will you? Lord Rutherford was convinced when he sent me to you that you could and would. Please, can you find me a situation, and soon? I will be happy when my life settles to normal again. And I will no longer be a burden to you.''

The dowager duchess viewed the distraught figure across from her and knew that the girl was not in any emotional state to listen to reason. Refusing Charles because she loved him indeed! And when Charles was so obviously head over ears in love with the gel, too. What disasters young people managed to make of their lives these days. Surely young ladies of her generation had had more sense.

"I suppose you want to go far away," she said. "I have a very dear friend in Yorkshire, my dear. Not far from Harrogate. She very likely will not have anything for you herself, but she will find something for you if I tell her that you come from me highly recommended.''

"Oh, thank you, ma'am," Jessica said, her face brightening, "but will it not be too much to ask?''

"I took in her and her daughter for ten days four or five years ago. When they arrived in tow to find their house unready," the dowager said. "She has been looking for a way to repay me ever since. Now, I suppose you will want to be on your way as soon as possible. But not today, Jessica dear. You could, of course, travel to London this afternoon and set out on your journey tomorrow morning. But there would be too many questions asked here. And I do not suppose you would like your grandfather to come blustering after you before you could even leave town.''

Jessica shook her head.

"What we will do," the dowager said, "is to order my carriage for very early tomorrow morning. Say five o'clock? Then you can go home, pack a trunk quickly, and be on your way long before anyone here has even realized you are gone. I shall send word that you are to travel in my best traveling carriage so that you will find the journey quite comfortable even if it is long and tedious. In the meantime, I shall also prepare a letter to send with you to Georgina.''

"You are so kind." Jessica put her hands over her face. "I was really wondering at luncheon what I was to do with myself. I wanted to leave, but it just seemed too far to walk to London. You will explain to Grandpapa tomorrow? Poor Grandpapa. He has traveled all this way just to see me. But it will not work out, ma'am. We just cannot see eye to eye.''

"You leave the marquess to me," the dowager said. "Now, dear, I need some advice on this new cushion cover I am about to embroider. Never did have much sense of color. Help me choose a pleasing combination. Come, we will move over to the window seat, where we will have daylight to help us.''

The Duke of Middleburgh announced the betrothal of his younger daughter to Sir Godfrey Hall at the end of dinner that evening. Most of his listeners were surprised in the sense that they had not expected Lady Hope to give up her single state so late in life. But several were at least not shocked. Sir Godfrey's devotion had been detected by a few of the closer

members of Lady Hope's family, and those members
had also suspected that her feelings were engaged far
more deeply than she herself realized.

There was probably not a person at table who was not
delighted by the announcement. One had only to glance
at the beaming face of Sir Godfrey and the glowing
expression of Lady Hope to know that theirs was to be a
love match. They sat next to each other, relieved that
their efforts to keep the secret through luncheon, the
long afternoon, and dinner could finally be relaxed.

Everyone was happy for them, even if everyone was
not happy. The Marquess of Heddingly appeared cross
and aloof, though he remained polite as befitted the
guest of honor at someone else's table. The dowager
duchess appeared somewhat preoccupied, though she
did rally and look remarkably pleased when her son
made his announcement. The Earl of Rutherford
appeared to be totally out of spirits. Two young cousins
seated close to him were quite unable to draw him into
conversation during the meal. Yet his smile and
congratulations to his friend and his sister were very
obviously genuine. Jessica too found herself able to
smile by making a concerted effort to forget her own
misery and identify with the gladness and glowing
happiness of her two friends.

Lord Rutherford had intended to disappear as soon
as he could after dinner. The afternoon had been hard
to live through though at least he had been able to
choose activities that were unlikely to bring him into
company with Jessica. The evening was a different
matter. The family tended to stay close during the
evenings.

In the event, though, he discovered that escape was
not easy. When he sat beside Hope and Godfrey in the
drawing room, he found them very unwilling to let him
go again. And Godfrey must have enlightened his sister,
Rutherford found. In the past she had scolded him
several times for taking Jess away from possible *tête-à-
têtes* with Godfrey. Now she almost immediately

beckoned to Jess to join them. Rutherford drew in a deep and steadying breath and wondered how soon he could decently move away.

"My dear Miss Moore," Lady Hope called out even before Jessica had quite come up with the group, "you really must congratulate me again. I absolutely insist on it. Do come and sit down beside Charles and let me hear you tell Sir Godfrey what a very fortunate man he is."

The two men rose and Rutherford had no choice but to indicate the empty place on the love seat next to his own. Jessica seated herself without looking at him and proceeded to give her congratulations.

"I really have been very clever," Lady Hope said. "Sir Godfrey has been saying for a long while that he intends to travel to the countries of Europe now that it seems safe to do so. Well, my dear Miss Moore, I have very cleverly arranged matters so that I will be going too. After all, he will not be able to leave his new bride behind, will he?"

She smiled fondly at her betrothed.

"You will have to be as clever as I, Miss Moore," she continued. "You must find another gentleman who either has not been abroad at all yet or has ambitions of going again. There must be many such gentlemen. Charles for one."

She laughed at her own ingenuity and subtlety.

Lord Rutherford and Jessica sat woodenly side by side as if afraid that if they moved a muscle they would touch.

"We should all go skating tomorrow again," Lady Hope said. "It would never do, Miss Moore, if that one occasion was your last. You must try again so that next year you will find it very much easier. You were really doing quite famously with Charles."

"Somehow, I do not believe that skating is Miss Moore's favorite activity," Sir Godfrey said gently, laying a hand over Lady Hope's. "We should not press her, dear. Perhaps in a few days' time she will regain her courage."

"How quiet you are, Charles!" Lady Hope said. "Anyone would think you were not pleased for me, dear."

"Hope!" he said. "You know that is not true. I am more hapy than I can say, especially to know that you have had the good sense to choose Godfrey. It is just that you bounce with energy when you are excited about something. And you are very excited about this. Allow the rest of us to be more sedately happy, please."

"Oh, but I do not believe I can!" she said, jumping to her feet. "I think the occasion calls for dancing. We have not had any at all this year, though there are any number of persons here to make up couples and sets. We must dance this evening. Nothing else will do. I shall go and talk to Papa immediately about having the carpet rolled up. Cousin Edith will play the pianoforte. We will start with a waltz, and I shall absolutely want the four of us to begin it with perhaps Faith and Aubrey as well."

And she was gone, making her way past smiling cousins and uncles and aunts to her father. Sir Godfrey grinned at his two silent friends.

"I always knew that your sister was a bundle of energy, Charles," he said. "I now begin to wonder if I shall be able to keep up with her."

"If I see Hope striding along in a few years' time dragging behind her a pale shadow of a man," Rutherford said, "I shall know what has happened, Godfrey."

They both laughed, but truth to tell Rutherford was feeling far from amused. He was feeling deuced uncomfortable and would quite cheerfully have throttled his sister at that moment. What was he to do about the silent figure beside him? He could not even plot how to move away from her. It seemed that they were doomed to waltz together as soon as Hope had organized the dancing. And that would not take long. All the people at one end of the long drawing room were already being herded out of the way so that a long line of footmen could roll up the Turkish carpet.

How could he dance with her? Touch her, look at her, speak to her?

"Will you mind dancing, Miss Moore?" Sir Godfrey was asking Jessica. "You really were not given much choice, were you?"

"I shall be delighted to dance for the occasion," she said. "And I am truly happy for you, sir. Lady Hope is a very special person."

It was fortunate that she was talking to Godfrey at that moment, Rutherford thought. When they were suddenly called upon to move from their places so that the footmen could clear their end of the room, it was quite natural for Godfrey to reach out a hand for hers. Rutherford stood slightly behind them for the next few minutes while they chatted amiably. He had not realized that those two were quite such friends. They joked and teased each other with great ease. He wished he could turn and leave the room.

"There!" Lady Hope said as she returned to the side of her betrothed. "All ready. You see, it was not such a great upheaval after all, was it? And Cousin Edith has been practicing already. Let us take our places. Charles? Miss Moore?"

Jessica turned to glance nervously at Lord Rutherford. He bowed formally and stretched out a hand for hers. He really did not want to be doing this, he thought as he led her out onto the floor. He was somewhat relieved to see that Faith and Aubrey and a few other couples were also preparing to dance.

Well, he thought, turning to face Jessica, this was the last time he would be close to her. Torture as it would be, he must make the most of it too. His eyes met hers as his one hand went to her small waist and hers rested on his shoulder. He clasped her other hand in his.

"I am sorry, Jess," he said. "I would not have deliberately put you through this."

She swallowed. "It is your sister's evening," she said. "We must help make her happy."

She fixed her eyes on his waistcoat as the music

played. He watched the shining curls on top of her head, remembering that the thought had occurred to him earlier that morning that perhaps two family betrothals would be being celebrated that evening. There was a dull ache somewhere in the region of his throat and chest.

"Jess," he said after a long interval of silence. She looked up at him, her eyes bright, so that for a moment he had an insane urge to bend his head and kiss her. "I shall be leaving here tomorrow. You need not fear that there will be awkward moments like this to live through in the coming days."

She stared at him and then nodded briefly.

"And you need not worry about coming face to face with me in town over the coming months," he said. "I will not be there. I shall retire to my own estate until the spring and then I am going to go abroad. Probably for a few years. It is unlikely that you will have to see me after tonight, Jess. Perhaps ever. You will be free of me."

She blinked twice and her eyes looked somewhat brighter than before. "Yes," her lips said, though he heard no sound.

He forced himself to smile. "I am sorry," he said. "I tried to order your life instead of asking what you wanted, did I not? You see the measure of my arrogance? It never really occurred to me until this morning that perhaps your own wishes just did not include me. I understand now. And I respect your choice. Will you forgive me? Can we at least part a little less than bitter enemies?"

She continued to stare at him with huge eyes before nodding her head briefly and looking sharply downward again. He took her through the motions of the waltz while every part of him ached to draw her closer, to move his arm right around her waist, to bring her head against his shoulder, and to sway to the rhythm of the waltz with her.

Jess. His hands touched her lightly, desperately trying to record the memory of her. His nostrils were deliberately conscious of the fragrance of her. Would he ever see her again? In years' time, when she was married with a few children, when he too maybe had taken a wife, would he see her again and feel nothing perhaps except the faintest pang of nostalgia?

Perhaps. But the prospect did nothing to ease the raw pain of today. Today she had told him that there was nothing about him that she could like, she had rejected his marriage offer. Today he had decided to go away from her rather than try again to persuade her to marry him. And today, now, he touched her, knowing that soon, at any minute, he must let her go and never touch her again. Today he had long months of emptiness and pain to look ahead to.

The music stopped before he was ready for it to do so. She looked up at him, a bewildered expression on her face.

"Good-bye, Jess," he said, raising her hand to his lips. He smiled down at her. "Be happy, my dear. I shall always wish for your happiness."

She did not immediately reply. He did not wait to see if she would have done so. He let go of her hand and hurried from the room.

# 15

JESSICA WAS STANDING IN her room at Berkeley Square, looking down at the small trunk and the valise at her feet. She thought she had everything. It had been easy packing her things when she was leaving the Barries. It had been merely a matter of taking with her all the scant belongings in the room. This time it was a little more difficult. There was so much to leave behind: everything, in fact, that the dowager duchess had bought for her. Only what she had brought with her would she take away again.

She looked down rather ruefully at the plain gray woolen dress she wore. She had thought when a maid had hung it with the others at the back of her wardrobe that perhaps she would never wear it again. Indeed, the dowager had urged her to give them all away. But she was very glad now that she had kept them. It would not do for a young lady to board the stagecoach and go in search of employment dressed up in expensive finery.

There seemed to be nothing left to do but pull on her gray cloak and bonnet and her black gloves and leave. Indeed, she must not delay for much longer. There was quite a distance to cover to the stagecoach terminal, and she must not miss the coach.

Jessica felt far more pain in looking around her this time than she had when leaving the Barries' home. She had been happy here. She had been treated well. She had felt loved. Once outside this building and she would be completely on her own again, all her dreams and hopes of the previous weeks finally dead. She would be a governess for the rest of her life, if she were fortunate.

She had said other good-byes much earlier that morning. The faithful Dowager Duchess of Middleburgh had not been content with merely summoning the carriage to bring Jessica from Hendon Park. She had got up to see her on her way. And it had been difficult to say good-bye. Jessica had hugged her very hard, feeling as desolate as if the old lady were her own grandmother. She had been grateful for one thing, at least. The dowager had made no attempt to persuade her to change her mind. Jessica had been somewhat surprised, but very relieved. She had been almost glad to be on her way.

She had said mental good-byes to those still sleeping at Hendon Park: to the duke and duchess who had accepted her as their guest with no apparent fuss, to Lord and Lady Bradley, who had always shown her quiet friendship, to Lady Hope, to Sir Godfrey. And to her grandfather. She had stood outside his bedchamber for a few silent moments before pushing under his door the note she had written the night before and running quietly downstairs to the waiting carriage. She wished things could have been different between them. She had been so very happy to see him just a few days before. And now she was leaving him almost without a word, never to see him again. If only he could have accepted her need to make her own decisions!

And she had said her mental good-byes to the Earl of Rutherford. All night long, in fact, while she tossed and turned on her bed, quite unable to snatch even a wink of sleep. She wished they had not been forced into company together the evening before. Without that encounter perhaps the bitterness of their morning interview might have sustained her for a few days, until she was far away and would find it easier to forget.

It had been agony to have to sit next to him in the drawing room at Lady Hope's request, to feel him close to her, to hear his voice. She had wondered how she would retain her composure long enough to waltz with him. His hand at her waist had seemed to burn a hole in her sash. She did not know quite how her hands had obeyed her will to touch his shoulder and clasp his hand. She had fixed her eyes somewhere on a level with his waistcoat, desperately resisting the urge to look up into his eyes or to lean forward to rest her forehead against his chest.

And she had cursed herself. She could have been celebrating her betrothal to him, as Lady Hope and Sir Godfrey were celebrating theirs. She could have been as glowing and happy as Lady Hope. Why had she said no? He had tried to talk to her, had tried to get her to explain why she would not marry him, and she had said nothing beyond agreeing with him when he had asked if there were nothing in him of which she could approve. That was not true. There was a great deal about him that she liked and admired. She could not love him else.

Why had she not explained? Perhaps if she had shown a willingness to talk, he would have spoken too. Perhaps she would have found that his reasons for wanting to marry her were not quite as shallow as they seemed, after all. He had spent three whole weeks— and during the winter, too—traveling the country trying to find out more about her and had brought her grandfather to London to be with her. Were those the actions of a man who merely had a lust for a woman? Or who merely felt duty-bound to offer for her?

But no, she had said nothing when he had given her the chance. She had stubbornly waited for him to speak first. She had wanted to hear him tell her how he had come to value her acquaintance, how he had come to respect her person. She had hoped somewhere in the unconscious part of herself that he would tell her that he loved her. She had not been willing to meet him halfway. She had wanted him to do all the bending.

So she had danced with him, aware of the fact that her misery was probably of her own making, wanting another chance, just one more, to work things out with him. But she had ruined all her chances. He must hate her now. She had released him from the obligation of duty. Her words and behavior must have killed any more tender feelings that might have been growing in him.

And then he had spoken and made her feel ten times worse. He had spoken with kindness. And he had spoken of going away so that she could be free of him. Why had it hurt almost more than she could bear to know that he was going away, that he would not be in London for the next few months, or even in England for the next few years? She was going away herself. His words just made the whole situation that much more final.

By the time the dance had come to an end Jessica had scarcely known how to place one foot in front of the other. It was fortunate, she had felt, that he made quite clear the fact that he was about to leave the room himself, else they might well have collided in the doorway. As it was, she had waited a few minutes before making her own escape.

He had said good-bye to her. He had told her to be happy. He wanted her to be happy, he had said.

Jessica came out of her reverie and picked up her valise in some haste. If she did not hurry, she would miss the stagecoach. The dowager duchess would be very upset with her for traveling by the public coach when she had arranged for her own traveling carriage to make the journey. But Jessica could not accept. The break must come now. And she must travel in a mode consistent with her station in life. She would accept a ride to the coach terminal simply because she had a trunk and she did not have time to sally forth in search of a hackney carriage. But that was all.

Jessica left her room and ran down the stairs to the hallway. She did not look back.

The Dowager Duchess of Middleburgh allowed her

maid to arrange her pillows behind her back and sank back comfortably against them. She laid her hands neatly on the silk cover of the bed and signaled the girl that Lord Rutherford might be admitted. She schooled her features into a polite smile.

"Ah, good morning, Charles m'boy," she said as he strode in. She turned her cheek for his kiss.

"Good morning, Grandmama," he said. "I hope I have not woken you too early. I have waited as long as I could since you left word that you wished to see me before I set out on my way. But I am eager to be gone."

"Is it some gel who has you so anxious to be back in town?" she asked. "Back to your wild oats, Charles?"

He grimaced. "By no means," he said. "Those days are over, you will be delighted to know, Grandmama. No, it is just that life grows dull here now that Christmas is over. It will be good to be busy again. I intend going down into the country by the end of the week, you know. It is time I looked over the estate again."

"Yes," she said, "young people must ever be busy, as I remember. And of course it would be dull for you here now that dear Jessica has gone away."

"Jessica?" he said. "Gone away? What are you talking about, Grandmama? I danced with her last evening."

"She left at five o'clock this morning," the dowager said, "in my carriage alone."

Lord Rutherford stared down at her in silence for a few moments. His face had turned paler. "She need not have gone," he said. "I told her last night that I myself would be leaving today. But perhaps she will feel more relaxed back at Berkeley Square. What the devil does she mean, though, by going back alone? And so early? Is the marquess not going too?"

"He does not know yet, m'boy," the dowager said with a sigh. "She is not staying at Berkeley Square, you know. She is going into Yorkshire. She carries a letter to

Georgina Hearst. Very old friend of mine, you know. She will find a situation for Jessica.''

"A situation?" he said faintly. "As a governess, you mean?"

"She seemed to think it was the only thing for her," the dowager said. "I spent all of yesterday afternoon pleading with her, Charles, but the gel was adamant. It seems that you had convinced her that her reputation was in shreds and that a Season in London was out of the question."

"But that is ridiculous!" he said. "Of course her reputation is not ruined. Does she not realize that she would not be received here if such were the case? No one knows about those past indiscretions except a few people who love her. None of those people is going to make the knowledge public."

"That is exactly what I told her," the dowager said. She was toying with a lace handkerchief in one hand. She seemed to be deliberating whether or not she should raise it to her eyes, but she evidently decided that a show of tears would be out of character. "It seems she believed you and her grandpapa rather than me, Charles, m'boy. You must have been very convincing."

Lord Rutherford was pacing back and forth at the foot of the bed. "Do you mean that Jess has gone to Yorkshire to be governess to some stranger all because she feels she cannot remain in the life to which she was born?" he asked.

"Foolish, is it not?" she said. "She could have a brilliant future ahead of her, Charles. She is already popular with any number of eligible gentlemen. With her grandfather newly arrived and the Season approaching, she could choose almost any unmarried gentleman she wished. Dear Jessica! I cannot help feeling that she will be very unhappy in service, especially now that she has tasted the pleasures of society."

"She must have that future," Lord Rutherford said. "She must be happy, Grandmama. Only so will I be able to find all this bearable. She cannot go back. You did not see her as she was before. I shudder to remember what a docile, gray little governess she was when I first set eyes on her. Not again. I cannot let that happen to Jess again."

"Do stop pacing, Charles," the dowager said. "You are giving me the headache. I really do not see what you can do about the situation, m'boy. I could not do anything yesterday. Of course, if you succeeded so well in persuading her that her reputation was in ruins, perhaps you will also find it possible to persuade her that it is just not true. It is a shame she has left already."

"She left at five o'clock?" he said. "That is more than four hours ago. Did she leave straight for Yorkshire, Grandmama?"

"She was to call at Berkeley Square first of all," she said, "to collect some of her belongings and to take my best traveling carriage. But she will be on her way by now, Charles. It is too late. Poor Jessica must be left to her fate. Perhaps she will meet a gentleman in Yorkshire who will appreciate her real worth. She is still young, after all, and very pretty even when wearing those very plain clothes. And knowing Jessica, I would be willing to wager that she is already dressed in gray again."

"It is not too late!" the Earl of Rutherford said decisively. "I can overtake your carriage very soon, Grandmama. I shall persuade Jess that she is being foolish, never fear. And I shall bring her back with me. By tonight. It is I who will be going away, not her. She will remain in London and settle to the life she should be leading. She is going to have a happy life. I swear it."

"I think it quite likely if you can but persuade her," the dowager agreed. "But if you intend to ride in this raw weather, Charles, do be sure to dress warmly, m'boy."

She was not at all sure that her grandson had heard her maternal advice. He had already stridden from the room. But the Dowager Duchess of Middleburgh did not seem unduly perturbed. She smiled smugly at one ornate bedpost and snuggled lower into her pillows.

The day's journey had not been nearly the nightmare of the previous one, Jessica thought with some relief later that evening. It had been every bit as uncomfortable, however, if not more so. The day had been bitterly cold and the coach drafty. Indeed, snow had begun to fall before they stopped for the night at an inn on the Great North Road. The coach seemed particularly ill-sprung, the passengers all very large and all carrying particularly bulky bundles. And there seemed to be an unreasonable number of unwashed bodies riding as inside passengers.

These discomforts aside, however, Jessica had found that she was not abused as she had been on that previous journey. Indeed, her right-hand neighbor, a woman whose abnormally large and stiff bonnet brim threatened to take Jessica's eye out every time she turned her head, was a plump, motherly person, whose hand regularly reached into her food basket and who constantly insisted on sharing its contents with other passengers, especially Jessica. The latter could well have done without the offerings, proffered as they were from a somewhat grubby hand. But she found herself reluctant to reject such obvious good nature. She accepted and even managed to eat a meat pasty and a jam tart.

The day wore on and Jessica's spirits drooped proportionately. What sort of a life was ahead of her? she wondered. Would the dowager duchess's friend be able to find her a suitable situation? Would it be a difficult job? Challenging? Lonely? Unfortunately, she was in no position to choose. She must accept whatever was offered to her.

And it would surely be a deal worse than it had been the last time. The last time everything had been new to her. She had had nothing with which to compare her life with the Barries except life at home with Papa. And although she had always been happy at home, she had

to admit that it had been a rather dull life of plodding
routine. Life at the Barries' had not been so very
different except that she had felt the absence of love.

Now she was aware of what her life could have
offered. Not just the fine homes and clothes, the
parties, the outings, and the suitors. But she knew what
her particular life might have been. She might have been
the Countess of Rutherford, the wife, the companion of
the man she had grown to love. She might have made
something of such a relationship even if his love did not
nearly match her own. At least she would have had a
chance to win his friendship, his esteem. The challenge
would have been exhilarating. Now she would never see
him again.

But she must not look back, Jessica told herself on
that first evening, must not regret rashly made
decisions. And she must not complain. Her first night
on the road was to be reasonably pleasant, at least. She
had actually been given a room of her own. Granted, it
was a tiny box of a room under the sloping roof of the
attic, in which it was necessary to edge one's way
around the rather lumpy bed. The only other furniture
was a cracked washstand and an equally cracked bowl
and water jug. But at least she would have some
privacy, and at least—and surprisingly—the sheets were
clean. And there was a dining room in this inn separate
from the taproom. She had been able to eat her dinner
without fearing at every moment that she was going to
be accosted

It was fairly early in the evening, far too early to go to
bed, Jessica decided. But she would not venture from
her room again. She took a book out of her valise and
perched as comfortably as she could on the edge of the
bed, huddled up inside her cloak. She would read until
the candle burned out, anyway.

It turned out to be a very frustrating day for the Earl
of Rutherford. When he left Hendon Park, he expected
that finding Jessica would be the least of his problems.

It was what he would say to her when he did so that occupied his mind all the way back into London. This time he must be very sure that he said the right thing. The whole of her future happiness would depend upon it.

For that very reason, perhaps, he was not quite as nervous as he had been the day before when he had proposed to her. Then it had been his own happiness he was trying to secure. Now he had merely to convince her that she must return to London and her grandfather's care. He must assure her that in the public eye her reputation was quite unsullied and would remain so. Although the Barries could cause her some embarrassment if they chose to do so, really the only persons who could do her reputation any real harm were himself, his grandmother, and her grandfather. Surely it would not be difficult to convince her that none of those three persons would ever be malicious enough to begin a whisper of gossip about her.

She must return to London, to the society where she belonged. The thought of her returning to the sort of life she had led when he first saw her filled the Earl of Rutherford with dread. Women ordering her around, treating her like dirt beneath their feet. Children treating her with as much insolence as they knew their parents would let them get away with. Men eyeing her with lust, scheming how to coax her into their beds. She would be fortunate indeed if she found her way into a house where she would be treated with the proper respect. And even then it would be no life for Jess. His beautiful Jess.

Perhaps she had not heard or had not believed his assurances of the night before that he was going away, that he would trouble her no more. Perhaps it was her fear of him as much as anything that was driving her away. He must repeat his assurances to her. He must convince her that he meant what he had said. She must know that she could return to London and begin her social life again without the constant fear that she would meet him at every turn. She must feel entirely free to encourage other suitors and choose an eligible husband from among them.

Rutherford felt physically sick at the thought, but he resolutely put his feelings from him. He had renounced Jess the previous day. He must train himself now always to think of her as quite beyond his reach. It must be her happiness, and only hers, that occupied him for the rest of this day's business. As soon as he found her, he would take her back to Hendon Park, or to Berkeley Square if she preferred, and then leave, never to see her again.

He decided not to stop in London. His grandmother had assured him that Jess would already have set out on her journey north even before he left Hendon Park. It would be an utter waste of time to go to Berkeley Square on the slim chance that she would still be there. After all, if she was bent on running away from her grandfather, she was not likely to spend a few hours relaxing at his grandmother's house.

He would save time, he decided, by taking immediately to the northern road. His grandmother's crested carriage was easily recognizable. He would overtake it within the hour, if he were lucky, or certainly not too much longer than that. He would be able to bring Jess back before the middle of the afternoon.

It was only as one hour turned into two that Lord Rutherford regretted not returning home for his curricle. It would have been a slightly more comfortable mode of travel. He had not realized that the carriage could have had such a start on him. Jess must have made almost no stop at all at Berkeley Square. It made sense, he supposed when he thought about it. He would wager that she would not take with her any of the finery that his grandmother had provided her with. Packing her belongings would not have taken her long.

As the afternoon wore on, he became downright uneasy. Could the carriage have possibly come this far? Was there any chance that he had passed it? But no, that was impossible. It was equally impossible that it could have taken a different route. Lord Rutherford began to come to the unwelcome conclusion that the carriage must still have been in London when he passed the city by and that it was somewhere on the road behind him.

But did he dare take a gamble and turn back? If by some chance she was still ahead of him and he went back now, he would never catch up to her.

He rode onward for another five miles before deciding that he must turn back. As it was, it seemed unlikely that he would get back to London that night. And the weather was turning bitterly cold. He had been trying to ignore it all afternoon, but his hands were numb even inside his gloves, and the heavy capes of his greatcoat were failing to keep out the cold. Stray flakes of snow were beginning to drift down from a leaden sky.

Lord Rutherford did not afterward know what inspired thought led him to consider that perhaps his grandmother's carriage was not on the road at all. Was it certain that that was how Jess was traveling? His grandmother had said so, of course. She had offered the carriage. But was it really certain that Jess would have accepted? Was it not far more consistent with her stubborn character and with her determination to return to her former life, for her to have decided to travel by the stagecoach? He had passed several since leaving London. She could have been on any one of them!

And so he made his way back, uneasy about his decision to do so, cold, worried about his tired horse, and determined to examine every stagecoach he passed to make sure that she was not on any of them. Soon, of course, most of them would stop for the night. He must look carefully at each inn to see if a stagecoach stood in its yard.

He hailed two stagecoaches on the road without success before spotting the one in an inn yard. Snow was falling. It was almost dark. He felt hopeless. He had lost her. Somehow he had missed her, and he would never

# 16

JESSICA STIFFENED WHEN THE knock sounded on her door. She might have known that her good fortune was too good to be true. She was going to have to share her room after all. The bed was certainly large enough to accommodate more than one person.

"Yes?" she called out hesitantly, wishing that she could pretend to be deaf.

There was no answer for a moment. Then her blood ran cold.

"Jess?" a familiar voice said.

Jessica leapt to her feet. Her book slid with a thud to the floor and her cloak slipped from her shoulders. "Who is it?" she called foolishly. There was only one person in the world it could possibly be. "What do you want?"

"May I talk to you for a minute?" the Earl of Rutherford asked.

"What about?" she said. "What do you want? I have nothing to say to you."

"Jess." He was speaking quietly through the thin door. "Will you please open the door? I have something of great importance that I must say to you. I give you my word of honor as a gentleman that I will not touch you."

"Go away," she said. Her voice was shaking, she noticed in some alarm. "Please go away."

"Jess, please listen to me," he said. "Please open the

door. The innkeeper will be up here soon wanting to know what all the commotion is about. Just listen to me. Hear me out. Please.''

She pulled the door open and immediately felt what a tactical error it was to have done so. He looked huge, clad still in his greatcoat and topboots. His hat and whip were in his hands. His hair was disheveled, his face rosy with cold. He looked impossibly handsome.

"My lord," she said breathlessly, "I do not know how you have found me here. But I will not be harassed any longer. I have left your father's house and your grandmother's. I am on my way to a new situation. I want nothing more to do with you. I thought I had made that plain. And I seem to recall that you promised just last night that you would leave me alone. Please go away.''

"Jess," he said, "let me in. Let us not entertain a whole inn with our quarrel. No, you are quite safe." He said this as he stepped inside, closed the door behind him, and threw his hat and whip onto the bed. "I have promised not to touch you.''

Jessica watched him warily and backed between the wall and the bed down toward the washstand.

"You must come back," he said. "This flight into Yorkshire and return to a life of service is madness, Jess. And totally unnecessary. You do not belong in such a life.''

"Your tune has changed drastically within a few weeks," Jessica said. She was beginning to feel more in command of herself. "Until you discovered my grandfather, this was exactly the life in which I belonged.''

"No," he said. "You forget that I offered you a very different life even before I discovered that you are Heddingly's granddaughter.''

"My life is none of your concern anyway, my lord," she said. "If I choose to take a situation as a governess, that is my business only. I do not owe you an explanation.''

"No, you do not," he agreed. "You owe me nothing,

Jess. Nothing at all. It is not for myself I plead. It is for you. I do not believe that you can be happy with such a life. And I have reason to believe that you are returning to it because of what I have said to you. But it is not true, Jess. It is not true that your reputation is ruined. You do not have to flee from society."

She looked at him, amazed. "Flee from society?" she said. "How absurd! Do you think I care what other people say of me?"

"Yes, I think you do," he said gently. "But other people are saying nothing, Jess. I made the situation sound very bleak yesterday morning, did I not, when I was trying to persuade you to accept my offer. I wished you to believe that you had no choice, that marriage to me was your only way of avoiding great scandal. But it is not so at all. I lied."

"Why?" she asked. She had moved around to the foot of the bed and held on to one of the bedposts.

He shrugged and smiled somewhat apologetically. "I don't know," he said. "I suppose I considered it a sure way of getting you to agree. Not very honorable, was it? And foolish, as it turned out."

"You should have been relieved that I released you from having to do the honorable thing," Jessica said.

"Relieved?" He laughed. "But it does not matter how I felt or feel, does it? That is not the question here. The point is, Jess, that you are running away from a situation that does not exist. And you belong back there. You belong with your grandfather, stubborn and wrongheaded as he can be. You need to marry and have a family with someone of your own class. Not this, Jess. Oh, not this shapeless gray dress, dear, and the severe hairstyle. And not the demure look, eyes cast down, that I saw at the Barries'. Not that, Jess. Please."

"Life was tranquil until just a couple of months ago," Jessica said. "It is only since that it has been full of feelings that have torn me apart. I have not been happy. And there is nothing to go back to. Only emptiness and heartache." She had laid her forehead against the bedpost and closed her eyes. "I want to be at peace again. I must go on."

She was aware of him throwing his greatcoat impatiently onto the mattress. He strode around the bed toward her but stopped a short distance away.

"I have promised not to touch you," he said. "Don't be so unhappy, Jess. Can you not see that I have been responsible for all your misery? I insulted you and harassed you when I first knew you, and I have pestered you with unwelcome attentions and with offers that you did not want. And the last one was unforgivable because I enlisted the help of a man whose wishes I thought you could not resist and used arguments that I thought would crumble all your resistance. Wherever you have turned, you have found me. And I now know that you have not wanted me in your life at all."

Jessica put one hand between her forehead and the bedpost so that he would not see her face.

"I am sorry," he said gently. "Love can make one very selfish and very blind. In my love for you, I was unconscious of the misery I was causing you. But the point is, dear, that it is a matter that can be put right. Once I have escorted you back to London—and I shall hire a carriage for you, Jess; I wil not ride with you— then I shall leave as I promised you last evening. And I shall not renege on my promise to leave the country in the spring and stay away for a few years. You will be happy once I am gone, Jess. I promise you will."

She was crying into her hand. But she could not move or say a word without betraying the fact to him.

"Would you prefer that I left now and sent someone else to accompany you tomorrow?" he asked. "Aubrey would come, or Godfrey, I know. Or would you prefer me to ask someone not connected with my family at all? Just promise me that you will stay here and not run away while I am gone."

Jessica was concentrating all her energies on not allowing a sob to escape her.

"Jess," he said suddenly. He sounded closer, though

he still did not touch her. "You are not crying, are you?"

She felt a light, hesitant hand on her hair when she still did not answer.

"Don't cry," he said. "Please don't cry, dear. I can't bear to see how miserable I have made you. Please, Jess."

She turned away from him and reached for a handkerchief in her pocket. She scrubbed at her eyes and blew her nose.

"You must not blame yourself," she said. "You have not been entirely the villain of this piece, you know."

"You will come back?" he asked.

She stared down at her hands, her back toward him, for a long moment. "Yes," she said, "I will come back."

He did not move. "With me?" he asked. "Or shall I send someone else?"

"With you," she said.

"Thank you." The tension had gone from his voice. "Thank you for trusting me, Jess. You have made the right decision, you will see. You will be happy once I am gone. For tonight I will not risk scandal. There is another inn two miles farther north. I shall stay there for the night and return for you in the morning. I shall hire a carriage for you. All you have to do is wait here. You will wait, Jess?" There was a note of anxiety in his voice again.

"No." She shook her head and turned to face him. "Don't leave."

"There is no room left here," he said. "I should have to sleep in the taproom. Not that that would matter. But we must not stay at the same inn. Tattlemongers might make something of that if word were to get out."

"There is a room," she said. "Here. I want you to stay here."

"What are you saying?" He watched her intently, a frown between his eyes.

She swallowed and flushed. "Do you still want me?"

she asked. "You used to want me. I am offering myself to you."

He did not move or change his expression. "I have not asked for anything, Jess," he said. "I have made no demands on you. I have come so that I might take you where you belong and set you free. I want you to be free, dear. You owe me nothing."

"Am I free to offer myself to you?" she asked. Her flush had deepened. Her hands twisted nervously against the sides of her woolen dress. "I do not feel constrained. I make the offer because I wish to do so."

"Jess?" He frowned and gazed at her uncertainly.

She took a deep breath and let it out raggedly. Then she stepped forward, laid a trembling hand against his coat, and lifted the other hand to join it. She unbuttoned the coat and then proceeded to do the same with his waistcoat. She spread her hands over the silk of his shirt and looked up into his eyes.

He had not moved, but he looked down at her in wonder.

"Don't you want me?" she asked, her eyes slipping from his.

"Don't I want you!" He caught her to him suddenly in a bruising hug and rocked her from side to side. "But I don't understand, Jess. I don't understand."

She raised her head from its position against his shoulder and found his eyes with hers once more. "Make love to me," she whispered. "Make love to me, my lord."

She gasped at first under the fierce onslaught of his kiss. His mouth covered hers hungrily and his tongue invaded its warm depths. But her passion matched his almost immediately. She put her arms up around his neck, arched her body against his, and gave herself. There would be no holding back this time, no last-second pangs of conscience. This time she was his for the taking, no matter what happened afterward. This time she offered the gift of herself in love and gratitude for the precious and selfless gift he had just given her: her freedom.

It did not matter that she no longer wanted that freedom. It was unimportant that she wanted nothing more than to be a prisoner of his love for the rest of her life. It mattered only that he had said that he loved her but had come to set her free. She would give him the most precious gift she possessed in return, and she would demand nothing, no security in advance.

His embrace soon gentled. And he was making love to her indeed, with sensitive, knowing hands, with warm lips and tongue, with murmured words whose sense was felt rather than heard, and with the firm touch of his body. And she touched him in return, kissed him, crooned words of love and desire.

"Come to bed," he said against her mouth eventually. "Come to bed with me, love, and let me unclothe you. Jess. Jess, my love, it will be good for you. I swear it will be good for you."

"Yes," she whispered. "Oh, yes."

And it would be good. She let him pull back the bed-clothes from the bed and lay her down. And she lay still as he undressed her with expert ease. She watched him through half-closed lashes, his face flushed, his hair even more rumpled than it had been when he came in. She was glad that the candle had not yet quite burned itself out.

And oh, yes, it would be good for her. Her body hummed with desire for him. And with impatience as his hands left her naked body in order to remove his own clothes. It would be good. She would feel pain. In a few minutes' time he would hurt her, according to all accounts. But it would be a welcome pain. She was eager for it. She wanted the moment of becoming his to be very memorable. She wanted it to hurt and hurt so that she would know her gift worthy of her need to give.

But there was no more time for thought. He came to her then, and his hands and his mouth began to work their slow, erotic magic again. And she took fire, reaching to take him closer and closer, arching to give more and more of herself. And she was gasping, moaning with the need and the frustration of being unable to give or take any more.

"Jess." He was speaking against her mouth, his hands in her hair. "Now, my love. Now. It will be good. I shall try not to hurt you."

But she did not shrink from the fear of the unknown. She opened eagerly and fully to his body as it moved across to cover hers, and tilted her pelvis so that his hands could come beneath her.

And then she was gasping against his mouth, clawing at his shoulders, tense with shock and pain and wonder. And finally, when his inward movement had stopped, she relaxed against him and smiled against his mouth with sheer joy.

"Beautiful. Oh, beautiful, Jess."

His voice was deep with passion. He buried his face against her hair. And then she began to lose herself in unimagined ecstasy as he started to move in her. Oh, totally unimagined. No need now to wonder at her earlier frustration. Of course she had not been able to give as she had wanted. Of course she had not felt quite satisfied with what he had given her.

It was this. Only this. This total and intimate giving and taking of lovers. She knew no anxiety even though satisfaction did not come immediately but only rather an unbearable ache. He would make it good for her. And finally she knew the way to give herself completely. She held herself open and relaxed for her lover and held no part of herself from him.

And finally the pounding rhythm of his body slowed and he moved his head to murmur against her mouth as she felt the warm merging of selves deep inside her.

He lay heavy on her for several minutes, but she did not feel the discomfort of his weight. She pulled the sheet up around his bare shoulders, wrapped her arms around him, and rested her head against his. She stared

up sleepily and happily into the darkness. She had not
noticed exactly when the candle had finally gone out.
She waited for whatever her future would be. But whatever it was, she would not regret what had just
happened. She could never regret that.

"Mm." He murmured drowsily against her ear
eventually and lifted himself away from her. "I fell
asleep, Jess. You must be squashed. I am sorry."

He gathered her into his arms, her head on his
shoulder, and tucked the blankets warmly around her.

"I did not mind," she said, her fingers feathering
over his chest.

"I hurt you," he said. "You winced. I did not want
to do that, Jess."

"But I am glad," she said. "I wanted there to be a
very definite moment, even a painful one, when I
became your woman."

"My woman," he said, his fingers touching her
cheeks. "Why, Jess? I still don't understand. I had
pledged not even to touch you. And then you offered
me this. Why?"

"Because I was free to do it entirely of my own will,"
she said. "I have loved you from the day of your arrival
at Lord Barrie's, I believe. And I have wanted you. I
wanted to be your mistress. I wanted to be your wife.
But there has always been pressure on me to do one of
those things, always a very good and practical reason
why I should do so. I was never free. I have never been
able to give myself to you. The best I could do was allow
you to take me. But not tonight. Tonight I was free to
give."

"I thought you hated me," he said against her hair.
"I thought I was the very last person on earth you
wanted. Jess, I have spent all of yesterday and today
trying to accustom myself to that thought."

"I wanted to know that I was free to choose," she
said. "I wanted to know that you needed something
from me too. Not just this. I wanted to know that you
loved me. Tonight you have said that you do. I do not

know quite what you meant by that. But you gave me something infinitely precious tonight. You gave me myself. Finally tonight I possessed something of value. I possessed myself, to give or to withhold as I chose.''

"And you chose to give, Jess?" His lips were nuzzling her ear.

"Yes, I chose to give, my lord," she said, turning her head so that their lips met warmly. "It was a gift. But a free gift. There will be no talk tomorrow of being obliged to offer for me because my reputation is in shreds. You are under no obligation to me for anything from this moment on. I did not use my freedom in order to put chains on you. I want you to know that."

He found her hand in the darkness. "Will you marry me, Jess," he said, "because I love you and because I think you will become the dearest friend I will ever know? And because life without you has seemed to me for the past two days and still seems the bleakest prospect I could ever be asked to face? Will you, Jess?"

"Yes, my lord," she said.

Lord Rutherford smiled down at his betrothed. He wanted to laugh, but he was afraid of waking her. There was some light filtering through the window from the inn yard below. Otherwise he might not have realized that she had fallen asleep. At just the moment when he was preparing to settle in for a long and satisfying talk. How could any woman listen to a marriage proposal, answer, "Yes, my lord," and promptly fall asleep?

He dared not move. He did not want to wake her. He did not want to wake himself. He was beginning to feel all the unreality of what was happening. She had refused him just the day before. He had said good-bye to her the evening before. She had run away that morning. He had come after her in the hope of taking her back home before taking himself away from her forever. Even an hour ago—less—he had been holding his breath almost, hoping against reason that she would let him accompany her home or at least allow him to go back and send someone else to her.

He had not dreamed, in the whole long day he had never once dreamed that he would be able to win her for himself. And yet here he was, lying in Jess's bed at the inn, holding her in his arms, watching her sleep as a result of their lovemaking. And betrothed to her. And all because finally he had done unwittingly what she had wanted all the time. He had given her the gift of her freedom, she had said. And consequently she had given him back that freedom as a free gift.

And how very sweetly and thoroughly she had done so. In all his experience he had never lain with a woman who had given her all with such abandon. It was as if she had wanted to keep nothing at all back for herself. And she would not even allow him to feel guilty about her pain. She had wanted the pain, she had said.

Dear Jess. He could not resist the temptation to kiss her lightly on the nose. She opened her eyes immediately and smiled dreamily at him.

"Have I been sleeping?" she asked.

"Amazingly, yes," he said. "I wonder what we would find if we opened this mattress, Jess. A couple of wooden crates and several lumps of coal, do you think?"

"Don't complain, my lord," she said. "You have me in here and I have you. What more could we ask for?"

"A few tons of goose feathers, perhaps," he said. "But your point is well taken, love. If I had to choose between you and the goose feathers, I don't suppose I would choose the feathers."

"Thank you, my lord," she said, smiling sleepily.

"Jess," he said, "I know the force of habit is strong, but do you think that at some time during the next fifty years or so you will be able to bring yourself to call me Charles?"

"Yes, I think so," she said, "Charles."

He kissed her on the nose again.

"Charles," she said, "are you going to make love to me again tonight?"

"Another free gift, love?" he asked, eyebrows raised.